CITIES

OF

MEN

CITIES

OF

MEN

A NOVEL

WILLIAM JENSEN

Turner Publishing Company
Nashville, Tennessee
New York, New York

www.turnerpublishing.com

Cities of Men, A Novel

Cover art: Kevin Tong
Package design: Maddie Cothren
Book design: Glen Edelstein

Library of Congress Cataloging-in-Publication Data TK

Names: Jensen, William, 1981- author.
Title: Cities of men : a novel / William Jensen.
Description: Nashville, Tennessee : Turner Publishing Company, 2017.
Identifiers: LCCN 2017002562 (print) | LCCN 2017010935 (ebook) | ISBN
   9781683366669 (pbk. : alk. paper) | ISBN 9781683366683 (e-book)
Subjects: LCSH: Missing persons--Fiction. | Fathers and sons--Fiction.
Classification: LCC PS3610.E5665 C58 2017 (print) | LCC PS3610.E5665 (ebook)
   | DDC 813/.6--dc23
LC record available at https://lccn.loc.gov/2017002562

9781683366669

Printed in the United States of America

17 18 19 20   10 9 8 7 6 5 4 3 2 1

I cannot rest from travel: I will drink
Life to the lees: All times I have enjoy'd
Greatly, have suffer'd greatly, both with those
That loved me, and alone, on shore, and when
Thro' scudding drifts the rainy Hyades
Vext the dim sea: I am become a name;
For always roaming with a hungry heart
Much have I seen and known; cities of men
And manners, climates, councils, governments,
Myself not least, but honour'd of them all;
And drunk delight of battle with my peers,
Far on the ringing plains of windy Troy.

—ALFRED, LORD TENNYSON

This book is dedicated to my parents,
Joseph Jensen and Kathryn Jensen.

Thank you for giving me books and a love for stories.

CITIES
OF
MEN

ONE

I SAW MY FATHER GET into only two fights. Both times he finished with scrapes on his elbows, blood in his mouth, and bruises that smeared his abdomen and sides. The first happened in a strip mall parking lot in 1983 when I was eight. We'd stopped at the Safeway so Dad could buy some ice cream. Mom and I waited in the car. It had rained throughout the day, and the night felt cold and damp. The roads were slick with puddles that shimmered across the blacktop, and the eucalyptus trees stood dark and soaked with their leaves still dripping.

I sat in the back seat. Mom had her window down. She smoked a cigarette, and the whiffs of cold air and tobacco floated back toward me. I saw her teal eyes reflected in the rearview mirror.

"You know why it rains, sugar?"

"For the flowers and the trees."

"That too. It's also a bath for mama earth, washes everything away. You know why there is a rainbow afterward?"

"No."

"That's God's sign that he won't use a flood to destroy us next time."

"Next time?"

"Next time he'll use fire."

Dad left the store, a grocery bag dangling by his thigh. He looked at the receipt in his hand as he walked. Fluorescent bulbs inside the store beamed out in a hot white behind him. These were the moments I secretly loved, the simple waiting in the car, the small pleasure of staying dry and warm.

It was late, and only a few cars dotted the parking lot. Dad passed a blue sedan with a woman in the driver's seat. A man leaned against the vehicle, talking to her. The man's moustache looked too big for his face. I waved, and Dad waved back. He wore jeans and a white T-shirt and his denim jacket with the fur collar. My father smiled. People entered and exited the supermarket. The doors slid open and shut.

It had been a normal day. A good, family weekend day. We had gone to a movie and then dinner at a small Mexican restaurant, and now we were going home. I don't remember who wanted the ice cream, but it was probably me. I was eager to get changed into my pajamas, eat some dessert, and maybe watch a little television before I had to go to bed.

When my father was halfway between us and the blue sedan and us, the woman started screaming. Everyone looked. The man yelled too. Dad stopped and turned. The man reached in through the window and pulled the woman's hair.

"I'll kill you, Denise," he said. "I love you, you bitch." It looked like he would have dragged her all the way out if he could have.

I don't know what the couple was arguing about. I don't know what the man planned on doing once he had the woman outside. Most people would have kept walking. But not my father.

At first I didn't realize what was going on—it was just a mess of arms and hair—and then Dad shoved the man away. I hadn't seen Dad turn around. I hadn't seen him go to the sedan. He was just there. It wasn't a hard or gentle push. Mom cursed under her breath. She flicked her cigarette out, and it hissed on the wet pavement. The man and my father stared at each other.

"Cooper, turn around," said Mom. "Don't look. I don't want you to look."

I know the man was talking, because I saw his lips move. I didn't hear what was said. The woman pointed at the man. He was taller than my father. Dad shook his head. Cars drove by, their tires splashing through the water. I could smell the clouds and the wet concrete. Everything seemed glossy from the rain.

Mom kept telling me not to look, but I did. I knew I had to. I kept my eyes focused. I needed to see.

The man swung at my father, and Dad swatted him away. The man tried again. Dad slammed him against the car. The woman rolled up her window. Dad dropped the plastic bag with the ice cream. People leaving the Safeway stood and gawked.

"Cooper," said my mother. "Look at me, sugar. I can't believe this."

I couldn't really hear her. Her voice sounded like it was drifting away at sea. I pressed my face and palms onto the glass, my breath fogging it over.

The woman started the engine. The man threw all his weight onto my dad. Both men fell to the ground, crushing the carton of ice cream. Butter pecan burst across the asphalt. They quickly got up, and the woman drove off.

I gasped when I saw the man take out a knife. It wasn't a big knife, but I saw the blade, and the sight of it froze my stomach and lungs. I didn't make any noise. I wanted to tell Mom. I wanted to shout, but all sound stopped in my throat. All I could do was stare.

First, the man slashed upward just inches away from my father's chest. Dad stepped back and sucked in his gut. The man yelled something, a yelp of not-words, an urban war cry, some vocalized adrenaline. His eyes grew wide. The man jabbed the blade's tip at my father. Dad jumped back. They almost looked like they were dancing, but they were clumsy and they stumbled. Their feet clomped in pools of rain, their jeans wet and streaked with grime. Their lungs heaved from the simple exertion. It began to drizzle.

My father was a big man, but he wasn't the type of big that looked dangerous. His size was that of a laborer. He held strength in his back and shoulders, but not much elsewhere. Dad's chest was weak, and his front was all flab from a diet of beer, chocolate, and too much fried food and red meat. His build was more weight than muscle. Still, he had once been athletic, if not graceful, and later he was a soldier, albeit reluctantly; so when the man rushed forward, my father shifted on the balls of his feet and punched the man in the face, shattering his nose.

The man collapsed. He then slowly rose to his knees. Blood covered his face, but the blood faded pink with the mist. I didn't feel afraid when I saw his nose cracked at the ridge. I was more in shock that Dad had been the one to do it. The man began to crawl away. I thought my father would leave, come back to the car. Let the man bleed in peace. That wasn't what happened. Dad jumped on the man's back. No one had the knife. They had to use their hands.

The shower turned heavy. They wrestled in the downpour. Dad kept his grip on the man's shoulders. He struck his knees into the man's rib cage. It was dark, and I don't remember any thunder or lightning. All I heard was my mother's breathing, my breathing, and the eucalyptus leaves swatting in the wind.

Dad sat on the man's chest. Mom told me to stop watching. Dad began hitting the man. First with his right fist and then the left. Then the right again. It wasn't a fight anymore. Now it was just a beating. The man pawed at Dad's neck and collar. When the man gave up, my father began panting. He stood, and his head fell back, letting the rain wash his cheeks and brow.

Dad staggered toward our car, kicking the half-empty carton as he dragged his feet. Observers stood near sliding doors and shopping carts like faceless statues. No one had gotten involved. Dad came around the hood. When I glanced back, the man was gone. I didn't see where he went.

My father swung the driver's side door open, and I heard the drops sprinkling outside. Dad peeled off his jacket. His shirt was transparent from the rain. He tossed the coat in the back beside me. It was crumpled, soaked, and dirty. Dad sat and closed the door. He put his hands on the wheel, and they stayed there. His knuckles were scratched and swollen. It would take days for them to scab and heal.

"Way to go, Percy."

"Not now."

Dad was still breathing heavy. His shoulders trembled as he exhaled. He started the car. Mom reminded him to turn on the lights. We pulled out slowly, almost as if nothing had happened. I turned in my seat and took one last look at the flattened ice cream carton sitting in the rain.

We drove home in silence. I saw Dad in the rearview mirror. I still couldn't believe what I'd seen, what he had done. It hadn't scared me. It hadn't impressed me. It just felt overwhelming. I had seen my father move furniture, lift lumber, and I'd witnessed him carry my mother in his arms, but I never suspected him capable of brutality. This was the man who had held me. This was the man who once helped me nurse a sick raccoon. This was the man who told me to never fight at school. It was the first of many contradictions I'd learn about the man.

I wanted to say something. I wished for someone to say anything, but no one did. Light from oncoming traffic blurred against the water on the windshield. With each passing car, there was a short burst of illumination. I saw my father's jacket next to me. It looked like a wounded animal, curled up and trying to appear small or dead. I reached out and touched the fur collar, and my fingers came back moist and smudged. Dad drove on. He took us straight home.

We lived on the eastern edges of San Diego, almost in

Lakeside, at the end of a cul-de-sac in a house by a hill. In the summer the wild grass along the slopes turned bronze and yellow as wheat, but in winter the sides grew green and lush and the leaves were always thick and fresh with dew. The soil went soft and dark in the rain. With the dry seasons the earth became gray, rugged, and white. The Interstate ran on the other side of the hill, and at night, if you listened, you'd hear the trucks roaming north toward the San Joaquin Valley. Coyotes lived on the hill, too. Sometimes they howled. But you almost never saw them except for when they were hungry and came down searching for food, and even then you saw them only early in the morning.

Other houses sat on our street. All of them small, practically cottages, with no fences or distinct property lines. The road was short and ended at our house by the hill. Our driveway lay beneath the branches of a eucalyptus tree. The pavement that led to the garage was speckled and blotted with oil. Mom kept her Volkswagen Rabbit in the garage. Dad's Dodge Charger stayed outside.

Dad parked under the tree. Mom got out. When her door opened, I smelled the clean scent that comes after a storm. Dad looked at me in the mirror. He didn't speak. I didn't know what I was supposed to do, if I was to do anything at all. We left the car and walked to the front steps. Dad's jacket stayed in the back seat. I didn't bother to remind him.

It was warm and bright inside the house. Mom sat at the kitchen table. She pulled out a cigarette and lit it. Dad marched past her.

"You're not in Nam anymore, Percy. You and I need to talk," she said.

"Later. I'm taking a shower."

Dad went into the bathroom and closed the door. I heard the water turn on. Mom tilted her head as if to look over her shoulder, but her eyes didn't move.

"You and I need to talk," she said again.

I sat at the table across from my mom. I watched her. She
smoked. My mother was pretty. Even as a child I recognized
this. She had red hair and pale skin, and she did everything
with grace. Her posture reminded me of royalty. I wanted her
to say something, even if it was only to tell me to go to bed. The
silence bothered me. She took a final drag. Her lips puckered as
she exhaled a thin stream of smoke. She stubbed out the butt
and smiled.

"Hi, Cooper."

I smiled back. My smile was forced. The house seemed
peaceful. Our home wasn't anything fancy, but it was a nice
three bedroom with wood floors in the living room and tile in
the kitchen. My father had laid the wood himself when I was
an infant. Last summer he'd ripped up the carpet in the extra
bedroom with hopes of putting down more wood there. He still
hadn't gotten around to it, so the floor was uninviting, bare,
and colorless particle board. It would stay that way for years.

I couldn't look at my mom. I glanced around the kitchen.
A pot's handle stuck out of the sink. Coffee mugs sat on the
counter. After a while I couldn't take the silence. I knew my
mother could. She could take anything.

"Is Dad okay?"

"I'm sure your father is fine. He and I will talk. You know
that wasn't your father tonight."

"I know," I said, but I didn't really know. I just wanted
to agree. In truth, I didn't understand how my father could
do such a thing. Part of me wanted to ask him about it, but
I feared what he might say. Deep down, another part of me
was afraid he might become like that again but toward me. I
decided to never address the topic with him.

Mom touched my cheek. Then her hand moved and laid
on my arm. I feel I should say now, before I get ahead of
myself, that I loved my parents, my father, my mother. I know
that might seem redundant, but I want you to know this from
the beginning. I always felt safe around my parents. My father

wasn't a distant type of man afraid to hug me or kiss me. My mother paid attention to me, too. She took me to the zoo and to museums and to parks and to the beach if the weather was good. I shared with her all my thoughts, feelings, secrets. We were happy. At least I remember us being happy.

My mother's hand felt soft and gentle. She gave me a look like she was trying to remain patient or understanding. She kept her hand near my wrist. After a while, she asked me to go check on my father. I said okay and left.

Steam enwrapped me when I opened the bathroom door. At first I saw nothing. It was all gray and hot. I heard the water pouring. The haze thinned, and I saw my father through the curtain. His arms stretched out with his palms pressed against the wall, and his head hung low so the spray hit his neck and ran down his back. His biceps looked beefy and white. The water's heat had turned his shoulders pink. I saw his right leg too. His calf appeared defined and toned.

"Yeah?" he said. "What is it?"

"Mom wants to talk."

"I bet. Tell her I'm on my way."

"Dad?"

"Yeah?"

"Nothing."

Mom told me to go to bed. I wasn't tired, but I did as she said. In my room I undressed in the dark, leaving on my underwear and T-shirt. The sheets felt cool and crisp, and then I began to grow warm. Moonlight shined through my window blinds, breaking into pale bars across my legs. I put my hands behind my head and waited for sleep.

I could still hear my parents.

"Where are you going?" said Mom.

"To put something on. And then I'm going to bed."

"Percy, do you even know what you did? Didn't you bother to think? He had a knife. What if he'd had a gun? What if you had gotten really hurt?"

"There isn't anything you can bring up that I didn't consider."

"Oh, really? It wasn't any of your business."

"That's such a cop-out."

"No, it's not. It's the real problem. You think you have to be some cowboy? Look where that gets you. Can't you try to have some class?"

"Arden, I'm tired. I'm stiff. I'm sore. Can we just go to bed, please?"

Then I heard a door slam, and the house went quiet. Soon I heard voices again, but they were low and muffled, and I couldn't distinguish precise words. My head fell to the side. I gazed out my window at the hill and the slice of moon above it. The world looked dim and smeared with shadows. Clouds hung behind the moon. I touched the pane with my fingertips. The glass was cold. An eighteen-wheeler roared by in the distance. I tried not to think of anything. If my mind stopped, then I could sleep. I didn't like it when my parents fought. I found it odd that Mom was upset. In television or in the movies, when a man fought, especially if he fought for a woman, he was rewarded. Dad didn't seem happy or proud. I believed he had won the fight, but I didn't think he felt that way.

I fell into a dreamless sleep. Later, I awoke and had to pee. I went to the bathroom, and as I headed back to bed, I noticed the light in my parents' room was still on. For some reason I thought I should go and see why. As I neared the door, I heard crying—not loud wails, just soft and simple weeping. Inside, I found my father sitting on the floor in his boxers. Mom lay in bed. Dad was crying. He saw me and pointed at me.

"Get out of here," he said.

I ran to my room. Seeing Dad cry scared me more than the night's violence. But I couldn't tell you why. I pulled the sheets up to my collar. I dug my face into my pillow, closed my eyes, and tried not to think.

I saw Dad fight only one other time. And that wouldn't happen until four years later, shortly after my mother disappeared.

TWO

MY MOTHER VANISHED LATE IN January 1987 when I was twelve. Dad and I had gone to a movie she wasn't interested in, and when we came home she wasn't there. It was just that simple. I knew something was different as the front door opened. The house lay dark and silent like a tomb, forgotten and now found. Dad must have sensed the difference, too. He stood still and then took slow steps forward. He held his keys loosely, shaking them as he walked. That was the only noise: his steps and the clattering jingle, like sleigh bells.

"Hello, Arden?"

The heater kicked on, and the walls hummed. I shut the door. There was no response. I took off my coat and draped it over a chair at the dining table. Dad started turning on the lights in the kitchen. I went to the garage, but my mother's car wasn't there. When I came back, I found Dad in front of the fridge.

"What are you looking at?"

"This."

An index card hung on the refrigerator. A magnet in the shape of California held the note in place. Dad took it down and handed it to me.

My mother's cursive, in blue ink, ran in two simple lines across the card: "Good-bye. I've gone off on an adventure." Nothing more. She had not even bothered to sign it.

Dad pulled off his denim jacket. His pumpkin-colored curls were turning thin and flat. I could already see a spreading bald spot on the back of his skull. He went toward his bedroom.

"What does this mean?"

"Who knows? Nothing we can do about it now."

"Should we call someone?"

"Someone? Like who?"

I followed him. In his room, he sat on the foot of his bed. He took off his shoes. Holes marked the heels of his socks. He leaned forward and placed his forearms across his knees. His gut fell over his belt.

"I don't know. The cops?"

Dad rubbed his eyes. He pinched his nose and sniffed.

"Coop. Think. What do we tell the cops? Thirty-six-year-old woman leaves house? She wrote a note. It's not kidnapping. Just typical Arden."

"What about missing persons?"

"You've been watching too much television. Your mother isn't missing. Not yet, anyway."

"Should we go look for her?"

"Where? How?"

I suddenly realized how absurd my ideas had been. I pictured us driving, the windows down, calling out as if she was a lost dog. I felt a twinge of anger at Dad for not wanting to do anything. The more I thought about it, the more I concluded there wasn't anything to do. But I didn't believe that. There was always something that could be done. At least that's what I told myself.

"Okay," I said. "So, now what?"

"Now? Now nothing. We wait. She'll come back. Go to bed. Get some sleep."

"I'm not tired."

"Then read a book. I'm heading for a coma for the next eight hours."

I took a deep breath. I was worried, but I was also annoyed. Dad said Mom would probably show up in the morning, maybe sooner, that she was just in one of her moods. I wanted to ask where she escaped to, but I knew Dad didn't know. I turned and left as my father undressed by the glow of his alarm clock. A few minutes later, I heard him snoring.

I waited a while to make sure Dad was really asleep. Then I left. If my father wasn't going to do anything, then I would.

I snuck my bicycle out of the garage as quietly as I could and then pedaled down the driveway, onto the street. A fog coated the hill. I sucked in the coolness, and I saw my breath when I exhaled. The world looked dark, wet, and deserted. The roads were calm, black streams. The streetlamps glowed through the mist and beckoned me farther.

Everything was quiet. The houses. The lawns. The roads. No pedestrians, no traffic. It was as if the world had been conquered by some sleeping death and now just the structures and the skeletons remained. I rode through the neighborhood as if I might find my mother on a pleasant midnight stroll. Keep your eyes open, I told myself. Maybe she's behind a stop sign or resting against a tree. Maybe you'll see her as she returns like a conquering hero.

I biked through my neighborhood all the way to Houston Street, turned right, and then came back to Columbus Avenue. I stopped at the corner and took in a few deep breaths. Columbus cut from the base of the hill to its peak in a charcoal scar. Sidewalks, eucalyptus trees, and front yards and driveways lined the road. The streetlamps glimmered like halos. At the bottom of the hill lay a strip mall, a post office, and a traffic light that guarded the true edge of town, the realm I thought of only as "out there," a land of brush and wild grass that surrounded the reservoir like some sprawling and powerful animal.

Though the road ran up and around the bend to my right, it vanished into a deep mist to my left. Part of me felt foolish trying to find my mother. She had a car. I had a bicycle. But I felt I had to at least try. I had to do something.

I pedaled across the avenue and steered down the slope. I quickly gained momentum and speed, and I zoomed across the blacktop like a rogue bullet. The cold wind shot into my eyes. I zipped away faster and faster, and I imagined the speed would rip my bicycle's frame apart. I had to use all my strength to hold the handles steady. It felt as if the rubber of the tire was about to shred off into bits and scabs, sending me into the air just to crash and skid along the pavement. The dark world around me blurred into a smear of bone, coffee, and jungle forest green.

I sliced through the fog and closer to the bottom of the hill. My eyes started to water. The water felt cold on my cheeks, and then my eyes became dry and frozen, and my insides tightened as I rushed onward.

Through the haze I finally saw the lights at the corner. The road curved and flattened out. I steered into the strip mall parking lot, and I had enough inertia going that I cruised halfway across without any effort. I pressed on the brakes, turned my front wheel to a hard left, and put my foot on the ground as I stopped. My lungs rocked inside my ribcage as if they wanted to escape. I rested there for a second, and my skin broke into a pale, clammy sweat.

I looked around for my mother's car. A few sedans, probably belonging to people working the night shift at the Ralph's, sat scattered around. Lamps on a grid across the lot shined down in blotches. Nothing moved. Mom's car wasn't there.

Suddenly, I felt stupid and small. I could almost hear my father's voice explaining there was nothing we could do. That we should just get some sleep. That we should simply wait. But I couldn't accept that. I wouldn't.

There was one other place I could go and look. One last place I thought she might be.

I pushed my foot off the ground and began to pedal away, past the grocery, the drugstore, the video rental place, and the hair salon. I dashed across the parking lot and drifted between a minivan and an El Camino toward the exit on the other side near the Taco Bell, where I came out on Deepwater Boulevard and then headed east toward the undeveloped hills.

My little town bordered a strange vastness of chaparral and coastal sage scrub. The landscape spread out like a lumpy quilt. Many birds lived there, but so did rattlesnakes that liked to rest on the warm rocks of summer and bathe in the sunshine.

I crossed the road and pedaled into the wilderness, where there were no paved paths or marked ways; there were only trampled social trails across the meadow. There had been a good amount of rain that winter, so the grass was up to my thighs. I couldn't really see where I was going. I didn't know what I was doing. I was just searching.

If you had asked me why I thought my mother would have been out there, hiding among the shrubs and tumbleweeds, I don't think I would have had an answer. It was just the desperation of a twelve-year-old boy.

I found a sandy track that looked lavender in the moonlight. My calves ached as I tried to ride through the grit. The land was littered with candy-bar wrappers, beer cans, and star-shaped grains of shattered glass. I knew teenagers liked to come there and vanish behind the California pepper trees and smoke cigarettes, and I'd heard rumors that some of them even had sex there on blankets and beach towels and on the soil itself. Vagrants and derelicts occasionally hid among the live oaks, but I never saw them. You saw only what they left behind: an old *Playboy*, a crushed cigarette pack, maybe an empty bottle of Mad Dog.

I had to raise off my seat as I pedaled, but I wasn't moving that fast. My throat burned with each breath. My spit turned into venom. A cool wind blew through the pepper trees, and the air tasted metallic. The moon vanished behind a veil of clouds, and the world became a black and dangerous beach. I felt the earth beneath me begin to shift and slope, and suddenly I found my bicycle taking me on a quick decline. I couldn't control the wheel. I couldn't see where I was going.

The rear tire slid out from under me just as the front tire snagged in the sand, and I flew over the handlebars. I crashed onto my shoulder and hip, and I immediately felt the sting of scraped skin on my left elbow. I lay there for a bit and kept my eyes closed as I caught my breath.

Everything on the outside and everything on the inside hurt. I crawled and pushed myself up. The clouds drifted away. The moon reappeared, coloring my skin a marble blue. I spat a couple of times to get rid of the taste of blood.

I looked around and couldn't see much but the outline of a hill and a few trees.

"You idiot," I said to no one.

I picked up my bike and shoved it up the slope and back to the flat grasslands. I knew Mom wasn't out there, but she had to be somewhere. I got on my seat, put my foot on the pedal, and pressed down. There was no resistance. The wheel didn't move. I'd knocked off my chain.

I guided my bicycle through the brush toward Deepwater Boulevard. Under a streetlamp, I got down on one knee and put the chain back on the gears. But it took only three seconds of riding for the chain to fall off again. I stopped and kneeled and put the chain in place. And like something out of a bad silent movie, I continued to repeat the entire experience. I couldn't get the chain to stay on that bicycle ever again.

I wasn't so much concerned about the bicycle as I was about having to haul it all the way back up the hill to my house. And there wasn't anything else I could do. I walked my bike to the corner, crossed the street, and began the slow climb.

The hike didn't hurt my legs that much. But my arms felt rubbery, stretched, and shredded from having to drag that bicycle all the way up. I hadn't developed any real upper body strength yet. I found myself gnashing my teeth and cursing my luck. All I had wanted to do was be a good son and find my mother, and now I was scratched and bruised and having to lug a cheap hunk of metal up a hill like some ancient slave.

With each step I took, with each painful gasp of air I sucked down, I promised myself that I'd see Mom again. But as much as I hoped to see her car in the driveway when I got home, I secretly prayed more to simply reach the top of the hill so I could put my bike back in the garage and be done with it all.

I pressed on.

By the time I saw my house, I thought I might cry. My arm was bleeding a little. My shin and knee were scraped, and my arms felt like loose guitar strings. My whole body was covered in the salt of dried sweat.

Mom's car wasn't there.

I put my bike away and told myself not to worry and that my father was right—there wasn't anything we could do. Still, the situation felt bizarre. After I closed the garage door, I stood in the driveway and scanned the surroundings. I knew if I told my schoolmates my mom was missing, they would have expected Dad and me to cry, sob, to call everyone we knew, start a search party, use helicopters, night vision, hound dogs, make a rescue squad to rush into the night. But that was not the case. At least not yet.

I have to admit my mother is an enigma to me, even after all these years. But I'm willing to bet she is an enigma to herself. She'd grown up in Arizona, a place she hated, and moved to California as soon as she finished high school in the late '60s. Lots of young people flocked to the West Coast then, and I'm sure my mother came for the same reasons as everyone else. She did one year at USC and dropped out and somehow made the trek south to San Diego, where she met my father a few years later.

The union of my parents has always seemed like a bad cocktail. My mother had a glamour about her. She kept her red hair styled and neat, and she consistently fixed her makeup.

Whenever she spoke to you she flashed a smirk, as if she knew something you didn't and wanted you to guess what it was. That was Mom. That was Arden Balsam, or Arden Holly before she married.

She liked, as they say, the finer things in life. Good food, museums, jazz. At night, before going to bed, I usually found her on the couch in silk pajamas, poring over a book of photographs or paintings by O'Keeffe, Bosch, or Dalí. She'd have her feet curled under her, and she'd be smoking her Virginia Slims and listening to Miles Davis. Oddly, my mother did not enjoy going to the movies, which my father and I did all the time. I believe she thought of most films as noisy and vulgar.

I respected these qualities of my mother. I admired her grace. To me she evoked a different era, one of long white gloves and champagne.

Of course there was another side to my mother, and it is this side that remains cloaked behind some velveteen shroud. I'm not sure if she tried to keep it hidden from the world, or only herself. Now that I'm older I can put some pieces together, but even those are speculative. I think my mother was conflicted and bitter. She probably viewed herself as a victim of circumstance. And in many ways, she was. I think there were a lot of things she wanted to do but felt she couldn't because of her gender, only to have society change its views later on, leaving her resentful but without anyone with whom to be angry.

I remember once—I must have been around ten (and I know it was summer because it was warm, and I wasn't in school, and Dad was at work)—I went in my parents' room to ask my mother something. She was lying on the bed in her underwear, smoking, and I could tell she had been drinking. She didn't acknowledge me at first. The room smelled of tobacco and the sharp burn of vodka. Sunlight came in through the window, and it was a bright afternoon. Red pubic hair curled out from under her panties. The makeup around her eyes had turned wet and runny and black. I said something, but she didn't look at me. She smoked and knocked off bits of ash into a saucer beside her on the bed.

"Come here," she said, her voice a raspy whisper. She stubbed out her cigarette, and I went and stood by her. I could smell her sweat and her moisturizer and the booze she had been drinking. I asked if she was okay. She smiled and nodded, and she touched my throat with her fingers and her thumb. She started weeping. I didn't like seeing her cry, and I asked her to stop. Her lips never moved. They stayed still and straight, neither a frown nor a smile nor a smirk.

"You're so lucky," she said so softly I could barely hear her. "I want you to have everything. Everything you can dream of."

She stroked my cheek. My body went tight. It was difficult to swallow, and my throat became sore and dry. Her thumb brushed against my lips, my chin.

"I want you to be happy," I said.

"Don't patronize me. I'm too old for that."

"What's wrong?"

"You need to leave. Go watch TV. You like TV."

And then she rolled over on her side with her back toward me. I left and gently shut the door. She was still in bed when Dad came home, so he and I went out for pizza. I asked him what was wrong.

"She just has a cold," he said, which I knew was a lie.

I realized early on that my parents were people, individuals with histories from long before I was born. Obviously, everyone understands this, but I knew it almost from the beginning. I knew my parents had backstories, some I'd never know, and I had to be okay with that. There wasn't anything I could do about it if I wasn't anyway.

I thought about this, all of this, that night as I stood outside staring at the empty roads and the night sky. I wondered about my parents and their lives and the secrets of everyone else, the people in all the houses, everybody sleeping, dreaming, their joys and regrets. I stood there and waited for Mom. I waited a long time.

THREE

DAD AND I SHOULD HAVE expected that something bad was going to happen. Not long before she ran away, Mom quit her job as a fragrance girl at a local department store. Totally unexpected. She'd been there a while, several years, and she hadn't said anything about leaving or taking a position somewhere else. And she never mentioned disliking her boss or coworkers.

My mother had held previous jobs—waitress, telemarketer, and she'd even been employed for a while at the DMV before I was born—but her role selling perfumes seemed like a perfect fit for her. She resembled the bottles of cologne and toilet water she sold. Fancy but mysterious. Intoxicating but impossible to hold.

The job was only part-time, but she acted as if it was a full-time career. By the way she dressed, you would've thought she worked on Madison Avenue. She wore slick dresses with expensive stockings, nice scarves, big earrings, colorful brooches to accent her makeup and hair, and her fingernails always matched the color of her lipstick and eye shadow. I think it would be safe to say that she was always better looking than the women who sampled and bought the bottles of Obsession, Giorgio, and various designer imposters.

Mom worked at a place called Harrison's. It used to be on the other side of the Interstate and a few miles west of my junior high and my father's shop. Harrison's shared a big, and usually empty, parking lot with a large movie theater—one of those older one-screen palaces that showed only a single film a week. Neither of those places are there now. The theater went out of business. The building later turned into a furniture rental shop, a music store with rows and rows of CDs and cult films on VHS, and finally a used-car lot. Harrison's was torn down a long time ago and became just a lot of dirt and rubble. Not even an extension of the parking lot.

Whenever I went to Harrison's—usually with my father to pick up my mother, or occasionally to buy something and use her store discount—I felt not so much like I was stepping into the past as I felt like I was entering a place frozen in time. Harrison's had been built in the early '60s, and nothing had been updated or revamped. Everything was colored orange and green. Atomic starbursts engraved the walls and decorated the carpet between the women's and men's wear sections.

I don't know if the store had ever been popular, but it was never busy when I visited. The only customers I saw looked like they might be middle-aged bachelors on their day off buying underwear and socks, or little old ladies who I suspected to be widows that lived on fixed incomes.

A few months before she quit—and not too long before she disappeared—my father and I met my mother at Harrison's on a Friday so we could go and have an end-of-the-week family dinner. Dad and I strolled through the big front doors and down the aisles of cheap necklaces, bracelets, earrings, and cuff links under glass. My mother stood hunched over her cash register at her station in the center of the health and beauty section. She had no customers. She rapped her fingernails on the countertop. My father and I walked side by side toward her, but she didn't see us, not even when my father waved. I don't think she realized we were there until we stepped right up to her station.

"Working hard, or hardly working?" said my father.

My mother shook a little as if she felt a chill and tugged on her blouse to straighten it. She quickly stood straight and smiled.

"You're early," she said and came out from behind her sales area. She gave my father a small hug while he kissed her cheek. She hugged me too, squeezing me tightly. My mother smelled of tweed and rose petals. She put a palm to my jawline. "I will need a few minutes. How about you boys go see if you can find yourself a tie?"

My father gave her a wink and guided me away and deeper into Harrison's. We wandered past the bras and panties and the half-nude, faceless mannequins. My father kept his hands in the pockets of his jacket. I stayed close by. The men's section of Harrison's sprawled out like a week-old slab of roadkill. The coatracks had random styles and sizes. They all looked baggy and ugly. Sweatpants and pajama bottoms hung between trousers and a few pairs of women's slacks. My father started combing through the shirts and would occasionally make a face as if sniffing a cheese or a wine.

I saw my mother fiddle with her cash register and rearrange some of the bottles. I figured the day had been a long one for her, and she looked like she was ready to leave and enjoy the rest of her Friday and the weekend. Family time. Before she could get all the way out of there, a woman in a fur coat approached her. I couldn't hear what she said. My mother began pulling all of the bottles back out. My father had given up on shirts and was now trying on a black silk robe. I decided to head back toward Mom.

"No, this is not the one I want," said the woman in the fur coat. "Are you dumb? A bit touched?"

"I'm sorry, ma'am," said my mother. "I am sure I can find the right fragrance."

"I've been coming to Harrison's for over twenty-five years," said the woman. "Do you know how many complaints I've had to make?"

My mother gave one of those thin and patient smiles but said nothing. Both of her hands lay flat on the counter.

"Not one," said the woman. "Not a single complaint in two decades and a half. And after all of that there's you. And you can't find the correct perfume. I want to speak with your manager."

"Yes, ma'am," said my mother. She gave a short nod and walked away. I stepped closer to her sales section. The woman in the fur coat held the straps of her purse close to her stomach. She and I made eye contact. She shook her head and let out a sigh. She muttered something, but I didn't catch her exact words. I drifted in front of the counter and looked at the various fragrances. I wanted to stay nearby in case my mother needed me. Why she would need my help, I didn't know. But I figured I should stay close to her regardless.

When my mother returned, she was followed by a bald man who wore a tie and glasses. The woman in the fur coat began describing her difficulties with my mother—how my mother couldn't find the right perfume, how she couldn't expound on the different plant and animal sources in each brand, and how my mother had been rude to her. The bald man listened and adjusted his glasses.

The woman in the fur coat appeared to be in her early sixties. The flesh under her chin drooped and swung as she spoke. She briefly pointed a finger at my mother. The bald man nodded.

"Yes, ma'am. I understand why you may be upset. I assure you that Mrs. Balsam was not trying to antagonize you."

"I've been a customer of Harrison's for two and a half decades. Kennedy was president when I first came here. And I've bought the same perfume all those years. Two and a half decades."

"Ma'am, I apologize for being out of your fragrance, but I will order it, and we should have it in a few days."

"And why haven't you done that already? L'eau de La Truie has been a staple of mine and many others."

"I'm afraid just not many women are wearing that these days."

"I'm honestly not surprised," said the woman in the fur coat. "Ever since boys started having long hair and women began burning their bras, it seems no one has any class or taste anymore. Look at this one." She motioned with her chin toward me.

By now, I was on the other side of the perfume section. The bald man and my mother moved their heads and saw me.

"I bet that one watches that MTV all day. Where are his parents? He's probably on drugs. Do you just let children roam wild here now? Shouldn't he be in school?"

My mother pushed the manager aside and stepped toward the woman in the fur coat. I watched my mother lean over the glass counter and put her face close to the woman's. My mother whispered something to her. I don't know what.

The woman in the fur coat took a few steps back. Her jaw dropped. She didn't say anything. She flashed a look toward the manager and then stared at my mother. My mother crossed her arms. The woman in the fur coat gave a snort and turned around. I watched her make her way to the exit and disappear.

"What did you say to her?" said the manager.

"Nothing she probably didn't know already."

"You've got to remember that the customer is always right, Mrs. Balsam. I'm going to have to write you up."

"Oh, go ahead, Alan. It doesn't make any difference to me."

The manager walked away. My mother put everything back again and came and found me hiding behind a rack of women's blazers with shoulder pads. Her purse dangled from her right shoulder. Her fingers opened and closed around her purse strap.

"Come on," she said. "Let's go eat something."

"What did you say to her?"

"Something not very nice."

"Because of me?"

"Because of both of us. Now where's your father? He hasn't gotten kidnapped by gypsies, has he?"

We found my father trying on tennis shoes. He asked what had taken so long, and my mother explained she'd had a last-minute customer. She didn't tell him anything else. She didn't say that the woman in the fur coat had been difficult or rude or that she had insulted me. My mother did not mention that her manager was going to write her up. And she did not mention how she had whispered something that was powerful enough to get the woman to immediately leave.

We left Harrison's that day and went to eat at a restaurant, just as we'd planned. But I noticed that while we ordered and ate, my mother did not say much. My father told stories about what had happened to Sebastian and him at the shop that day; my mother just smiled in silence. The restaurant was dim and crowded. We sat in a booth in the corner, and the three of us drank diet soda and ate pizza.

"Does anyone want to go see *Crocodile Dundee* this weekend?" said Dad.

"I've read good things about *Blue Velvet*," said my mother.

"I really, really don't want to see that. Sorry."

"Maybe we can do something else. Coop, how would you feel about the ballet?"

"Sounds lame."

"Have you been to a ballet?"

"Do monkeys drive cars?"

"How can you say the ballet is 'lame' if you've never even been to a single performance?"

"Leave the kid alone," said Dad. "He wants to have a few laughs. Nothing wrong with that."

The bill came, and my father paid. The waiter left, and we waited for him to return with the change. My father finished the soda in his glass. My mother leaned over and ran her fingers through my hair.

"Just be careful," she said in a low and quiet voice. "You

don't want to turn into one of those kids who rots away watching MTV."

She winked at me, but I could not tell if she was trying to be funny or scary.

DAD WENT TO WORK THE morning after Mom left. It was Saturday, and he had to open his shop. When I awoke, I heard him walking through the house, slapping his palms, coughing, cooking breakfast. I smelled coffee, bacon, and oil. I stayed in bed. It was cold outside the covers, and I liked the way my pillow felt against my cheek and brow. Then came the slam of the door. The house went silent.

I found a note on the fridge in my father's handwriting saying he'd work until four, his normal hours. I knew I could walk down and see him if I wanted, but I didn't feel like it. I didn't want to see anyone. And I thought someone should stay at the house in case Mom returned. The fact that she hadn't yet made me tense. I hated the waiting, the feeling of helplessness that came with the waiting. I told myself to stay calm. There was nothing else I could do.

After making some toast, I sat on the couch and read my paperback of *Hawaii.* I wanted to visit the islands someday. I wanted to travel and see exotic places, but I knew I probably wouldn't get to. The book was long, but I was determined to finish it.

At first I couldn't concentrate. Every time I heard a truck drive by or a car door open and close, I looked up or ran to the window thinking, wishing, Mom was back. It was never her. After a while I settled in and got lost in the saga of the South Pacific. I stretched out and read. The morning passed like that.

In the early afternoon, I went outside to see if there was any mail yet. I'd hoped there would be a catalog because I liked looking at the pictures of people and imagining what they were doing, why they were smiling, and what they did when not showing up in glossy photographs. They all looked happy, healthy, and lucky. The mailbox was empty.

I was about to head back inside when I heard a voice call my name. The sound startled me. A shot of adrenaline, hot and spiky, flushed my skin. I spun around and saw Donald. He lumbered toward me. He didn't wave.

Donald was about two years older than me. I was never sure if he wanted to be friends or enemies. He had a flattened nose and sharp, crooked teeth. Though barely in his teens, his body was already pear-shaped. I didn't understand Donald. He once told me he liked to verbally attack a teacher in the middle of class because he knew it would get him suspended for a few days. "Think of how much Nintendo you get to play," he'd said, smiling. I would label him something of a bully—he pushed me around and called me stupid and pulled my hair if I didn't follow him where he wanted to go—but I'd seen older kids bully him. He wanted to be rough, but I think deep down he knew he wasn't smart, or tough, or handsome, and that the world would have its way with him eventually.

"Hey there," I said.

"Hey, toilet-licker. What are you doing out here?"

"Checking the mail."

"You're such a dumb-dumb. Mail doesn't come on the weekends. You got oatmeal for brains. You want to play?"

"The mail comes on Saturdays."

"No, it doesn't. It's the weekend. Week. End. No mail. That shit is closed."

"I need to go."

"Don't be a pillow-biter. You want to hang out?"

"Not really."

I wasn't going to tell him about Mom. Donald had, on more than one occasion, mentioned that he found my mother attractive. He'd once gone on a quick tirade describing what he wanted to do to her before I ran away, covering my ears.

"Bull. Come on. I want to show you something cool. You're coming, or I'll stomp your balls off."

Donald yanked me by my shirt, and I trailed behind him. It would be easier to endure his antics than to avoid them. We went down the sidewalk and across the street to his house. Donald's house was a lot like ours as far as size and construction, both small stucco buildings with wooden shingle roofs. We went through the garage, which Donald's father had transformed into a Spartan-type dungeon gym. There was an old weight bench, the bar rusted, the bench's vinyl ripped and torn, with the egg yolk–colored stuffing protruding like fat tissue. Dumbbells lay scattered about nearby like the weight bench's turds.

When we walked inside, Donald's father, Jake, was sitting at the table smoking cigarettes. He was in just his boxers and a black tank top. The place smelled of grease and syrup. A television was on with the volume up high. Jake resembled a Viking blacksmith. He could have entered bodybuilding contests, except for the fact that he was hairy and maintained a hefty roll of flab around his waist despite his exercise regime.

"Hey, Daddy, can I make Cooper some Kool-Aid? He said he was thirsty."

"You're thirsty, little man?"

Jake smoked his cigarette and read his newspaper. He knocked his ash into an empty beer can. I never figured out what the man did for a living, if he even worked at all. I was always a little afraid of him, though he was always nice to me. One time he drove by as I was walking home from the drugstore after buying some comic books, and he gave me a ride even though he was going in the opposite direction.

"Actually," I said, "I should be going."

"Don't be so rude, Cooper."

Donald winked at me. Seeing Donald try to act smooth was revolting. I rolled my eyes. I knew it would be easier to comply than to rebel. I sat at the kitchen nook with Jake. Donald went to make us the Kool-Aid. I never liked the stuff, but Donald drank it by the gallon. Always grape-flavored.

I never felt comfortable at Donald's. This was in part because of my fear of his father. It was also because the place always smelled like stale crackers and mustard. Crumbs from chips and bread lay everywhere, never cleared, simply brushed away.

I heard an infomercial trying to sell something on the television. Jake rested one elbow on the table. His bicep looked like it might be the size of my head. After Donald fixed two glasses of Kool-Aid, he sat between me and his father. He handed me a McDonald's souvenir glass filled with the purple sugar water. Jake shoved his cigarette butt into the beer can and then grabbed his pack, shook out a new one, and lit it with a plastic lighter. The man's beard was thick and coarse. He didn't look at his son or at me. He just smoked.

I tried to be like a statue. Jake looked over his shoulder (seemingly at nothing) and then back to his paper. Donald drank his Kool-Aid. I sipped mine. After he finished his glass, Donald wiped his lips with the back of his hand and asked if he could have a beer. Jake shook his head and told him no.

"Please."

"No dice. And stop your bitching before it starts. You ask again, and I'll give you something to bitch about. And I'll do it right here in front of your little friend."

Jake smiled, and then he and Donald laughed as if they had seen something hysterical that I'd missed. Jake tousled his son's hair. Donald swatted his father's paw away, and they laughed again. Jake shot me a look and grinned.

I heard a soft rumbling and saw Donald's mother. She wore a blue bathrobe with a frayed collar. I assumed she'd been watching television. Donald looked a lot like his mom, but he had none of her personality. Her name was Karen. She was nice and patient and nurturing, and she listened when you talked. Her Westie trailed her heels.

"What are all you boys doing?"

"Waiting on you, troublemaker," said Jake.

"I'm not a troublemaker. Not anymore. You boys want some pancakes? I can make some pancakes."

"We're okay, Mommy."

"Let me make you some pancakes. It won't be any trouble. What about Coop? You didn't ask him. You want some pancakes, Cooper? Goodness, you look like a cat at a dog show. You okay?"

"I'm fine, ma'am. But thank you."

Donald's mother put one hand on her husband's shoulder and one on her son's. Donald's mother had light-blue eyes, almost like ice. I reached down to pet the dog.

"How've you been, Cooper? I haven't seen much of you. Are you playing any sports?"

"No, ma'am."

"Why not?" said Jake.

"Don't know. No real reason."

Donald's father scooped up the little dog. It sat in his lap. He scratched the animal's ears and let it lick his cheek.

"Next year," said Donald, "when I enter high school, I'm going out for the swim team."

"Like hell," said Jake. The Westie jumped away.

"I'm going to give it a shot."

I quickly pictured Donald, pale and blubbery, standing near a pool, wearing a Speedo, goggles, and a skullcap, his love handles pouring over the sides of his trunks. I was unsure if he was joking or being serious. I almost laughed but was able to keep my face devoid of expression.

Jake dropped the butt into his beer can. "We'll have to carve them titties off you and get you some muscle."

"I'm all muscle," said Donald.

"You're all butter and flour."

"No," said Donald's mother. "He's all sunshine and smiles."

"Christ, Mommy."

"Don't you swear."

Donald told his mother we were going to play Nintendo, and we went to his room. I hated being in Donald's room. I always had the feeling rats nested in the corners. Donald sat on his bed and pulled out a copy of *Fangoria*. He grinned.

"Check it out," he said and opened it to a picture of a woman with her throat slit. My stomach churned. "It's from the latest Jason movie. Isn't it cool?"

"Yeah, pretty cool," I said, but I didn't think so. I only said it because I knew I had to say something, and it seemed like the thing Donald wanted to hear. He showed me some more pictures. All knife and axe wounds and dead teenagers and blood. I never liked horror movies, and I always thought people who did were a little strange. Donald loved slasher films. He enjoyed the carnage. Occasionally, he got me to watch one with him, and he'd cheer for the maniac to chop and slice away. I always had to cover my eyes, and he'd tease me until I watched. It wasn't so much that I was scared as I was simply depressed by the cruelty.

"Look, this one came with a poster of *The Fly* remake. Daddy took me to see it over the summer. It's extra gory."

"That's great."

Donald tossed the magazine to the side and clasped his hands together.

"You okay? You look kinda sick."

"I'm fine."

"Good. Because I've got news. Big stuff. My daddy just got a crowbar. We need to go smash some stuff. Am I right?"

This was typical Donald. He enjoyed breaking things. Demolition and destruction were fun to him. I always worried what would happen if he ever got his hands on some dynamite.

"I don't want to smash anything."

"Sure you do. Sometime soon, too. I say we sneak out at night and break up the plants in somebody's garden. We won't get caught."

"That's not the reason."

"What do you mean?"

"I've got to go."

"No, Cooper, seriously," he said. "This crowbar is amazing."

"Amazing?"

"Yeah, amazing. It's heavy, yet light . . . I don't know how to explain it. When you hold it, you feel big, real big."

"Great. I've got to go."

I turned and left. Donald followed me. His parents were still sitting at the kitchen table. They smoked and drank soda. Donald's mother asked us what we were up to, and Donald told her I was leaving.

"So soon?"

"I have to see if my mom is back," I said and winced. I hadn't meant to say anything, but I had. I tried to recover. I went with the first thing I could imagine. "She's just out. Garage sales and stuff."

"Okay, is your dad at his shop?"

"Yes, ma'am. Until four."

Then Jake and Karen looked at each other the way couples do when they are thinking the same thing but not speaking.

"You need to stay with us for the day, big guy?" said Jake. He stubbed out his cigarette.

"No, I'm okay," I said. Jake and Karen looked at each other again.

"You're just hanging out over there all by yourself?" said Jake.

"Yes. I've been reading."

"All right," said Karen. "You come on by if you need anything."

Donald and I walked outside, but as we left I heard Jake mutter "They're raising that boy like a couple of crackheads."

FOUR

I MARCHED HOME. A BURNING sensation grew across my chest and faded only if I clenched my jaw. Mom's car wasn't in the driveway. I didn't understand why my father was so calm. I knew there had to be more we could do. My mind flashed to Mom's body by the side of the road with a lightning bolt of blood trailing down her chin—car wrecks, psychos, accidents where no one is ever found.

When I got home, I wandered through the house. I didn't turn on any of the lights. No television. No music. Sunlight spilled through the windows and blinds in thin streaks of corn silk. Cars shifted gears as they sped up Columbus Avenue, the long and sloping street behind our house. From the kitchen you could look out across our tiny back yard to the winding road that ascended into the woods of sycamore and eucalyptus to the top of the hills where California pepper trees grew wild. The road was black and smooth because it had been repaved just last summer, and the yellow lines down the middle reminded me of bumblebees.

I drifted into my parents' room. The bed wasn't made. Dad had kicked all the sheets and the blankets to the foot. The room felt cold and almost damp. The lone window's view was blocked by a hibiscus tree that blossomed red as blood in the spring. The clothes my father had worn yesterday lay on the floor next to a pile of newspapers, junk mail, and magazines: *Sports Illustrated* and *Car and Driver*.

I crawled on the bed and put my face on my mother's pillow. The fabric didn't smell like her, as I'd hoped. It had an odor of dead skin, hair, and fabric conditioner, not of her lotion or perfume or shampoo. A lone strawberry strand ran across the bedsheet. I sat up and held the hair in front of my face. It dangled and twirled, and then I wrapped the hair around my pointer finger so tight it cut off the circulation. I went to my parents' closet. They didn't know I did this, but sometimes I liked going through their things. I pushed back my mother's dresses, my father's jackets and his one good suit, using both hands as if trekking through jungles or tall grasses of wilderness. Shoes cluttered the floor. Stilettos, kitten heels, and loafers. Boots and sandals. The ugly carpet inside the closet smelled of dirt and dander from the cat we'd once had. A car on Columbus Avenue ran her over and just kept driving. I kicked some of my father's tennis shoes away. The cigar box waited for me in the back against the wall. I was never sure if Dad wanted to hide the box or if there was any reason for its seclusion. I sat with my back against the foot of the bed and opened the Dutch Masters box.

I'd done this before. At least half a dozen times.

Inside were my father's medals. There were photos, buttons, and patches. He had one black-and-white picture of a group of guys standing around a jeep, all of them bare-chested, drinking beer in the hot midday sun, loafing about in some Vietnam camp in between patrols. Most of them wore aviators; a few others had on thick, black-rimmed, Buddy Holly–type glasses. One man in the picture stood in the back. He must not have known someone was taking a picture—or he just didn't care. He was slurping his Budweiser when the camera clicked, so no one could really see his face. He had large arms, broad shoulders, and strong, pronounced abs. Though I couldn't clearly see his face, I knew he was my father. I could tell by how his stance shrugged off the attention, the celebration, or whatever it was that was happening right then.

My fingers rummaged through the box. I didn't know the names of the medals, though one was obviously a purple heart. One medal's ribbon was yellow with green stripes on the sides and three red lines in the center. One was crimson with two bold white bars near the edges. Another medal was red with a blue line with white borders in the middle. That one had several oak leaf clusters pinned into it.

I returned the cigar box to where I'd found it. I made sure to cover it with some of Dad's socks that lay on the floor. The sun was going down, and my father would be home soon. I wanted to find something—anything—that might clue us in to where Mom was. Dad believed she'd return when she was ready, but that wasn't good enough for me.

There had to be an address or a name that would tell me where to find her. I looked through the dresser for an address book but couldn't find one. There was just underwear, a jewelry box, some cuff links, and a few ugly ties rolled into tight coils. I knew my parents had boxes in the attic, so I decided to look there instead.

Our attic was the only part of the house I wasn't supposed to go into. It wasn't the safest place, with only a sole dangling lightbulb, pink insulation everywhere, not to mention the wobbly excuse for a floorboard. I didn't like going there. The pull-down ladder always felt as if it was about to snap beneath you, and the dark corners seemed to be where nightmares came from. My father had warned me about black widows, too.

When I crawled into the attic, I climbed into a pit of warm, stale air. I pulled the string to turn on the light. A dull yellow glow washed over a few feet, but no farther. I grabbed at a couple of cardboard boxes and discovered Christmas decorations, old sheets, some of my childhood toys, and some old auto mechanic books my father had devoured as a young man.

One box had "Arden" written in large black letters across the side. I yanked it toward me with both hands. There wasn't too much of interest inside. A graduation cap and gown. An old pink teddy bear. A petite gavel. Photos of my mother as a teenager, with her hair styled similar to Jackie Onassis's.

Underneath a few old blouses was a cookbook titled *Saucepans and the Single Girl* and an old penny notebook filled with my mother's cursive. I snagged this and started flipping through it. There were notes about high school things: dances, classmates, upcoming exams. One page caught my eye. It read:

Sometimes I love the world so much I want to scream. I feel as if I am a child locked away in the county fair. I hope to ride all the rides and eat all the cotton candy before I die. There is Europe, poetry, art, and the great wall of China. All the things that Alburn has shown me. Oh, so sweet. I want it all. I want all the wonder in the sea. Too much for my little heart to take. I feel sorry for my friends. Me? I won't end up like them. God, why do some people even keep on breathing? If you can't be happy, then you shouldn't be at all. One needs to drink all the wine. Even if it belongs to someone else.

The other night we drove out into the reservation and sat in the back of John McKallan's pickup truck. Alburn wouldn't come with us. I know he'd rather stay in his room. His records. His books. Interesting worlds and words.

After we got far away from the road, we looked at all the stars. Little Dipper. Big Dipper. Orion's Belt. Everyone talked about dances, gossip, the rodeo. I remember liking those things. But now I'm about to be a junior, and I feel differently. I know I deserve more.

I read the last sentence several times. Though I had seen pictures of my mother as a young woman, she had never spoken to me about her youth. I tried to picture her in the late '60s as a hippie or a flower child, some teenager who thought she'd never die. It didn't make sense. But those last words stayed with me. *I know I deserve more.*

I wondered who Alburn was.

I unwrapped the hair from around my finger. The skin had

turned cold. I put the strand in the gutter of the notebook and closed it. Blood and warmth returned to my finger. I carried the journal under my arm and left the attic. I thought about Mom and if she had not wanted me, if I was some accident, if I had been the ball and chain that kept her from doing what she had always wanted to do. I wondered if she hated me.

I took the journal and retreated from the attic, careful to leave everything as I'd found it. The boxes remained stacked, the light was turned off, and the dust was returned to darkness. With the journal clamped under my arm, I went to my room and dove onto my mattress.

I started reading random passages. The more I flipped through the pages, the more I wondered about my mother— the things that drove her, inspired her, scared her. Of course, what I really wanted to know was where she had gone and if she was coming back.

I told myself that upon her return, she and I would drive into the mountains and stop in the little town of Julian. There were apples there, always fresh and crisp, and the shops smelled of cider and cinnamon and wood. My parents had taken me there in October. During that trip, we sipped hot chocolate and wandered the small streets decorated with pumpkins and corn. My mother walked with me beside her, keeping her arm draped over my shoulder so she could pull me in close. We drifted like twins in and out of the diners and stores. My mother's jacket was made of a heavy wool and reeked of her cigarettes and sweat and perfume. Dad trailed us like some friendly but protective bear.

The best part of that day was that it was cold. And it wasn't cold just by a drop in temperature. It was a seasonal briskness with a crackling wind that snapped in the air. We followed the main street all the way down and back again, and by the end of the day our cheeks felt brittle from the chill. The three of us drove to Dudley's bakery in Santa Ysabel and shared a loaf of bread. There was Danish apple nut, western wheat, and pecan maple, but we settled on date nut raisin because Mom said it was her favorite. I'd never tasted anything like it, and I watched Mom dip her crust in her cocoa. After walking around outside most of the day, sitting at that bakery in between my mother and my father felt like the warmest I ever had been or ever would be.

I tried to remember that day as best I could.

I closed my mother's journal and looked at it. I admit I felt a little ashamed reading it. But only slightly. I decided to hide it under my mattress because I didn't want my father to know I had it. I didn't want anyone else to know about it.

Dad came home about an hour later. Sebastian, his only employee, walked into the house with him. Dad looked me up and down as he took off his jacket. He tossed it onto the couch and slapped his hands together as if knocking soil off his palms. It was a habit of his. I didn't know where he had picked it up or what it was all about. I found myself doing the same thing a few years later.

"Hey there, Captain Tsunami," said Sebastian.

I liked Sebastian. I never understood his nickname for me, but I enjoyed it anyway. Sebastian was at least twenty years older than my father, and he resembled a wizard who had spent a lot of time in Haight-Ashbury. His long hair had turned a dark silver, and he kept it pulled back in a ponytail. He had a beard and a handlebar moustache. He had crazy stories of living on the road, seeing Bob Dylan in Greenwich Village, and meeting Timothy Leary at a Kool-Aid party. Dad and Sebastian took me camping the previous summer, and Sebastian had taught me how to tie a dozen different types of knots. There had been other employees, but they were all young men who never stayed long, just a summer before college or a year until they figured they wanted to do something else.

"You hungry, Coop? Sebastian and I are thinking tacos."

"Mom hasn't come home. You said she would come home."

"She will."

"We need to do something."

"You're right. We need to get tacos."

"Tacos, tacos, tacos," said Sebastian. He gave tiny fist pumps as he chanted. His eyes looked hungry and wild.

"Damn it, Dad—"

"Don't yell at me," he said. He looked over his left shoulder. Sebastian stood close to the door, and he didn't say anything. Dad glanced at me and nodded in a way that made me feel like an asshole. I bit my lower lip. "I bet she comes home later tonight. Okay?"

"What if she doesn't?"

And then we stood there, locked in some strange and quiet stare as if we wanted to read each other's mind, manipulate the other's limbs like puppets. I knew what I wanted to say to him, but I had no idea how to say it. This happened to me occasionally. Sometimes I wanted to yell or scream, but I knew that would only work against me. I took in a deep breath through my nose and gently exhaled out my mouth. This calmed me slightly. Still, all I could think of was noise and roars and metal crushing into metal.

"Coop, I promise if she isn't back by Monday, then I'll call some people."

"People? What people?"

"Look, you're frustrated and hungry. Now how about you come with me and Sebastian and get a bite. Or if you want to stay here, then you can do that, too."

"Come with us, Captain Tsunami," said Sebastian. "The world is a far greater place when seen with a full stomach."

I looked at my feet. I hated it when someone patronized me. Dad and Sebastian waited for me to say something.

"You coming? Or are you going to sulk?"

"I'm coming," I said. "Let me get my coat."

We all piled into my father's 1972 Dodge Charger. He'd grown up with his own father fixing trucks and sedans, and he'd worked on the Charger a lot over the years. He'd picked it up as a battered husk of metal and transformed it into a pristine and powerful machine. After he started the engine, he'd let it idle for a while, and the engine would growl with confidence. The interior was clean and well kept, too. Sebastian sat up front, and I sprawled out in the back. Dad turned on the heat and headlights. He slowly backed out and began heading down the hills into Casa de Oro.

We ate at a small Mexican place next to a Laundromat. The three of us chomped down carne asada burritos and chips and salsa. Mariachi music played on a boom box in the kitchen, but it was loud enough to hear in the small dining area where we sat in a wooden booth by the window. Palm trees stood outside like stoic soldiers awaiting orders. A little boy played Donkey Kong on the machine in the corner. Sebastian sucked horchata through a straw.

I was pretty upset, so I didn't talk. Dad and Sebastian joked about work stuff and reminisced about old movies. Sebastian complained about Reagan. After a while, Dad got up to use the restroom. I watched him walk away and waited until he was gone.

"You've got to help me, Sebastian," I said.

"I try not to get involved in other people's mistakes, migraines, monsters, or marriages. I fear I may end up with some of my own."

"My mom is missing, Sebastian. Dad doesn't even care."

Sebastian tossed his napkin onto his plate. He put his fists on the table and looked at the door to the men's room. The little boy playing the video game started yelling in Spanish and kicking the machine.

"Guess the poor kid lost all his quarters. The rest of us just lose our marbles."

"Are you going to help me?"

Sebastian sang out, "Help, I need somebody. Help, not just anybody."

"Forget it."

The kid punched the arcade game's screen.

"You cheat! You cheating stupid thing!" His voice broke and screeched as he yelled.

Dad came out of the bathroom. He didn't see the kid or the video game. He didn't see the kid pick up the chair. He didn't see the kid bash the chair into the side of the machine. But my father definitely heard it. There was a loud crash, and, almost as if someone flipped a switch in his brain, my father dove to the floor and covered the back of his head and neck with his hands.

"Everybody get down!"

Dad crawled toward the corner. His boots screeched on the linoleum as he moved. The kid stepped back and stared at my father. He didn't say anything. Dad's face flushed pink when he hit the ground, but his cheeks quickly became pale and gray as ash. He rolled over and scooted so his back pressed against the wall with one knee pulled to his chest. His other leg lay crooked on the floor. He began hyperventilating. His eyes turned larger than I'd ever seen and blankly glared ahead.

"Down, down . . . just stay down," he muttered. His chest kept heaving. The little kid ran outside. Dad flinched when the boy dashed by. His right hand patted his side, his hip, and along the floor. The mariachi music continued playing from the kitchen.

I didn't move. I didn't even think. All I could do was observe in some type of muted stupor. Sebastian slowly stood and held out his hands. He said my father's name several times in a calm voice. My father watched him. Sebastian took one step forward. Dad's body tensed up.

"Easy, Percy. You're okay. You're having a flashback. It's not real. You're with me and your son. Look around. You're at a Mexican restaurant. You're not in-country, man."

Dad's eyes stayed focused on Sebastian.

"Just breathe, partner. Just breathe."

Sebastian took two small steps forward. Dad's eyes returned

to their normal size. He began sweating. Sebastian kneeled
beside my father. Dad started blinking and covered his lips and
nose with his hands.

I just sat there, unsure of what to do. I had never seen my
father act that way. I had never seen anything like that. Part of
me was startled, but another part of me was embarrassed. I'm
ashamed to say that now, but it's true. I didn't even really understand what was going on, and I wouldn't understand for years.

Sebastian talked to Dad for a while. I didn't hear what
Sebastian said, but I saw my father nod a lot. Sebastian helped my
father up, and they went outside where Dad could walk around
a bit. While Dad caught his breath and calmed down, Sebastian
poked his head back inside and told me we were leaving.

I tossed our leftovers and put the plastic baskets on top of
the trash cans. The chair the kid had slammed into the video
game still lay on the floor. I set it upright and left.

Sebastian drove us home that night. It was one of those
tense and silent trips. I looked at my father from the back seat,
and I could tell he was clenching his jaw. When we got to the
house, my father asked Sebastian to stick around. I went straight
to my room. I didn't like it when Dad got quiet like that.

I retrieved Mom's journal, crawled into bed, and started
reading. A few minutes later, Dad knocked on my door. At first I
didn't say anything. I hid my mother's journal and looked at the
door, expecting him to enter. But he didn't. Finally, I said, "Come
in," and my father slowly turned the knob and opened the door.

"It's me," he said. His voice sounded hoarse and distant
and tired. The man's eyes looked dull.

"Are you okay?"

"Yeah," he said without looking at me. He sat on the foot of
my bed. He leaned forward with his forearms across his knees.

Then he shook his head. "You know what? No. Not really.
But I will be."

"You scared *me* tonight."

"I scared me, too," he said. He turned his head so our eyes

met. He had slim eyebrows and a pronounced chin. The hair on his forearms was light and fair. He gave one of those smiles that looked more like a shrug, the kind where the lips just go flat and straight. "But hey, I don't want you to worry. It's all okay now."

"You don't sound so sure about that."

"Well, you know how you have a nightmare? Sometimes all you have to do is wake up."

He reached out and touched my leg. I got the feeling he was talking more to himself than to me. I didn't really understand what he meant by any of it. He rose and slapped his hands the way he did.

"Is Mom having a nightmare?"

Dad scratched his cheek. He put his hands on his hips and nodded.

"You know what? I think she is. I bet that's all there is to it. Don't worry, Coop. Besides, there isn't much worrying can do about it at this point."

He talked to me for a little bit longer but not about anything that really seemed to matter. He told me Sebastian was going to be spending the night, and tomorrow we could all go out for breakfast if the weather was clear. When he left my room, he pulled the door behind him, but it didn't shut all the way. I listened to his footsteps drift away. Light from the hallway spilled into my room. But then Dad flicked the switch, and the house went dark.

I fell asleep not long afterward, but I didn't have any dreams. Then, sometime in the middle of the night, Donald tapped on my window and woke me. His skin had a tint of green in the starlight, and he stood like a gargoyle. Donald mouthed, "Open up." He held the crowbar in his right hand.

I didn't know exactly what he wanted to do, but I was sure it wasn't anything good. I shook my head side to side. Donald snarled.

"Don't be such a tampon. We've got plans."

"You've got plans. I've got sleep."

"I'm going to start screaming in three seconds."

"Donald, don't."

"One."

"I don't want to. Just go home."

"Two."

Donald took a deep breath. He wasn't bluffing. I was afraid he'd wake my father, wake up the other neighbors. He'd put the blame on me somehow.

"Okay, fine," I whispered in a hiss. I slid open the window. Cold air rushed in and over my face, chest, and arms. My skin broke into goose bumps. The wind smelled of eucalyptus leaves and damp soil.

"Let's go."

"Give me a second."

"You take longer than a woman."

I put on some clothes and shoes. Donald told me to hurry up. I snuck out but left the window open a crack for me to get back in later.

Donald offered me some gum: Big Red. It wasn't like Donald. I accepted a piece. At first the cinnamon burned, but the flavor faded quickly. Donald put a hand on my back and guided me away.

"We're doing night patrols, Coop. We're a Lee Marvin type of bad, brother. You're lucky you got someone like me to look after you."

I didn't know where we were going. We crossed through my small back yard and down the slope of ice plant to Columbus Avenue. Donald began marching ahead of me. He walked with the confidence of a victorious general.

A thin mist rolled up the road but seemed to clear as we moved closer. I followed Donald along the sidewalk until it came to an end and there was just road and the dirt by the side of the pavement. Donald noticed I'd stopped.

"I think we should turn back," I said.

"Don't get all Don Knotts on me."

Donald jogged a little ahead, turned right, and disappeared behind a row of Italian cypress. I shoved my hands into my pockets and peered over my shoulder. The world was dark and cold and quiet. I couldn't see Donald anymore, and I felt a tiny shock of fear run into my throat. I didn't like standing there alone. I called his name but didn't hear a response. I trudged after him into the night and tried to catch up.

Donald made his way up a gravel driveway to a large stone house. I knew the place. Whoever lived there had three dwarf apple trees in the front yard. Sometimes, I admit, I had trespassed and stolen a few Galas right off the branches.

I hiked the slope. The only noise was the crunching sound of my feet on the pebbles and grit. My spit tasted like tinfoil. I worried Donald might be hiding somewhere up ahead, waiting to jump out and scare me. I moved on.

Donald stood at the top. He crossed his arms in front of his chest as he watched me stumble toward him. He didn't say anything. He didn't need to. I saw the three trees and knew what he wanted to do. I secretly prayed some light inside the house would switch on, right then and there, and scare Donald off. I felt hollow as a jack-o'-lantern and couldn't look him in the eye.

"You take too long. You're a slowpoke. Just watch this."

Donald moved as a shadow across the yard. He didn't look human—just a streak of gray on black. With an athletic grace I'd never seen in Donald, he picked up speed and ran toward the apple trees with the crowbar in his hands. The trees didn't have any fruit or leaves. Donald used the crowbar like an axe. He swung and smashed the thin base of one of the trees. At first the tree didn't waver. But Donald swung again and brought the metal down on top of the tree, splitting it.

Donald used the crowbar, and then he just used his feet and stomped on the wood and the pulp of the plant. He didn't make any noise save for his gasping for air. Even in the dark you could see the fat shake on his sides when he moved. After a while, he stopped. He waved me over to join him.

I didn't move, and Donald waved again. I couldn't see his face, just his body and the outline of his arms and shoulders. Something inside me felt sorry for the apples that would never grow, for the people who lived there who had cared for those little trees. They were going to wake up and see the destruction and feel an ache that I didn't want to think about. I turned around and left to go back down the gravel driveway to the street. I took the gum out of my mouth and tossed it to the ground.

Donald hissed my name as I walked away. He'd tease me about it later, I was sure. But it had been a long day, and I didn't care much about getting teased anymore. I just wanted to crawl into bed and sleep and, perhaps, dream of Mom.

After I nudged my window open and pulled myself through, I kicked away my sneakers and peeled off my jacket. My room seemed hot after being outside, so I went to the kitchen to get a drink of water.

"You're up late," Sebastian said from the couch in the living room.

"Sorry if I woke you." I'd forgotten he was staying the night.

"Didn't wake me. Come here."

All the lights were off, so I went toward his voice. Blots of moonlight, pale and dim, fell through the window and onto his face and shoulders. He had his shirt off and had let his hair loose from his ponytail. His skin looked like limestone. When I got close he reached out and grabbed my forearm, almost as if in warning.

"Can't sleep?"

"No," I said. "I guess not."

"Insomnia is the curse of the thinking class. What have you been thinking about?"

"Nothing," I said.

"You're too young for nihilism. And you're too good a person to be a good liar. Now tell me the truth."

"I don't want to talk about it."

Sebastian let go of my arm. He put his hands on his lap and shrugged.

"I'm not going to force you, Captain Tsunami. But you should know that all things—even the worst of the worst—end eventually."

"Same for the good things?"

"Especially the good things. Sadly."

"Thanks for the pep talk."

"Wait," he said as I began to turn around. "I've got something for you."

Sebastian leaned over the couch and pawed at his jacket on the floor. He mumbled and hummed as he dug through the coat's pockets. Loose change and receipts fell to the floor. He sat upright and brushed the hair out of his face. Sebastian shot me a half smile.

"I want you to have this," he said. He extended his right hand and gave me a pocket flashlight. It was white and heavier than I thought it would be. A green snake was painted around the sides. Some of the paint was chipped and flaking off. I pressed the button, and the little bulb turned on, illuminating the room in a bright clear beam.

I turned it off and shrugged.

"Thanks," I said, not really knowing what else to say. Sebastian could be a weird guy like that. He always said he didn't like property or ownership. I'd seen him give money away to the homeless at the beach, and I'd been with him when he had donated clothes and furniture to the Goodwill—not because he was trying to get rid of anything; he just felt others could use the stuff.

"You like it?"

"Sure," I said while still looking at the thing. I gave Sebastian a polite smile and put the flashlight in my pocket. I didn't think I would ever use it.

"A few things a man should always carry," said Sebastian. "A watch, a handkerchief or bandanna, a knife, and a flashlight."

"A lot of things to haul around."

"You were never a Boy Scout, were you?"

"Nah. Not my thing."

I knew some other boys at school who had done Cub Scouts and now were doing Boy Scouts. I thought all that stuff was pretty lame. And their outfits made them all look like dorky mama's boys.

"The Boy Scout motto is always be prepared. You ever hear of that?"

"No."

"Well, you have now. I was a Boy Scout."

"You?"

"Eagle Scout, actually."

I couldn't picture Sebastian ever wearing the neckerchief, the khaki shorts, or the campaign hat. Of course, I could never imagine Sebastian in his youth, either. There was something about him that was perpetually old. Even when he was young, I think he would have been middle-aged, almost as if he'd been born with gray hair and wrinkles.

"So what's your point?" I said.

"My point? Let me tell you my point. The point is what you saw tonight has to do with your pops and not you."

"I know that."

"You don't know what side to butter your toast. Your dad had a bad night. That's all."

"Why did he do all that stuff?"

"Let's just say he was having a really strong memory. He probably doesn't want to talk to you about it. He probably doesn't want me talking to you about it either. Just remember, your old man is doing the best he can."

"That sounds like something he would say."

"You still worried about your mom?"

"What do you think?"

"I think I need some shut-eye. Got to get my beauty sleep. You should, too. It's late."

Sebastian nodded at me and lay back down and pulled the blanket up over his torso. He rolled onto his side. I wanted to keep talking with him, keep asking him questions. I thought about nudging him and keeping him awake, but I figured that would only annoy him.

Back in my room, I sat on my bed and then took out the flashlight and turned it on. For a small bulb, it was pretty bright. I turned it off and put it on the chair next to my bed. I slid Mom's notebook out from beneath my mattress. I read one undated passage:

This land is a desert in more ways than one. The people here are dry inside. Their thoughts are dust. Their souls are stone. Nothing grows here. A promise to myself to keep: I will get away—far, far away. Like Alice in her little blue dress. And when I do, I will kiss ever so deeply. Softly. Me and the Cadillac. There is more to enjoy than open skies. Yes? No? Yes!

The other night, Alburn cried in front of me. Such a fragile creature. Almost like the bones of a bird. He knows more than the sky or the sea. I've read his poetry. He taught me Donne and Frost. He should run away the first chance he gets. No more tragedy. No more waste.

I had no idea what any of it meant.

FIVE

A FEW WEEKS BEFORE MOM went missing, she took me out to eat, just mother and son. We drove into the city and parked in a garage downtown. We walked along the busy streets to an Italian restaurant where meats and cheeses hung in the windows and the tables all had red-and-white checkered covers. Outside, the gas lamps came on and glowed like holy candles.

Mom had a glass of wine. I drank Coca-Cola. When the waiter came I ordered ravioli, and Mom asked for gamberi ripieni with a small salad. The waiter told us we had made excellent choices, and then he went away.

Mom looked nice. She wore makeup, earrings, and perfume. Her red hair was pulled up in the back, while a wave of bangs swiped to the right of her forehead. I had my shirt tucked in and had wanted to wear a tie, but I didn't own one and my father's were too big for me.

"What do you think of this place?" Mom said. "And be honest."

"I like it," I said. "It has a nice charm to it."

"Charm . . . I'm not sure if that's the word I'd use, but yes. I guess it does have a certain charm. I love this restaurant. After we eat, I want you to try their cannoli. It is so good and rich and creamy, you'll swear off any other type of dessert."

"It's that good?"

"Yes. It's got a worldly flavor. You're getting older. You should be expanding your palate, trying new things. You and your father eat too much processed stuff. All that fast food will clog your heart."

It was nice seeing my mother enjoying herself, and I enjoyed being a part of that, sitting with her while she had a good time. I don't think my mother took pleasure in many things, so I tried to be on my best behavior and be agreeable. I wanted her approval, too; that is true. I remember I stared at my fork and knife with a breathless panic, hoping I would use them correctly.

Our food came, and Mom ordered another glass of wine. She smiled and used the waiter's name when talking to him. I liked having dinner with my mother. She enjoyed the conversation and treated a night out with a nice meal as a type of ritual. There should be wine and salad and then dessert and port.

I knew my father wouldn't like the place. He might eat there and smile, but he wouldn't have enjoyed it. That was Dad. He could be polite, but he didn't like being anywhere that expected more than jeans and a T-shirt, maybe a ball cap pulled down low on his brow, covering his sweat-matted curls. Mom loved getting into a fuss about what to wear and using proper etiquette.

"Do you like school, Coop?"

I didn't know what to say. I remember I was asked this all the time growing up—did I like school, did I enjoy school, what was my favorite subject. The truth was I didn't really like school, but I knew no one wanted to hear that answer. I told her that some days were better than others. I shrugged and poked at my pasta.

"You should try to pay attention in school. Then someday you can get a scholarship and you can go to college. Wouldn't you like that?"

"I guess."

Mom kept her arm extended with her hand gripping her wine glass. She tapped the side of her glass with her fingernails. I glanced at the other people dining near us. I was clearly the youngest person in the room. The men were round and balding, and they wore suits and ties. Their wives all had short hair, and their shirts had shoulder pads.

"Think about it. Coop, my Cooper the college student. You could go to Harvard or Princeton and be on a crew team. I'd love for you to be on a crew team."

"Crew sounds boring."

"It's an honorable and physical sport. You'd enjoy it."

"I'm not that into sports."

"That's fine, Coop. You can be an intellectual. You'll read poetry to all the co-eds, and then you can take the train into the city."

"I could go to San Diego State."

"You don't want to do that. You want to go someplace nice. You'll need some place where you can meet a good girl. You can meet her parents. And you can take her out to eat, to a place like this. And then you can spend Thanksgiving with her and her family, and you'll be happy then."

"I'm happy now."

I cut a piece of ravioli in two with my fork and then ate a half. It was good and buttery, with lots of zest in the meat. I reached across to grab some bread to wipe up the sauce. Mom slapped my knuckles, and I snatched back my hand.

"No, you're not."

"No?"

"I can tell who is happy and who isn't. Trust me. Mothers know these things. Women know these things. Do you have a girlfriend you're not telling me about?"

"No."

"Absolutely sure?"

"Yes. Of course."

"I want to tell you something about girls," she said.

I immediately felt nervous. I already knew, more or less, about sex, and I did not want to have to hear my mother talk to me about it. I had questions, but they were not the kind of questions I would ask anyone—especially her. But she didn't talk to me about sex or pregnancy or STDs.

"Don't trust any of them, Coop. You're too good for all of them. And they're all going to be bitches to you, honey. All of them bitches. Men are idiots, but women are bitches."

I didn't know what to say, how to respond. So I didn't say anything. I took another sip of my Coke. I wondered if she was joking. But she wasn't. And then she didn't say anything for a while. When the waiter came by, Mom asked for the check. All she said to me was "Come on. We'll get the dessert another time."

We got on Highway 94 and drove east toward home. At one point, Mom reached out and rubbed my cheek, touched my ear, but that was it. I stared out the window as we traveled over the 805 and through Lemon Grove. It was the middle of winter, and all of Southern California lay quiet and peaceful. The streetlamps had rings of mist around them.

When we arrived home, Dad was on the couch watching television. He wore jeans but didn't have a shirt on, and his feet were bare. Dad asked us how dinner was, but Mom didn't say anything. She went straight to her bedroom and locked the door, leaving me and Dad alone, silent save for the television's rackety commercials and theme music.

"What was that all about? Did you say something to upset her?"

"All I said was that I'd be okay with going to San Diego State."

Dad sat up and turned around to try to look around the corner to see if Mom was coming back out. She wasn't. I just stood there. I didn't want to make things more complicated, even though I wasn't sure what was going on.

"Sit down. Watch some *A-Team* with me."

"Okay."

"First, could you bring me a beer?"

"Yeah."

"What a guy."

I sat beside Dad and gave him his beer. I kicked off my shoes and watched B. A. Baracus lift up the A-Team's van. It was a silly show, but I liked it and Dad liked it. My father had to sleep on the couch that night, but that happened every now and again. He could deal with it.

I should say something about my father. This is as much about him as it is me. He was born in 1949 in Los Angeles and moved with his family throughout Southern California during the '50s. His parents had lived on ranches and farms most of their lives, but after the war there was better work in factories and on sound stages in Hollywood. He'd told me his father briefly worked as a grip on *Dragnet* and once did stunts for Robert Mitchum. But by the decade's end, Dad's family had settled in San Diego. My grandfather took a civilian's job as a mechanic for the navy. My father played football in high school but wasn't, in his words, "anything special." After graduation, he enrolled in community college, but he dropped out after one semester because his father had a heart attack and wasn't able to work. So my father took a job at the A&W to help out. In the summer of 1968, he was drafted and sent to Vietnam.

This is where my father's history blurs. He never spoke to me about the army or the war. The few times I built up the courage to ask, he would merely shrug and say he didn't remember much except it was hot and humid and green and that he spent most of the time simply waiting.

People respected my father. He knew how to make them feel at ease. When he talked to you, he spoke in a calm but curt manner and you sensed he wanted to be honest and not waste your time. This made him a good salesman, but he lacked a certain drive, an aggressiveness, which kept him from being a great salesman. Yet oddly this probably aided him with his specific customers, regular men and women who needed trucks and cars fixed. And even though he owned the place, he still wore a work shirt with his name on the left breast like a regular employee. My dad liked being his own boss. He liked being a husband and a father. That may sound common, but I've known plenty who truly did not like being in those positions.

For the most part, I would describe my father as a hardworking optimist. But I also believe my father carried a great deal of stress. Every now and again I came home and found him drinking. Dad liked scotch. My father almost never drank alone, so seeing him sit on the couch with a bottle of Cutty Sark and a blank stare was similar to seeing a bull's nostrils flare or hearing a snake's rattle. My father never hit me. He never hit my mother. And outside of the two fights I saw him get into, I would have guessed him incapable of violence.

When he was angry with me, he didn't yell—he whispered. He'd put his face close to mine, our noses almost touching, stare me in the eye, and speak so softly I had to hold my breath to hear him. If I was upset or crying, he would wait for me to hush. I always turned mute when he leaned in. I listened to his murmurs and did as instructed.

When I was a child, it frightened me. As I grew older, I came to admire this about him. I found my father's control, his restraint, to be a noble virtue. Even more so as most virtues lost their meaning to me. Though I knew he underwent various strains, he always managed to endure—and I believe that to be triumph enough.

SIX

WHEN MOM HADN'T SHOWN UP by Monday, Dad phoned some people. Nobody knew where she was. We talked with the police and filed a report, but the cops said there wasn't much that could be done for a voluntarily missing adult. We even tried Mom's former employer, Harrison's.

My father and I marched into the department store like we were ready to rob it—fists, sneers, and big shoulders. We made our way through the jewelry and women's wear sections accompanied by the elevator music that played from cheap speakers in the corners. It all sounded the same to me. Stuff that Lawrence Welk would have found boring.

At the perfume section, there was a new fragrance girl. She was young and pretty with big brown hair. Her bangs stood stiff from gels and sprays. Red plastic hoops dangled from her ears.

"Hello," she said. "May I help you two gentlemen?"

"Yeah," said my father. "I need to talk to your manager."

"Is there a problem?"

"No. You're fine. I just need to see him. What's his name? Alex? Alan?"

"Just a moment."

The new fragrance girl left her sales station. I stood

there beside my father and waited. I could see the sports and health section from where we were, and all they had on display were roller skates and those cheap skateboards that children got for Christmas but used only once. I knew that for sure, because I had received just such a skateboard for last Christmas.

The fragrance girl reappeared with the manager following her. He was the same guy from when my mother had been criticized by the woman in the fur coat. He looked like he was even wearing the same clothes and same tie. He carried a clipboard with him. I wasn't sure if he resembled more an FBI agent or an overworked accountant. He came and stood in front of me, next to the perfume counter.

"My name is Alan. I'm the manager. Is there a problem?"

My father sighed and rubbed his eyes.

"No," he said. "It's not like that. My name is Percy. This is my son, Cooper. My wife used to work here—Mrs. Arden Balsam. Did she explain why she quit?"

"Shouldn't that be something to ask your wife?"

"She's missing," I said.

The manager moved the clipboard to his chest and squinted. The fragrance girl waited on the other side of the counter. The manager looked at her, and she smiled and went away. She went to the dress section and talked with a woman with a toddler. The woman's hair wasn't combed. It tufted up and spiked out in patches. Her kid wore a light-blue jacket. The woman held the toddler's hand and wouldn't let him run away, though he kept pulling at her arm as he tried.

"So," said my father. "Did she say anything? We're trying to figure out where she might have gone."

"Not really," said the manager. "We were happy with her. But I don't think she enjoyed being here."

"Why do you say that?"

The toddler in the blue coat started crying. Not just weeping—he wailed like a fire alarm in the middle of the night.

He pointed at something and screamed. His mother picked him up, but he fought her as she did so.

"Take a look around. Harrison's isn't where the elite meet, at least not anymore. Between you and me, I don't even know if this place will see 1990. Your wife always pressed the good stuff on the customers—and we appreciated her efforts—but eventually you have to know your clientele. Big bottles around Mother's Day and Christmas. That's the only real market time for us in the fragrance section. Your wife probably couldn't afford some of those bottles on what we paid her—even with her discount."

The fragrance girl was still talking to the lady with the toddler. The kid kept sobbing. I couldn't see his mother's face, but the look on the fragrance girl's was one of those forced plastic smiles. The kid slapped his tiny fists against his mother's head. The mother finally carried her baby away and out of the store. The fragrance girl looked at me and then kept wandering around to see if anyone needed assistance.

"Do you have any Hawaiian shirts?" I said to the manager.

The manager lowered his clipboard and looked at me.

"Hawaiian shirts? No. I don't think so."

"You should carry some."

"I'll look into it."

"How did she quit?" said Dad.

"She just said she'd been thinking for a long time and had decided it was time for her to leave. We shook hands. She left on good terms."

"Thinking for a long time? She said that?"

"Yes. I believe so."

"Thanks."

My father and I left the store and walked into the parking lot. The manager hadn't told us much new information, except that now we knew my mother had planned on quitting for a while. That meant she must have been ready to take off for a while, too.

Eventually we dialed my grandmother, my mother's mother, in Arizona. I talked to her first.

"No," she said. "Arden hasn't been here. She hasn't called me either."

"Where did she go?" I said.

"Don't know what to tell you, kid. Your mother never liked eating brussels sprouts or taking orders. Stay calm. Just wait it out. She'll head back once she's done doing whatever she thinks she needs to do."

"That sounds like what Dad says." I listened to my grandmother smoke a cigarette, the strange, dry puffing sound she made whenever she took a drag. I wanted my grandmother to say something reassuring, but she was too much of a realist.

"Listen to your papa. Now let me talk to him. Put your father on."

I handed the receiver to Dad, who had been standing by the kitchen sink watching me. Dad put the phone to his ear and said hello. I scooted into my parents' room and picked up the second phone so I could hear what Dad and Grandma Liz said. I covered the mouthpiece with one hand so they wouldn't hear me breathing.

"It isn't like that," said Dad.

"Your son is worried, and you're not? You should feel ashamed."

"Of course I'm worried. I'm just not stupid."

"You need to do something."

"You don't get to talk to me like that. I came to you once, and you wouldn't have given a drowning man a towel."

"She could have done so much better."

"You got some magic ball I don't know about?"

"She used to brag about how smart you were. I still don't see it."

"You can cut out the wicked mother-in-law of the west routine."

"You better find her. You have to."

"I'd love to. Any ideas, Nancy Drew?"

"Arden isn't exactly one to go slumming. She must be spending money someplace."

Then no one said anything. Dad was breathing heavily. I suspected he might have known I was listening, so I chewed on the inside of my cheek to stay extra quiet. I heard Grandma Liz take a drag off her cigarette and wipe her lips, probably with her shirt collar the way she always did.

"I'll call a few more people."

"Check her credit cards. If you don't find Arden, I'll sell my house and move in with you. And I know you would just love that."

"She'll be back. You'll see."

Dad and Grandma Liz talked for a little longer but not about anything important, so I stopped listening. When I hung up, everything seemed pointless and stupid.

I hated the house. I hated the furniture. I hated the eucalyptus tree in our front yard. We didn't deserve this, I thought. But maybe we did.

My grandmother didn't visit us often. And we didn't drive to see her much, either. But I liked my grandmother and enjoyed it when she stayed with us, which was probably about once a year.

The last time she made the drive from Camp Clark, Arizona, to our little house in California, she brought me a red Hawaiian shirt decorated with hula dancers. The blouse was too big for me—it almost looked like a nightshirt—but my grandmother told me that I would grow into it.

"Please don't wear that in public," said my mother. "At least not if you're with me."

"I think it's great," I said.

"Please stop bringing him these things," said my mother. "They're gaudy and . . . they just don't have any class."

"Not everything is about being classy," said my grandmother. "Some things are about having fun."

Grandma Liz sat on the couch and smoked a cigarette. My

mother waited beside her on the armrest. My father wasn't there. I undid the buttons and slid my arms through the sleeves and wore it like a trench coat or some type of cape. I told myself that by the time I was old enough to visit the islands, I would already have the wardrobe.

"Coop, take that thing off," said my mother. She wiggled her fingers at me and grimaced, and her eyes squinted a little. Grandma Liz shook her head and stubbed out her cigarette.

"Do I have to?"

"You can wear it another day. Go put it in your closet for now. And don't just toss it on your bed or the floor."

"Thank you, Grandma."

"You're welcome, Cooper."

I walked to my room. As I went away, I heard my mother and grandmother talking.

"Stop bringing him stuff like that."

"I can spoil my only grandchild if I want."

"Then spoil him right. I don't want my son to be some cigar-chomping, beer-guzzling slob in a Hawaiian shirt."

I went to my room and closed the door. I took off the shirt and laid it on my bed. I buttoned it to the collar and smoothed out all the creases. It looked pretty nice. And then I balled it up and threw it into the corner of my closet.

And the shirt stayed there until the night my father and I called Grandma Liz to ask about my mother. After I hung up the phone, I went to my room and dug through the dirty laundry, forgotten toys, and old Halloween costumes scattered in the back of my closet and found the blouse all scrunched and twisted. I fluttered it out and shook off the dust. The fabric smelled of dirt. I undid the buttons and slipped on the shirt. It felt good on me. I would wash it with the next load of laundry—something my mother usually did for me, but now I had started doing it on my own—and would wear it when and wherever I wanted.

For the next couple of days, Dad started going through the mail left on the dining table and ripping open every envelope sent from the bank. He sat on the couch and examined all the phone bills and credit card notices to see if anything stuck out. Dad didn't say anything while he did this. He simply read to himself, occasionally circling something with a red pen and then nodding as if listening to instructions from an invisible trainer.

He didn't have the TV on. He didn't listen to music. He didn't eat anything or keep a bottle of Michelob or a glass of Cutty Sark nearby. And I made sure not to bother him. The one time I sat next to him and flipped on the television, he turned his head like a falcon and stared at me until I switched off the set and went back to my room without either of us speaking.

I'd hide in my room and read my copy of *Hawaii* or browse my mom's high school journal. Some passages I found myself rereading.

There'll come a day when I leave and never look back. Away from all the smallness. Something sweeter? Yes. No more grease and deep fried for this girl. This woman. I want to eat caviar. I don't know what it tastes like, but I'm sure I'll love it. And if not, then I'll learn to love it. When I move to New York, I'll drink only champagne. Nothing but the best for me and my Cadillac. The boys at school can't get anything but PBR or Old Milwaukee. Occasionally, they'll sneak a pint of Old Crow into the dances, but that stuff is vile. I wonder why anyone would consume such a beverage. Alburn says chilled white wine is the only drink for him.

Maybe Paris instead of New York? I have plenty of time to decide. Read more about Shanghai. Sounds interesting.

I could hardly imagine my mother as a teenager, let alone one who felt she belonged in New York or Paris. She didn't write much about her classes or teachers or friends. Almost every entry was about her dreams of escaping Camp Clark, Arizona. I couldn't help but wonder if she and I would have been friends if we'd gone to school together. Probably not. As much as I loved her, I have to admit I found her journal to be a little snooty. But I also found myself wanting to say, "Yes, I know just what you mean!" I thought of all the times I'd wished I could visit the jungle and the

Bahamas and the unmapped islands of the East, and I wondered what journeys I'd be able to take and which ones I wouldn't.

One evening, I was browsing my mother's journal in my room after dinner. Dad pounded at my door and called my name. I hid the journal. Dad knocked again, and I answered.

"Get your coat," he said. He wasn't smiling or frowning. He didn't blink. "We're going on a little trip."

"Where?"

"Downtown. I think I've found something."

A few minutes later, we were in Dad's Charger and heading west on State Route 94. Dad shifted gears as he sped ahead and changed lanes. The sun was going down fast, so the road and the cars all looked dim. Dad explained that Mom had used a credit card at some shop, and we were going to go and ask some questions.

The freeway stretched out before us like an empty gray vein. The sunset stained the sky colors of sherbet: purple, orange, raspberry. We drove on.

We shot into downtown and caught I-5 north for about twelve miles before Dad took an exit. I could tell he wasn't quite sure where he was going, because he slowed down to a slug's pace and tried to read street names. He kept glancing back at the credit card bill in his right hand.

"Are we going to find Mom?"

"Well, we're not out here to get ice cream."

We rolled past bars and old shops lit up with neon signs. A lot of people wandered outside and jaywalked across the streets. Everyone looked young and energetic. Dad turned left onto a thin road, almost an alley. The sun vanished somewhere into the ocean, and the world went dark.

Dad parked the car, and we got out. I could see down to the main drag. There were people moving and laughing and talking. Dad buttoned up his coat and told me to follow him. We went past a few dumpsters and a tattoo parlor. Dad kept a fast pace, and I tried to keep up.

I can't tell you the name of the road we were on, but I can tell you most of the buildings were vacant or trying their best to look that way. Their windows were blacked out with cardboard and yellow newspaper. Only one place had a sign hanging out front, and this sign was just an electric red light that read "Leather." And this was the shop my father entered.

It was clean inside but cramped and reeked of cowhides. Usually I enjoy how leather smells, but this store had so much of it that it made my stomach want to crawl into my throat. It was as if the ghosts of a hundred slaughtered herds were having their revenge. Black biker jackets hung in clumps to the right with dozens of zippers in fanged grins. An unmanned counter waited to the left. In the far right corner stood a mannequin clad in tight patent leather. There was even a mask that covered every bit of the head, including the eyes. A zipper ran across where the mouth would be.

Dad stepped up to the counter and called out to see if anyone was there. You could see past the counter into the back room, where the work was done. Slabs of leather, aniline and pigmented, lay across a large table. An ashtray with a smoking cigarette lay next to a head knife on the table. A small television sat on the opposite end. I could see Woody Woodpecker on the screen. Dad shouted out again, and we waited while the cartoon music played in the background.

I heard a door open and close in the back somewhere. This was followed by heavy footsteps. I was surprised when a skinny bald man came up to the other side of the counter. He wore glasses, dark-navy slacks with no belt, and a cheap dress shirt buttoned up all the way but with no tie. His sleeves were buttoned at his wrists. Though he had no hair on his head, he had several days' worth of scruff on his cheeks and chin. A tattoo of a green spider web clung to the left side of his neck, just creeping out from beneath his collar. The man stood on the other side of the counter and looked at me and then at my father.

"I don't do stuff with kids," he said.

Dad pushed the credit card bill toward him. The man's eyes peeked at it, and then he put his sight back on my father.

"I think my wife bought something here. Her name is Arden Balsam."

The man drummed his fingers on the counter. His eyes slid toward me.

"Do you have a receipt? Are you here to pick up your wife's order?"

"What did she buy?"

"It doesn't work like that. I can't share my clients' information—even with their spouses."

Dad smiled. He picked up the credit card bill and put it in his pocket. He looked at me. He let out a sigh and clenched his jaw. I heard Woody Woodpecker laugh his frantic and staccato chuckle.

"See this boy?" Dad said, pointing to me.

The man nodded and adjusted his glasses. Woody Woodpecker danced and hopped about a barbershop.

"That's my son. My wife, his mother, is missing. Now, I have a credit card bill that states she made a purchase at this store. What did my wife buy?"

"My clients come to me because they know I respect their privacy."

"You're not a priest. I'm not asking you about who else comes in here and buys freaky stuff," said Dad while he motioned with a jerk of his thumb toward the mannequin in the shiny outfit. "I just want to know what my wife bought right before she fell off the face of the goddamn planet. Are you going to help me, or what?"

On the television, Woody Woodpecker was trying to give a burly guy a shave and a haircut. He sang an aria from an Italian opera while he worked. I stood back and tried to stay quiet. I wasn't sure what was about to happen, but I could tell Dad was losing patience.

"You're a very rude man, aren't you? Maybe you should leave."

Dad took the credit card bill back out of his pocket and held it up in front of the man's face. The man scratched the tattoo on his neck.

"See here? That's your shop, right? What the fuck did my wife buy that you won't show me?"

"Maybe it's an anniversary present. You wouldn't want me to ruin her surprise, would you?"

Dad nodded slowly but kept his gaze on the man. The man began to smile. Woody Woodpecker continued to break just about everything in the barbershop, scaring the customer all the while.

"You mind shutting off that damn TV? Cartoons freak me out."

The man grinned but didn't say anything. He turned and went to the television set and turned up the volume. Now Woody Woodpecker screamed and shouted across the store. The man sauntered back to us.

"I like Woody," he said. "And it's my store."

"You like this, don't you?"

The man smiled.

"You've got a nice shop," said Dad. "You make a lot of money doing this?"

"I get by."

"You want to get by a bit further?"

Dad took out his wallet and removed several twenty-dollar bills and put them on the counter. The man sneered at the money. Dad bit his lip and put a few more twenties down. The man reached out to grab the cash. Dad snatched the man's wrist and squeezed. The man's fingers curled up and went white.

"No," said Dad. "Not yet."

"That hurts."

"Arden Balsam. What did she buy here?"

Dad slid the money to the edge of the counter and told me

to come and take it, to hold on to it until the man answered his questions. Woody Woodpecker ended up getting tossed into a shelf stocked with shaving mugs. He gave his manic and signature giggle one last time.

I did as I was told. Dad pulled on the man's arm—not hard, but enough to get the man's attention. I stood back with the money against my chest like lilies. I watched. He tugged the man's arm again.

Dad didn't hurt the man—but he could have.

The only other time I'd seen Dad do anything like that had been several years before, when he'd gotten in the fight outside the supermarket. I stood there and watched. It was a little bit surreal, more like I was watching a movie or actors rehearsing a scene. I have to admit a sliver of me was excited. This guy had antagonized my father and now was getting his comeuppance. But another part of me felt just the opposite: small, afraid, and disgusted. I also felt sorry for the man behind the counter. There had to be something a little humiliating about being manhandled like that in your own place of business.

"Let me go. She paid in advance. She never picked it up. It's in the back."

Dad released his grip. The man sulked away into the back room. I stared at my dad. He wouldn't look at me.

The man reappeared a minute later. He had something in a long plastic bag. He laid it halfway across the counter.

"See," he said. "Nothing weird."

"Unzip it."

The man didn't say anything. He wouldn't make eye contact with my father. He unzipped the bag and took out a beautiful pink leather jacket.

The man held it up for us to gawk at. It was small with one zipper down the middle; two smaller zippers cut across each breast. There was no collar.

"You made this?"

"I make everything here."

"That's nice work."

"I know."

"You're sure my wife bought this?"

"She commissioned it."

"It's kinda small," said Dad.

"I went with the figures she gave me."

"She buy anything else here?"

"No."

"Okay. Come on, Coop."

Dad gathered up the jacket and bundled it under his arm. He moved toward the door. Another cartoon started, and Woody Woodpecker laughed once more.

"Hey," said the man. "Tell your kid to give me the money."

Dad looked over his shoulder at the man.

"You already said you were paid in advance. Let's get out of here, Coop. I feel like getting a burrito."

Dad pushed the door open and marched out. I shot after him. The man behind the counter shouted something at me, but I didn't really hear what he said. Outside, Dad didn't wait for me. He stomped to the car and wouldn't stop when I yelled out to him.

He unlocked the driver's-side door and tossed the jacket into the back. He got in and slammed the door shut. I ran around to the other side. It was locked, so I tapped on the window. Dad just sat there.

"Dad," I said. "Let me in."

He didn't move.

"I think that guy is going to come out here. Will you please let me in?"

Traffic down the way sounded like waves on the beach. People laughed as they left restaurants and bars. The Pacific air felt brisk, raw, but the street and the gutter reeked of piss.

Dad moved his head and blinked a few times. He leaned over and opened the door. I sat down and buckled up, even though Dad hadn't started the engine. He hadn't even put his key in the ignition.

"That was stupid," he said. "I wish I hadn't done that."

I still had the cash. I handed it to him, and he took it. He didn't count it. He held on to the bills like a talisman.

"Shit. You think I should go back in and give this to him?"

"What? No. That guy was a jerk. He had it coming."

"Don't talk like that. We're not thugs, Cooper. Don't start thinking . . ."

"What?"

"Forget it."

Dad shoved the money into his coat pocket. He started the car and drove home.

We didn't know what to do with the pink jacket. Later that night, Dad sat on the couch and examined it. He held it up to the light like a possible counterfeit bill. He gnawed on his lower lip. He shook his head as if in disbelief and handed it to me. It was a nice-looking coat.

"Doesn't make sense. The thing wouldn't fit her."

Dad flipped on the television, and I snuck to my room with the jacket under my arm. I closed the door behind me and went and sat on my bed in the dark with the jacket on my lap. I ran my hands over the leather, the zippers, the lone silver button at the top where there should have been a collar. I tried on the jacket, and it was too small even for me. I stretched out my hands and looked at my palms. The cuffs reached only halfway down my forearms.

Standing there, wearing that pink leather jacket, my abs, back, and shoulders tensed up and ached. It was a cold feeling—almost like a stone bruise—and then the sensation drifted away. I took off the jacket and hung it in my closet. It looked like a fresh scab among the dark shirts and pants.

I knew my mother was out there somewhere. I imagined her dancing. I imagined her crying in a motel bed. I imagined her stepping onto a train bound for places unknown, and I imagined her sitting alone in some bar and gazing into her wine. I imagined her driving south on the Pacific Coast Highway, speeding through the night to get back home and back to me.

SEVEN

AN ENTIRE WEEK WENT BY. No Mom. No calls. No idea where to look. Nothing to be done but try to remain stoic. It didn't take long for everything to fall into chaos. Dad and I couldn't function well without her. We all did our share of chores, but it was Mom who reminded us to do them. We were not good at domestic tasks; with no one to please, we turned primitive and quiet. Dishes, pans, and coffee mugs filled the sink. One stuffed garbage bag sat beside the trash can, waiting to be taken out. Crushed soda cans cluttered the kitchen counter. All the cabinet doors stayed open. The house lay stuffy and crude. We ate in front of the television. We washed plates and silverware individually and only as needed.

One day, Dad was drunk when I got home. He sat on the couch in his briefs and undershirt, drinking Cutty Sark and water. The television played *Moonlighting.* Dad's eyes, glassy and pink, glanced at me without turning his head. He raised his eyebrows and kept watching the show.

"No Mom?"

"No sir, kiddo."

"Okay."

I sat beside him. A commercial came on. Dad mumbled

and waved a hand at the screen. He smelled of scotch and soil and sweat, almost sweet and woodsy.

"School go today?"

"It went."

"An education is a hell of a thing."

"If you say so."

"Hungry?"

"Haven't eaten since lunch."

He stood in a wobble. He finished what remained in his glass.

"Okay. Let me fix some grub."

Dad lumbered into the kitchen, turned on the oven, and tossed in two frozen dinners. He came back saying we'd have supper in a bit. The night moved on. We ate our frozen dinners with the tiny side of vegetables and little bit of mashed potatoes that tasted like cardboard. We watched *Moonlighting.* At one point, a bad guy shot a machine gun and missed everybody.

"Horrible shot," I said.

"Such bullshit. You don't miss with that type of firepower. You just aim and spray. Kills everything. Dead gooks everywhere."

I asked Dad what he meant, but he had fallen asleep.

What my father did not know was that I had been calling my grandmother. I waited until Dad was distracted by some television show or had gone to sleep early, and then I quietly snuck to the phone and dialed long distance and whispered with my mother's mother.

I had lots of questions regarding my mother's journal. Who were these people? What were her friends like? Why did she hate Arizona so much? What was my mother like as a girl? Grandma Liz did not have many answers for me.

I listened as Grandma Liz smoked and dried the corner of her mouth with her shirt collar. Sometimes she would hack a little, and I could hear her light a new cigarette.

"Cooper, your mama was not like anyone else in this town. Sometimes that worked for her, sometimes it didn't. When all her classmates were wearing jeans, she wore dresses—almost exclusively. Like she wanted homecoming to be every day."

It seemed like the more I asked about my mother, the more distant and abstract she felt. At least to me. My grandmother told me about how my mother auditioned for her high school's production of *Our Town* and made the cast, but she dropped out before the first rehearsal. She told me my mother got hired at the grocery store but that she would wear a wig to work. She told me that she talked about New York City all the time and then suddenly decided to move to California at the last minute. None of it made much sense to me. But then I wasn't sure if any of it was supposed to make sense.

I kept to myself at school. I didn't really mind the actual learning part of history or math or English, but I couldn't stand dealing with the other students. The problem was simply that there were too many clashes of personality without any unifying goal. In a workplace environment there may be a bunch of people who normally wouldn't get along, but they are all there to make a living and are willing to make nice to get that paycheck. In school it is just hours of being in a place no one wants to be, with people who don't like one another. I learned early on to sit in the back, be quiet, and not draw attention to myself. I usually made good, but not amazing grades, which helped. The smart kids and the dumb kids set off an equal number of flags to the teachers.

On Wednesday, my math teacher, Ms. McMurtry, asked me to stay after class. I had her right before lunch, and I was eager to find a place to sit and eat and read and not be bothered. But Ms. McMurtry was nice and I didn't want to be rude, so I stayed behind while everyone else ran to buy ice cream sandwiches and sloppy joes from the cafeteria.

"Coop, your last few quizzes have been quite poor."

"I'm sorry, Ms. McMurtry."

"You don't have to apologize to me, Coop."

Ms. McMurtry sat behind her desk, and I stood in front of

it. The door was open. A brisk wind blew inside. The morning's
rain had stopped and the midday sun had come out, but there
were still puddles and mud.

I didn't look at her; I looked at my feet. Ms. McMurtry was
young and pretty in an Emily Dickinson type of way. She never
wore makeup, but her skin was always clean. Her brown hair
stayed bundled up behind her head, and her neck looked long
and fragile like a bird's.

"I'll do better next time."

"Coop, usually when a student's grades drop as sharply as
this, in my experience, it means something is wrong. Is everything okay? Has something happened recently?"

"No, ma'am."

"Please don't call me ma'am."

"Sorry, Ms. McMurtry."

"Well, if you need to talk, you can come see me. Okay?"

"Yes."

"Coop?"

"Yes?"

"What do you want to do?"

Then I looked at her. I was taken aback by her question. No
one had asked me such a direct and straightforward question.
Adults had never seemed to truly care about my opinion. I
wasn't sure if Ms. McMurtry did care, but the asking itself
was enough to make me stumble. Ms. McMurtry leaned in her
chair. Her hands rested on her stomach. Her blouse was a silky
off-white, and her wrists and forearms looked incredibly thin.

"I want to travel," I said.

"To where?"

"I'd like to see Hawaii, the tropics, and the Far East. Everywhere, I guess."

"Why do you want to travel?"

"What do you mean?"

"I think it is a pretty basic question, Coop."

"I don't know," I said, which was the truth. I didn't know.

"Well," she said. "Think about it. Will you do that for me?"

"Sure."

I left Ms. McMurtry's room, not understanding what had just happened. I went to lunch and ate alone. Though I tried to read, I couldn't concentrate, so I let my mind wander and think about what she had said. Of course I wanted to travel, I thought. Who didn't want to travel?

Later that afternoon, when I was home but Dad was still at work, someone phoned for Mom. I expected it to be a telemarketer or a wrong number—the only calls we received.

"Hello?" I said.

"Yeah, is Arden there? Put her on, will ya."

The voice belonged to a female, but it was deep, almost masculine. It wasn't anyone I recognized. Whoever it was, she was chewing gum.

"I'm sorry, she isn't here. She's been gone for over a week."

"A week, my foot."

"Has she called you? My dad and I are worried and can't locate her."

"Wait, you're her kid?"

"Yes," I said. "I'm her son."

"That lying bitch. You tell her that Roxy called."

"I told you, she isn't here. We don't know where she is."

"Yeah, yeah. Don't give me no soap operas. You tell her I'm coming for her."

Then the phone went dead. I figured it had to be a prank call. I didn't know from whom. The world was filled with crazy people, mean people. To them another person's suffering was just entertainment. People devouring people.

Dad came home with cheeseburgers from In-N-Out. Sitting in front of the tube, we ripped the bags apart and used the grease-stained paper and wrappings as plates. Dad ate all the fries. I asked if he knew anyone named Roxy. He stared at the screen and shook his head. We didn't talk. There wasn't much to say. We stayed like that, lit by the gray glow of the television in the dark room, waiting for bedtime and another day to begin.

That night I walked outside, and I stared at the moon. People in Hawaii were looking at that same moon. And then I wondered if Mom, wherever she was, was looking at it too. Thinking about Mom made me feel bad. I told myself to cut it out. Nobody liked someone filled with self-pity. Okay, I thought, don't think about her; she probably isn't thinking about you. And that settled it.

Someone called my name, and it startled me. It was Donald.

"Hey, where have you been?"

"Nowhere."

"Follow me. I want to show you something."

Donald and I went to his house. The garage door was open, and the light was on. Donald jogged to the corner where his father kept his tool cabinet. He returned with the crowbar. He held it in both hands like one might present a sword, the Excalibur of crowbars.

"We're going to smash some stuff tonight."

"I'm going home."

"Bullshit. You're coming."

I didn't want to go. But I knew if I refused, Donald would start yelling and punch me, and I knew he outweighed me and I'd lose the fight. And on top of that, Donald would never let me forget it. It was easier to give in. That was the thing I hated about Donald; if he didn't get his way, he became a bully or he whined until you caved. It was not mature, but it was effective. Part of me wanted to snatch the crowbar away from him and smash his face in, but I reluctantly followed him anyway.

Looking back, I'm not sure why I was so passive around Donald. I have to admit that sometimes I had fun with him. I think we got along mostly out of the limitations of our environment—in other words, we had to. There were simply not many other kids for us to play with. There were the Merril sisters, but they were girls and hadn't ever wanted to play with us, or at least wouldn't play with Donald. There were the two brothers, Hunter and Quint, who lived nearby, but Hunter had already beat up Donald a few times and Quint followed his brother around like a little assistant. Teddy Hacker, a twenty-one-year-old who lived down the block, was always nice and willing to show us his ninja stars and take us for rides in his Firebird, but my father had given me direct orders to stay away from him for some reason. So Donald and I had gotten used to each other.

Before I knew what was happening, Donald was tugging on my shirt with his right hand, pulling me along. We trailed out of the garage, onto the driveway, and then down the sidewalk. The night was noiseless and cold. I could see my breath. Everything tasted damp and metallic.

I followed Donald to Columbus Avenue, the main drag that cut through our neighborhood. The street curved like a blacksnake around the bend of the hill. Down and to the north there were the little league fields, the post office across from the liquor store, and the Taco Bell. If you followed the avenue up far enough, you came to homes with horse stables and the one Victorian with peacocks in the back yard. If you went even farther still, you would come down on the other side, near the reservoir. The houses there had all been built between the world wars. They sat close together, and there were no sidewalks and few trees. The population there was predominantly Hispanic.

The avenue looked like a river, dark as coffee, but without any swells or rapids or muddy banks to stand on. Cars had parked along the sides, their windows masked with dew. Streetlamps lined the sidewalks beside the small slopes of rosemary and ice plant. The lights gleamed through the mist. The street was busy only during certain hours: in the morning when people left for school or work, and in the hour or two before dusk when those same people returned. The rest of the time, it was more or less a silent stretch of pavement.

Donald and I jogged across Columbus, through someone's

back yard, and came to a cul-de-sac. In the summer the people who lived in one of the houses there left their windows open, and if I woke early and went outside, I would hear them snoring. The houses didn't look that different from mine or Donald's, except these had red tile roofs. Their sedans and trucks sat in their driveways. Their front lawns looked neat and orderly, not rugged and overgrown like mine. I wondered if anyone was watching us. Donald's heavy breathing, almost panting, was the only noise. He gripped the crowbar with both hands as if it were a baseball bat.

"Let's have a rodeo," he said.

Donald smashed the first mailbox with one good swing. He crushed it in the middle. He hit it two more times after that. The next mailbox was stronger. It took Donald three tries to bash it in.

There wasn't much noise. There was just the dull thudding followed by the brief crumpling of aluminum. When he finished, Donald bent over at the waist and caught his breath. Then he came and handed me the crowbar.

"You go," he said.

"No," I said.

"What? Scared?"

I was scared. I didn't want to be caught. And I didn't want to wreck someone's mailbox. But then I felt the weight of the crowbar, and it was heavier than I expected. There was something powerful about it, something primal that made me feel awake and strong. Donald stood close to me. He didn't say anything; he just stood there watching me, waiting for me. I knew I should have just handed the tool back to him and walked away. I knew that there was something stupid and mean-spirited about his love for vandalism and that I should have said no. But then part of me wanted to break something. Part of me craved destruction. I desired the energy of demolition, the explosive adrenaline of havoc. I wanted to make someone hurt.

I knocked the mailbox off its post with my first swing. It fell to the ground, and I went after it. I clubbed it like a caveman beating at wild game. I was all muscle and power. I was order and discipline, the king whom everyone obeyed. The metal reverberated in my grip, bruising my palms. It felt good. I thought of my mother and how there was nothing I could do, how I wouldn't even be out if she was home, how much I hated the world. Donald silently cheered me on. He pumped a fist and punched the air in time with my swinging.

I kept at it. Everything was silent and numb. I knocked over another mailbox. I crushed it just like the last one. It made me feel better, but only for a little while.

EIGHT

DAD INSTRUCTED ME NOT TO tell anyone about my mother. He said it was our business and no one else's. So I kept my mouth shut.

Sometimes instead of going straight home after school, I stopped by my father's shop if he wasn't busy. The properties near him had high turnover, and there were always several empty spots up for lease. But some stores had been there as long as I could remember; the ice cream parlor, the bicycle mechanic, and the comic-book gallery had all become small local staples. They looked the same from the outside: large windows and glass doors with mail slots by the brass handles. Some had neon signs flashing their names, but most did not. A row of sycamore trees cut across the parking lot. All their branches were bony and naked for the winter. In the summer they flourished a chameleon green. But I loved them most in the fall, when their leaves changed to the colors of fire, looking warm and welcoming and gentle– like they came from somewhere else, somewhere far away.

If the place was busy, or if Dad was with a customer, I'd keep walking and follow Houston Street toward home. But sometimes I looked in and saw it was just my father and Sebastian.

The second Thursday after Mom disappeared, both
Dad and Sebastian sat behind the counter. The bell rang as
I entered, and suddenly all I could smell was the plastic and
rubber chemical odor of an auto-parts store, the faint whiff of
bleach beneath everything. Dad and Sebastian looked at me.

"If it isn't Captain Tsunami," said Sebastian.

I put my backpack on the counter. Sebastian asked me what
I was reading, and I told him I was working through *Hawaii*.

"I've been there," he said.

"Don't listen to him," said Dad. "He fell asleep once while
watching *From Here to Eternity*."

"That doesn't count."

"Did you wake up next to Deborah Kerr?"

"Is she a big black woman?"

"Nope."

"Then maybe I'm confusing Hawaii with Detroit."

"Happens to me all the time."

"Coop, anyone ever tell you your old man is a real
smart-ass?"

"Better than a dumb-ass," said Dad.

"Well, everybody likes a good piece of ass."

Dad and Sebastian were sipping bottles of cola, but I
could smell the rum on my father's breath, and his eyes were
bloodshot and glassy. He'd been drinking but wasn't drunk.
Both men laughed and then sighed.

It was one thing when Dad drank his scotch at home, but I
didn't like being around him when he drank in public. Thank-
fully, he didn't do it often. It took only a few drinks to make him
messy and brutish. He swore and slurred. He'd sweat and grow
flushed, and then he'd get sleepy.

I told Dad and Sebastian that I couldn't stay. This was a lie.
But I'd rather go home and be alone than watch Dad get wasted
in front of people trying to buy oil and windshield wipers. Dad
leaned back. He drank and smacked his lips. Sebastian waved
at me as I walked out.

Later that day, around dusk, I was on the couch reading
Hawaii. I'd been lost in the saga, and I think I was near the
halfway mark when I heard a car pull up to our house. My first
thought was that it had to be Mom. But it wasn't her. It was an
orange VW Bug, Sebastian's car. I watched Sebastian help my
dad out and walk him to the door. Dad's feet slid and kicked
at the dirt. Sebastian looked like he was having a hard time. I
opened the door for them. Once inside, Sebastian dropped my
father on the couch.

After Sebastian caught his breath, he said, "He'll be okay.
He just needed to let off some steam."

Dad kicked off his shoes. He mumbled something, rolled
onto his back, and tossed an arm over his face so the inside of
his elbow masked his eyes.

"That beautiful bitch," said Dad.

"Make sure he gets some water and some aspirin if you
have it," said Sebastian.

"Thanks for bringing him home."

Sebastian nodded.

Dad tried to sit up but couldn't, so he lay down again.
"This isn't the first time," he said. "She's done it before. She'll
do it again. Never this long, though. Jesus."

Sebastian and I glanced at each other. He went and got
Dad a glass of water. I shook Dad's leg and told him to stay
awake.

"The first was the worst. God, she scared me."

"Drink this," said Sebastian. Dad sat up, took the glass,
and drank.

"Right after we got married, we rented this crappy
apartment by Dog Beach. I was working—both of us had these
shit jobs—and I came home, and she wasn't there. I figure a
girl's night out. No big deal. I fix dinner, watch *Carol Burnett*,
and I fall asleep. I wake up, and Arden is still gone. Now, I'm
not happy, but I don't want to overreact. I know the bars are
still open. She's been out a while, but still no reason to call the

cops. So I move to the bed and figure, hope, she'll slip in beside me during the night. I wake up, still no wifey. Now I'm freaking out. I'm picturing car crashes, murder, rape, kidnapping, all types of B-picture stuff. I'm calling our friends, I'm calling the cops. Nobody can help me. I just have to hold steady and wait."

"Jesus," said Sebastian. He took the glass out of Dad's hand.

"How long was Mom gone?"

"Four days."

I could tell Sebastian was looking at me. I could feel his gaze. I don't know why he was looking at me. I looked at my father; his eyes stayed focused straight ahead. There was something calm yet scary in his tone. He was being honest with me and not trying to soften the conversation. He spoke to me as if I was a grown-up. This startled me, because I still did not know how a grown-up should respond.

"When she showed up, it was as if nothing had happened. At least not in her mind. I asked where she had been, I told her how afraid I'd been, and she just looked at me like I was saying all the wrong things. It was as if we were on stage in a play, but we had different scripts, and we kept waiting for the other to realize it."

"Where did she go, Percy?"

"I never found out. When I asked, she got mad. So I stopped asking."

Dad shrugged. He went silent.

"But she went off again?" I said.

"Never as long as that first time."

"And you never knew where?"

"No. Women need space. I think she just needed a break from me. From the world. Silence and peace. Space to think in."

"But she's coming back."

"Of course."

"What if she doesn't?"

"Then she doesn't. Coop, some things are out of your control. You have to accept that."

And with that he relapsed into the diction of an adult addressing a child. I didn't like that. I wanted him to be honest. He still wasn't looking at me or anything, just staring straight ahead between me and Sebastian in an undead gaze. His jaw looked too heavy for his face. I realized I was holding my breath.

I walked Sebastian to his car. Dusk had turned to night, and now the streetlamps glowed in a cold yellow. Sebastian sat on the hood. I couldn't look at him. I couldn't force myself to look at anybody.

"I never knew all that," I said.

"Don't worry. Your mother is a different type of woman. A hellcat. But she loves you. She'll be back."

"I'm not sure I believe that."

"You know what I believe? Love is ceaseless. You never run out of it. You always have enough to give someone else."

"I have no idea what that's supposed to mean."

"Me neither. I've been married three times and divorced just as many. What do I know? Keep your chin up. We'll go and try that watermelon gum to cheer ourselves up."

"Watermelon gum?"

"Looks pretty neat."

"Sounds kinda gross."

"Sounds delicious to me."

Sebastian patted me on the arm and got in the car. He drove away, and I was sad to see him go. I went back inside and draped a blanket over Dad and then went into my room to read. A while later, I heard Dad get up, use the toilet, and go to his room. I tried to keep reading. I was getting tired. The book was good, and it made me want to visit the islands even more. I wanted to see jungles and wear Hawaiian shirts. Eventually I fell asleep.

I awoke to Donald tapping at my window. His eyes looked big and wild. He got that look whenever he was about to do something stupid. Donald motioned for me to come outside. I knew he wanted me to go with him and vandalize something else. He started to talk, but I put a finger to my lips to tell him to be quiet. He nodded and stepped back.

I snuck out my window. Donald had the crowbar. Since we'd smashed mailboxes on the other side of Columbus, we decided to go the opposite way, toward Houston Street. A faint mist fell over us. We walked side by side, ready to break, smash, and pulverize. Everybody had better watch out.

Donald paused by a grove of trees. The air smelled of rain and pine. Donald gave me the crowbar to hold. He dug into his pockets and took out a pack of cigarettes and shook one free. His eyes met mine, and he held the pack toward me.

"Want one?" he said.

"Yeah," I answered. He tapped another one up and handed it to me. Donald fumbled with a BIC and lit up. I'd never smoked before. I had seen Yul Brynner's commercials asking people not to smoke—with his freaky bald head and eyes looking as if they were always taking aim—but I was curious. More than that, I knew it was something I wasn't supposed to do. It didn't surprise me that Donald had stolen some of his father's Camels. But I surprised myself when I accepted one.

I liked the way the cigarette smelled, woodsy and of the earth. It reminded me of the sawdust in our garage in summer, of camping trips with Dad and Sebastian in the mountains and the deserts just east of San Diego. Donald took back the crowbar and held out the flame for me. I put the cig between my lips and leaned in. That first drag tasted like heavy poison. My mouth, throat, and lungs burned. It felt as if my insides had been taken into the street, beaten with a baseball bat, and shoved back into my chest. I couldn't stop coughing. My eyes went red and watery. Donald laughed.

"Popped your cherry," he said. I bent over and coughed some more. I couldn't stop. I prayed for it to stop. I thought for a second I might throw up. It didn't make sense that this

could be addicting, I thought. Who did that to himself? I felt
light-headed and strange. I stumbled to my left and sat against
a tree. When I closed my eyes, it was like the world fell away
and I was drifting into some darkened limbo. My brow began
to sweat. My mouth went dry.

"Are you trying to kill me?"

"Hey, I didn't force you. Try it again. It gets better."

"Why should I believe you?"

"Hey, you want to be like the Marlboro Man or what?"

I still had the cigarette clenched between my fingers. I wiped
the tears away and took a second drag. Donald was right. This
time it wasn't as bad. It didn't really feel good, but it didn't feel
like an eighteen-wheeler was trying to parallel park within my
lungs anymore. The smoke tasted good. I wheezed and hacked
a little, but I was able to finish smoking the cigarette.

Donald flicked his butt into the street. Smoke poured out
his nose. He told me to hurry up. I ground the cig into the dirt
to make sure the fire was completely extinguished.

"If you like that," said Donald, "then you'll love what else
I've got."

I didn't know what he meant by that, but it didn't sound
good. He gave me a hand as I got up. I dusted myself off and
followed Donald. My tongue felt fuzzy and too large for my
mouth, but it slowly returned to normal. I couldn't smell the
pine anymore, just the warm tobacco on my lips.

Almost all the residential roads were cul-de-sacs. The few
that weren't were connected to either Columbus Avenue or
Houston Street. Nobody had their lights on. I didn't hear any
traffic. We dashed across Houston's four lanes and into another
cluster of stucco homes with red tile roofs. I didn't know anyone
who lived there. Donald and I walked down a sloping sidewalk,
and I tried not to trip over myself.

We turned onto another road and walked for a while. I
may not have known the destination, but Donald didn't need
to tell me when we got there. We stood in front of a house

with a front yard decorated with garden gnomes—happy, tiny garden gnomes. They all wore pointy caps and had smiling faces, and I hated all of them. I hated their stupid happy faces and their cutesy outfits. Some held lanterns. A few of them held hands. I didn't know who lived there, but I was sure they were content and didn't have problems or ever get hurt, and I hated them too.

"Ready?" said Donald.

"Ready," I said.

Donald broke the first one. It was a bearded gnome dressed all in green. Donald swung the crowbar like a golf club, and the little guy shattered. Donald strolled back and passed off the bar. I used both hands and smashed a lady gnome in a red skirt. Donald broke a couple of flowerpots. When it was my turn again, I picked up a gnome in blue who smoked a pipe, threw him in the air, and hit it like a baseball. Ceramic shards went everywhere. After a while, we stopped taking turns with the crowbar and just began breaking stuff; we stomped on plants and tossed yard decorations onto the street. We made sure every gnome was demolished.

It felt good. It made me believe I was big. Nobody could touch me. I was Rambo, the Terminator, Dirty Harry, and Optimus Prime. I wasn't just a twelve-year-old kid; I was the Wolfman.

It wasn't long before a light went on within the house. Donald and I sprinted away. We didn't yell or shout or cheer. The only sounds came from our tennis shoes pushing off the pavement.

We trailed down the street, across someone's yard, and then across Columbus and into a cluster of eucalyptus trees on the side of a large hill. I had hiked the hill in the summer and had ridden my bike around the secret dirt paths to the canyon on the other side. A water tank sat at the top like a giant pale emerald that no one wanted to claim. Donald and I climbed the slope a bit, just high enough that we could stare into the branches of the trees and not see the roads or the houses or anything of the valley. Donald tossed the crowbar onto the ground, and we both collapsed and rested. My lungs heaved. I was still on an adrenaline high from killing the gnomes and the flowerpots. It was a foolish thing to do, but I'd enjoyed it.

Donald took out his cigarettes, and we smoked. It was easier for me to smoke that time. It still made me feel light-headed and good. The smoke made a course through my lungs and into my muscles and blood, and my body relaxed and went soft. If I had just been an action movie destroyer, now I was a noir detective hero, waiting for another dame, another case. Sam Spade. Philip Marlowe. Jake Gittes.

"You sure know how to throw a party," said Donald.

I didn't say anything. Smoke from my cigarette floated into my eyes. I tried not to drool on myself. Donald dug into the back pocket of his jeans. He pulled out a half-pint of Kentucky Gentleman. Donald unscrewed the cap and made a silent toast to the air before he took a sip. He puckered and exhaled as if he'd tasted something hot or sour. Then he bit his lower lip, squinted, and nodded. He coughed a little as he passed the bottle to me.

"I don't know," I said.

"It'll put hair on your nuts."

I smelled the liquor. The scent alone turned my stomach. I glanced sideways at Donald and could tell he was watching me, waiting. If I didn't drink, then he'd just hound me, call me a baby. I put the bottle to my lips and let the whiskey pool in my mouth so I could swallow a bit at a time. It burned and tasted of corn and wildfire. My throat felt stripped of lining and tissue.

"Look at you," said Donald. "You're gonna hurl. You're such a virgin."

Saliva started to fill my mouth. My gut rollicked in and out. I thought Donald was right—I was going to throw up. I breathed slowly through my nose and closed my eyes. After a while, it all stopped. Donald took the bottle away from me and sneered. He was disappointed that I had not thrown up. I think the first time he tasted bourbon, he must have vomited all night, and now he hoped to inflict the same experience on someone else.

Donald drank. He stared off into the darkness of the trees. I lay down on the grass and soil of the hill with my hands behind my head. I finished smoking my cigarette, which made my stomach begin to convulse again. I stubbed out the cig and focused on my breathing. I'd be damned if I would give Donald the satisfaction of seeing me throw up.

"You know what?" said Donald. He took a drag. "Someday everyone is going to be sorry. I'm going to be famous, you know. You can be one of my captains—when I take over, I mean."

"You plan on going into politics?"

"Something like that. I'm going to be like Hitler, but you know, not like killing Jews. I'm going to be the good Hitler."

Donald pounded his left breast twice with his right fist. He kept the bottle in his other hand. I turned my head to look at him.

"That doesn't make sense," I said.

"I'm going to bring everyone together and run things."

"The 'good Hitler'?"

"Damn right. Then I'll get so much pussy . . . It'll be beautiful. They'll want to lick it and everything."

Donald rested his forearms over his knees. He seemed deep in thought, almost as if in a type of trance from his delusions of grandeur.

"That's gross."

I sat up. I swatted at the back of my head to knock the leaves and grass out of my hair.

"What do you know?" said Donald. He moved his head but not the rest of his body. He looked me up and down and took on a type of drill-sergeant tone. "Have you ever even seen a woman naked? I bet you haven't. You're too young. You're a baby."

I didn't know what to think. I understood the basic mechanics of sex, but a lot of it was still just rumor and mystery to me. But I knew it was supposed to be private, and I felt a little embarrassed that Donald was talking about it. I had never seen him with any girls, so I figured he was lying.

"And you have?" I said.

"You bet. I've pushed in the bush, I've slapped the hot dog into the bun, and I've creamed into the ham wallet."

"Gross."

"Fucking isn't gross. It's awesome, and you're just jealous because you haven't gotten your pee-pee wet."

"I don't know what that means."

"I know you don't."

"Who have you done it with?"

"No one you know."

"Oh," I said. Donald liked to exaggerate his experiences. I wasn't going to press him about whom he'd had sex with. I didn't believe him, but I didn't think he cared if I did or not.

Donald stood and dusted off his arms, even though his sleeves were clean. It was just some gesture he'd seen other people do and wanted to emulate. He held out his hand to help me up. I reached for it, but he pulled it back and snapped his fingers and laughed.

I got up, and we started trekking home. We drifted between the eucalyptus trees along the hill; the leaves perfumed the air. Donald dug one hand into his pocket while his other hand used the crowbar like a cane. I heard his teeth chattering. We couldn't see any of the streetlamps or houses from the hill. We didn't hear any cars on Columbus or Houston. Everything felt damp and covered in a shroud.

I took out the little flashlight that Sebastian had given me. The light wasn't much, but it shined enough for us to avoid tripping on protruding roots and gopher holes. We made our way along the slope to the chaparral, ice plant, and rosemary near the base by a dead-end road. I wanted to get back home.

I aimed the light along the sidewalk back to the main road and up to where we lived. The cars parked on the street already had a frost on their windshields. The road looked gray as fog.

Outside his house, Donald rested the crowbar over his shoulder and hawked a loogie. I pointed the flashlight at his face. He swatted it away.

"Tomorrow," said Donald. "We'll really let 'em have it."

"Who is 'them'?"

"You just show up tomorrow night. Time for the revolution. Time to separate the boys from the men. I'm sure you're tired of being a boy. We'll smash some stuff, get drunk, get laid. We're going to be Top Gun and Delta Force."

"You're an idiot."

Donald punched me in the shoulder. Hard. The pain screamed down my arm and inward to the bone and across my chest. I had to gnash my teeth to stop from crying.

"Tomorrow night. Got it?"

I didn't know what Donald had planned. I just nodded and said okay.

NINE

THE NEXT DAY WAS FRIDAY, and I walked home from school with my head down. I turned onto Houston Street at the liquor store and started up the hill. A car with some other students drove past me, and all the kids in the back seat pointed at me and laughed that I was walking. It didn't faze me; I just thought it a little odd. The street ran underneath the freeway and then up alongside the hill. Telephone poles lined the road, but a huge winter storm had blown some of them down and broken others in half. Some of them would never be fully repaired. I passed the poles and the houses and the elementary school with the principal who still paddled children. I hadn't gone there, but I knew others who had. They all spoke of the man like he was Dracula.

I trespassed through someone's back yard into the cluster of homes where my family lived. Most of the houses were stucco, but there were a few that were brick. They had been built close together. Their front yards, small and square, were spotted with an odd mix of eucalyptus, sycamore, and pine. It was a quiet neighborhood. A safe place for trick-or-treating in the fall. Sometimes me and other boys who lived nearby— Donald or Quint and his older brother, Hunter—would chase rabbits or build forts in the California pepper trees.

We were close to everything and nothing. The schools, stores, churches, and swimming pool were all within walking distance. But the movie theaters, museums, and good restaurants might as well have been in another state. My mother had always complained about this.

When I got home, I saw someone sitting by our front door. At first glance, it just looked like a smudge with hands. As I got closer, I saw it was someone with dark hair who was dressed all in black. It wasn't anyone I knew. The person watched me come up.

"Who are you?" said the person.

"I'm Cooper. Who are you?"

"Jesus Christ."

I recognized the voice from the strange phone call the other day. Roxy.

Some people look like their names, and Roxy was one of those people. There was something masculine about her, something reminiscent of rockets, rage, and rock 'n' roll. She looked like a stouter version of Joan Jett. Roxy stood and snapped her fingers. Faint smears of violet ran across her cheeks. I told her that Mom wasn't there.

"No?" said Roxy. "I guess she's a Houdini."

"She's missing."

"Elvis is missing. Arden is just being a bitch."

"Elvis is dead."

"You take that back."

"What?"

"Kings don't die, and Roxy don't buy. Now stop looking like Gilligan, and let me inside."

"I don't think I should."

Roxy rolled her eyes. She put her hands on her hips and started tapping one foot. Then she tilted her head to the side and let her tongue droop out of her mouth to look as if she had been hanged. I wasn't sure who Roxy was, but I knew for certain she wasn't like anyone I'd ever met before.

"I think you should leave," I said.

Roxy snarled and took two steps toward me.. Her jaw went tight, and she scrunched her brow. Her nostrils flared. I wasn't sure if she was about to slap me or bite me. She reminded me of the junkyard dogs that snarled from behind barbed-wire fences, the Rottweilers and the Doberman pinschers, always hungry and alert.

"Keys," she said. "Now."

The way she ordered me turned my bones into arctic timber. I tried not to show any fear, and I hoped my face looked as blank as I wanted it to be. Roxy put out her hand, palm up, and waited. She didn't break eye contact. I dug into my pockets and removed my blue rabbit's-foot keychain with the house key and gave it to her. Her fingers closed around it, making her hand a tiny fist. Roxy snarled, and I heard her grind her teeth.

"That's a good puppy," she said. I tried not to swallow, but my throat suddenly felt dry. Roxy unlocked the door and let herself in. I followed her and shut the door.

"Mom isn't here."

"I'll wait."

"She's been gone two weeks."

"She was with me all last week and then poof! Gone Suzy-Q, gone. I hope your couch is a pullout."

"She was with you?"

"You got pillows in your ears? Yeah, she was at my place, and then she wasn't. A real abracadabra, that one."

Roxy strutted around our living room, her fingertips glossing over our furniture, almost as if she learned through touch and was researching my family. She scanned our walls and observed the photographs. When she came to a picture of me and Mom, she stopped and smiled. Then she stopped smiling and hung her head low, and she closed her eyes for a second as if concentrating. Roxy let out a sigh and rubbed her neck.

"Nope. Nope. Is it beer thirty yet?"

Roxy went to our refrigerator and opened it. She bent over and peered inside and started poking around, moving our condiments, readjusting the leftovers. She grabbed one of my father's Michelobs and twisted off the cap. Roxy kicked the door shut and tossed the cap in the sink.

I set my backpack on the table and watched her, unsure what to do. She didn't believe me when I told her about Mom, and I couldn't think of how else to handle the situation. Some people would have left, but I didn't think I should leave this woman alone in my house. Other people would have tried to remove her by force, but I knew if I tried that she'd tear out my insides. I guess I could have called the police, but she was too close to the phone for me to get to it without her stopping me. Roxy looked at me. She leaned against the kitchen counter. She drank.

"You don't look like her," she said. "You really her kid?"

"Yes."

"You sure?"

"Pretty sure."

"She ever tell you about me?"

"No."

"Typical. What a bitch. She would be that type. A real bitch."

Roxy crossed her arms, and her ring finger tapped the side of the bottle. Her face changed. Everything about her went from tight to soft. For a second I thought she was even about to cry.

"Just my luck," she said. "Typical. Bitch."

"How do you know my mom?"

Roxy glanced at me, and her eyes went wide. She drank her beer and looked off and to the side.

"We were going to move to Hillcrest," said Roxy. "Lying bitch."

"Hillcrest?"

"Boys. So dumb."

Roxy finished her beer and put the empty bottle in the sink with the dishes and the frying pan. She walked over to

me and put her face close to mine. I could smell the soap and
the shampoo she used. I tried to stay as still as possible. She
wasn't much taller than me, so her breasts almost touched my
collarbone. Her eyes, dark and brown, stared into my eyes with
a sad intensity I had never seen. She moved her lips as if about
to speak but then only sighed.

"You're no Jerry Lee Lewis," she finally said.

"Guess not."

"So what makes you so great?"

"I'm not great at all."

"Exactly. And you better believe it. I guess Arden treats
us both like a couple of opening acts. Arden told me she was
married, but I didn't care. She told me about how macho your
papa bear was. Made him sound like a real swinging dick."

"My dad works in an auto-parts store," I said. "He's a good
man."

"Macho bullshit. All of you. Arden told me he once almost
beat a man into his grave. A real silverback gorilla?"

"It wasn't like that."

"You Clint Eastwood? Charlie Bronson? Big balls all over
the place to impress the little ladies?"

"I was there. He was trying to help a woman. She was in
her car, and a man pulled her hair."

"John Wayne to the rescue. Swinging in like Tarzan because
you all think women are dumb and helpless."

"You weren't there."

"The picture is painted on the wall," said Roxy. "Tell me,
you got your daddy's big balls too?"

Roxy grabbed my crotch in a grip tight enough to make me
know just how much blinding pain she could inflict upon me if she
wanted to. She held my genitals, and I clenched my jaw, suddenly
aware of how fragile testicles really are. A cold shiver jetted up
from my privates. She and I didn't break eye contact.

"Feel that?"

"Yes."

"Damn right. All balls and no brains. Aren't you? Admit it. Say it."

"I'm all balls and no brains, no brains."

Roxy squeezed a little, as if to see if an orange was ripe. I winced at the thought of her going full out and bursting me into pulp. Part of her hand rubbed against my prick through my jeans, and I grew hard. I hadn't meant to have the erection; it just sort of happened. Roxy felt it too. She smiled and leaned in, pressing her wrist against my penis, now stiff and bulging against my pants.

She put her lips close to my ear. Her hand stayed hooked on my scrotum. I tried not to move. The world around me went blurry. Roxy's skin smelled waxy with makeup and lotion. When she exhaled, I felt her breath, hot and muggy, across my neck.

"Feel me now, Mr. Big Balls?" Roxy whispered. "I've got you, and I can do anything I want with you. Are you still Chuck Norris? Are you still Hulk Hogan? Everything that you think makes you so great is just another weakness. Never forget that."

Roxy gave my scrotum a tug, and then she bit my earlobe. Only then did she let me go. Roxy backed away, pressed a finger to her lips, and giggled. Both of my hands went to my groin as if to make sure everything down there was still all right and to block a second attack. I was scared and humiliated. I'd never been touched like that, and I didn't really know what I was supposed to feel. I couldn't look at Roxy, and I didn't want her to look at me.

"Relax," she said. "Everything is working fine."

She took out a pack of cigarettes from her coat and lit up. I felt my erection go away. Only after I'd gone soft could I look at her. She smoked and grinned.

"Look," she said, "I'm sorry. Sometimes I get a little out of control. That's just how Roxy rolls."

She took a drag, and smoke poured out of her nostrils, making her look like a dragon or some mad cartoon bull. She stubbed out her cigarette. The house was soundless and neither cool nor warm, and it was just the two of us and the low hum of the refrigerator running.

"If you see your mom," said Roxy, "tell her I loved her." I didn't say anything. I was trying not to cry in front of her. She grabbed a pen and an old newspaper off the table. She scribbled something on the corner of the front of the sports page and then tore it off. Roxy held the slice of paper between her pointer and middle fingers like a business card. "But then," she said, "I guess Arden doesn't love anyone."

Roxy tilted her hand so she pointed the paper at me. Her eyes motioned at me to take it. I did. An address and a phone number were scribbled on it.

"No," I said. "She loves me. She loves my father."

"Kid, grow up. You know the first time I saw old Arden, I told myself that her cunt had to taste like cotton candy. It didn't. She tasted like a razor. That's where she can find me. I won't be at the old place."

Roxy turned and went out the front door. After she left, I stepped outside and watched her walk down the street until she came to the corner, turned, and went out of sight. I stood there dazed, for a moment. I looked down at the torn newspaper with her number and address. I put it in my pocket and decided to hold on to it.

I made up my mind right then and there that, like the mailboxes and the garden gnomes, I'd never tell anyone about what had just happened. I didn't want anyone to know about Roxy or about how she'd grabbed me.

I went into the bathroom and pulled down my pants and shorts. I looked at my privates and, as Roxy had said, everything was intact. I gave a sigh of relief and then almost started to weep. I wanted to cry, but I wouldn't let myself; I would not allow it. It felt as if the world had suddenly been picked up and shaken like a snow globe. I wanted to yell. But there was no one to yell at, so I took a deep breath and exhaled slowly with my eyes closed. I forced all of the frustration and anger and confusion to go soft and mute. That's how you do it, I said to myself. You just need to breathe and stay calm and not let it all overwhelm you. If you let that happen, then it is over and you are just a sorry baby that no one feels sorry for. People will just try to avoid you or call you a freak and get rid of you.

What nobody ever bothered to say was that no matter how bad or crazy the world got, you still needed to get going, to wake up and eat breakfast, tie your shoelaces, go to school, go to work, put gas in the car, pick up the dry cleaning, finish your homework, and try not to murder anyone while you did it.

After I zipped myself up, I went to my room and found the pink leather jacket in my closet. I ripped it off the hanger and took it to the kitchen, where I found a knife. I knew that jacket had been for Roxy—and she didn't deserve it.

I dropped to my knees and started stabbing the jacket. The leather was thin, so it wasn't that difficult. I jabbed the blade into the front, the back, and into the sleeves. By the time I was done, the thing looked like flamingo swiss cheese. I wasn't crying, but I was panting and gnashing my teeth. The knife fell and clanged on the floor, and I grabbed my head with both hands.

"Fuck you, fuck you, fuck you!"

Eventually I caught my breath. My lungs felt like bags of stones inside my chest. I put the knife back. The jacket, once beautiful, now lay in my hands as shreds and trash. There wasn't anything left to do. I shoved it deep into the garbage can in the garage. No one was ever going to wear that thing, I told myself. None of it really mattered.

I crept into the living room and sat down. I didn't do anything. I didn't watch television. I didn't read my copy of *Hawaii*. I sat and let my mind go blank.

Dad and Sebastian came home a couple of hours later. I hadn't moved. Outside, the world had turned purple. The sky looked like skinned plums of winter. I heard Dad's Charger pull up onto the driveway. Dad found me on the couch. Sebastian stood behind him.

"You okay, Coop? You look like a zombie."

"I'm fine."

"Captain Tsunami! Don't be wiped out so early. The iddy-biddy and the mighty-fighty await your presence, sir."

I had no idea what Sebastian meant by that. Dad slapped me on the shoulder and told me to get up, that we were going out to eat. He went to use the bathroom. Sebastian watched me as I stood. We looked at each other but said nothing. Sebastian's eyes were dark and deep with a small glint that made them seem lighter than they really were. When Dad came back, he guided us out to the car. I sat in the back.

That night the three of us ate at a country-western place with long tables and a big dance floor. A loud band played Hank Williams and Bob Wills. Everything smelled of lager and denim. I watched couples two-step. Neon beer signs and faded black-and-white photographs of cattle barons and ranches adorned the walls. Not too many people connect cowboys with Southern California, but there are a lot of places around San Diego that embrace Stetsons, belt buckles, and mechanical bulls. This is especially true the farther east you go. Places like Lakeside and El Cajon are filled with bars and liquor stores where the men wear boots and large hats. There are lots of horses and ranches too. It goes way back. The first cowboys were Spanish. The Spanish were in California early on, and they laid the foundation. People are quick to forget stuff like that.

Dad ordered chicken. Sebastian and I had country-fried steak, smothered in gravy, served with corn, beans, and potatoes. The food tasted hot and good, and I wanted to keep eating after I was full. Sebastian asked me if I knew how to dance. I told him no, but I wanted to learn. I figured if Mom was around, then she could teach me. All I could do was look at the men and women on the floor. Sebastian encouraged me to go find a girl and ask her to dance. I decided against this even though I wanted to be out there, a part of all of them— my hand on the small of a woman's back, smiling and twirling, surrounded by friends, music, drink. I was afraid of embarrassing myself. I was afraid of getting frustrated at my feet and poor sense of rhythm. It was better to simply watch. I didn't see any other twelve-year-olds dancing, and I was not going to be the first.

The song finished. Everyone stopped dancing and clapped. Men in the band raised their hats in thanks. I sipped my sarsaparilla. Every now and again, I reached down to my crotch when my mind returned to Roxy and how she'd almost neutered me with her bare hands. I knew I should tell Dad about her, but I was too ashamed, too nervous to mention her. I couldn't bring myself to talk about her. Besides, I told myself, even Roxy didn't know where Mom was. Roxy was looking for her, too.

Dad downed his beer and said he was going to get another one from the bar. He asked Sebastian if he wanted anything, and he said no. Dad pushed back his chair and got up. He bumped into a man as he left and apologized.

"Just watch it next time, asshole," said the man.

"Take it easy. It was a simple accident."

"Accident? Why is it only cocksuckers like you have accidents? Notice that? You come here with your boyfriend, act like a jerk, thinking you're better than everybody else and have a few accidents, just fuck everything up."

"I said I'm sorry."

"Maybe that ain't good enough."

Dad sighed. Sebastian continued eating without paying attention. I stared out of the corner of my eye. The man stood no taller than my father, but he was pudgy and small-shouldered. His speech slurred, and his head wobbled when he spoke.

"What else do you want?"

"Maybe I want a piece of you, buddy."

"Let me buy you a beer if you're that sore."

"No, sir."

"Afraid that's all I can do then, partner."

"I ain't your partner, partner."

Dad threw his hands in the air, turned, and began to walk away. The man stumbled behind him. He wore jeans and a Van Halen shirt. His hair was already a little gray on the sides, which made him look older than I suspected he really was. I'd guess he was a couple of years younger than my father. I asked Sebastian if I should do something.

"No," he said. "Let him handle it. Your pops knows a thing or two about a thing or two."

I turned around in my seat. Dad kept walking, crossing the dance floor to the bar. The man pointed at him as he shadowed him. He kept telling my father to stop, to come here, to listen up. Dad ignored him. People began to notice. Heads turned and gawked.

Dad ordered a beer. The bartender poured a draft into a clear plastic cup. Men and women strolled across the dance floor to their seats. The man tried to block Dad.

"Do you mind? Back off."

"No, this is just you and me."

The man slapped the beer out of my father's hand, and the plastic cup hit the ground. Beer splashed and began to puddle around Dad's feet. In movies you always hear the music stop, like someone yanking the needle off a record, and then everyone turns and looks at the commotion. But that wasn't what happened. It was a small scuffle in a crowd, and though a few turned to look, no one rose or yelled or gasped. Waylon Jennings sang through the speakers, and the conversations of the crowd continued in mumbles, laughter, and noise. It was almost as if nothing had happened.

I expected Dad to punch the man. It felt humiliating seeing Dad get pushed around by some loser who probably peaked in high school and had grown bitter about it. The worst part was that I knew Dad could clobber him. I remembered how he'd fought in the parking lot years earlier. Dad understood how to duck, kick, and wrestle. He wasn't a weakling or a coward, yet he let this bumbling drunk taunt him.

Dad stepped over the cup and the beer. He walked away. The man in the Van Halen shirt continued to insult my father, but he didn't follow him. Two of the man's friends came and said something about fresh air and black coffee. They escorted him away. Dad came back and sat down.

"What was that?" I said.

"Just some yokel who had too much to drink. Don't worry about it."

"But, Dad—"

"Cooper," said Sebastian. "Finish your dinner, or else you can't have any cobbler."

I ate what was left on my plate. But I didn't want any dessert. Sebastian finished eating, too, and he ate everything. While my plate still had crumbs and juice, his was bare. The band started to play again. The couples returned to the center of the hall to two-step. Dad paid our bill, and then we left and dropped Sebastian at the auto parts store so he could pick up his car.

Back home, I followed Dad to his room and watched him sit on the bed and take off his shoes.

"Why didn't you fight him?"

Dad looked at me while he massaged the ball of his foot. He stroked his toes and the spaces between his toes.

"You think I should have?"

I didn't say anything. His response stunned me.

"Listen," he said. "The guy was looking for a rumble. I didn't want to give him that type of present. I'm not Santa Claus for drunks. Besides, what would be the point?"

"But he was messing with you."

"If I fought every jerk who messed with me, I'd constantly

be beaten up or in jail. I've seen enough of that bullcrap."

"So you think you should just take it?"

"I didn't say that."

"You're a wimp," I said and immediately regretted it. I was shocked that I'd said it. I zipped my lips, but my eyes shot wide open. Dad would scold me for sure.

"Cooper, what do you expect from me? This isn't television. There are times when you have to call it a day."

"What about Mom?"

"What about her?"

Dad lay atop the covers. He still wore his jeans and under-shirt. He rubbed his eyes but didn't speak. I wanted answers but knew I wasn't going to get any. He closed his eyes and didn't say anything. I waited for him to speak. He began to snore. I turned out the lights as I left.

I went to my room and pulled out Roxy's number. I thought about calling and screaming at her. I didn't know how she'd respond, but I figured it wouldn't get me anywhere. I felt like yelling at someone, anyone. Dad should've beat up that guy, should have ripped his face off in some barbaric triumph. But he didn't.

Dad wasn't doing what I thought he should be doing. Of course, there wasn't much he could do.

I put the piece of paper with Roxy's information in a paperback copy of *Jaws*, the last book I'd read, and then I put the book on the trunk at the foot of my bed so it would be easy to remember and easy to find.

I lay on my bed and tried to read some of *Hawaii*, but I really wanted to read more of my mom's journal. I finally gave in and dog-eared the novel and set it aside and found the penny notebook. The journal fell open to a random page.

Time moves so quickly. Yesterday was yesterday. Today is almost gone. I worry too much. But then there is a lot to worry about. Everyone seems so angry or nervous or just plain weird. Alburn says change is inevitable. He thinks more about those things than I do. I will try to pay more attention.

I went to the drive-in with Stanley the other night and saw Bonnie
and Clyde—*so violent. And I hate violence. All of it. And there's just
more and more of it. The world is changing. Stanley's older brother is
in Vietnam. Stanley doesn't seem too worried. He tried to put his fingers
inside me. I told him no. Men are so clumsy. At least Stanley keeps his hair
trimmed. And his fingernails.*

I closed the journal. My guts felt foul and soggy. I hid
the journal under my mattress and got up. I knew I had to
meet Donald for some surprise. I figured we were going to
break some more mailboxes or garden gnomes. I wanted
to break something.

Around midnight, I went outside.

I walked down my street and saw Donald in his garage. He
was duct-taping an old butcher's knife to a piece of PVC pipe.
Donald noticed me and waved me over. He ran to the corner
of the garage and came back with the crowbar. When I got
there, he held it above his head in one hand like a commanding
caveman's spear.

"You ready?"

"Yes," I said. I wanted to bust something open.

"Let's go smash some stuff. Follow me."

Donald and I didn't talk as we moved. We traveled west,
prowling avenues away from houses. Dogs, chained and tied
up, barked and snapped at our shadows. Thick clouds hung
like veils. Each breath I took felt sharp and cold. Donald and I
tramped our way down Houston Street. We crept into town. All
the stores and shops had closed; only the gas stations remained
lit and open. There was almost no traffic. At first I didn't know
where we were headed, but then it became obvious. We were
going toward the school.

Bancroft Middle School had been built in the early '50s
and had not been well maintained. It wasn't falling apart, but it
resembled the era it came from just as much as an automobile
would. It consisted of a main office, a cafeteria that doubled as
an auditorium, two long parallel promenades of classrooms,

and a square library that smelled of wood, yellowing paper leaves, and the odd old-woman odor of the librarian, Mrs. Jacobsen, who still wore a beehive and had worked at the school since its construction. There was a small locker room where we changed before and after gym. The tiled walls and floors always reeked of steam, urine, and bleach. All exercises were done outside. And when it rained, gym was canceled.

Donald held the crowbar against his side, and he covered it with the length of his arm. We crossed the street toward the front of the school. I was in sixth grade; Donald was in eighth. We didn't share any classes. Sometimes I saw him at lunch, but usually I snuck off and ate alone on the outskirts of the large dirt field where we ran laps. I liked the solitude and the shade of the eucalyptus trees.

The school doors were locked at night, but one could still stroll the grounds. Only a long brown chain blocked the parking lot, and anyone could step over that.

Donald and I stood by the cafeteria and observed the surroundings. The place felt different at night. The buildings looked like dull silver, and the walkways appeared long and large when void of students. I didn't want to be there. I didn't enjoy being there in the day, and I definitely didn't enjoy being there at night.

"Let's leave," I said. "We shouldn't be here. You know that."

"Don't be such a puss-puss. What are you afraid of?"

"I'm not afraid. This is just stupid."

"Always a limp dick, aren't you? We're going to show these fuckos who's the big dog."

"Donald—"

But it was too late.

Donald gripped the crowbar with both hands. He turned and ran toward the classrooms. Mr. O'Connor's history. Mrs. Montejano's Spanish. Mr. Utley's English. Ms. Barron's geography. I thought for a quick frozen second that he would chicken out. I believed even Donald would stop himself from doing something so reckless. I did not understand his motive, but then I quickly realized that there was no motive; there was just a desire for the excitement of destruction. I had felt it when I had vandalized the mailboxes with him. But I regretted my actions. Donald did not. Now the school was merely an easy and daring target.

The first window shattered—and not in any type of slow motion or dramatic breaking. He hit the center with the crowbar, and then large triangular shards fell. Donald moved on. He smashed each one like that. He went down the row and hit them in the center. They all fell that way.

Donald broke four windows and paused. He then went to Ms. McMurtry's room and smashed in her window. Broken panes fell into the room and onto the paved walkway. Jagged slivers protruded up from the bottom window casing like shark teeth. A dull and sinking type of ache ran across my chest. Ms. McMurtry didn't deserve that. None of the teachers had deserved that. Not that it was their property to begin with, but I still felt like a bastard for watching Donald do it.

Donald turned around and held his arms up as if he'd just scored a goal in soccer. I stood there with my arms crossed. I wasn't impressed. If anything, I was embarrassed and maybe a bit ashamed. Donald jogged back to me. He held out the crowbar.

"Your turn. Show them you don't care. Do it, you cocksucker."

Donald pushed the crowbar at me. He shook it once, signaling for me to grab it. I looked at the beads of broken glass on the walkway, practically shimmering. I didn't want to, but I was certain Donald was going to make me do it. I looked at the glass. I looked at the crowbar. Donald stared at me.

Then a light hit us, and we spun around to see a middle-aged security guard. I hadn't even known our school had a security guard. I saw the edges of his stomach and chest, clad in a distinct uniform. His face hid behind the white blaze of his Maglite. My limbs shot numb. My blood stopped pumping. I didn't move. I couldn't move.

The guard spoke. I didn't hear what he said, but I can assume it was something like "Halt!" or "Who's there?"

Donald didn't say anything. He shoved the crowbar at me and ran off. It must have been pure instinct. The light hit him, he turned, he sprinted away. It was, perhaps, the only time he had not whined about me following him. But then I realized I was left standing there, holding the crowbar. And there were five broken windows. The guard began to approach me.

My brain had a half-second discussion about what to do, the consequences, and the reasons behind my predicament. And in that half second, my mind concluded that there was simply no way I was going to accept punishment for Donald's bad ideas.

I turned and ran as fast as I could.

The guard chased me. I rushed through the parking lot, jumped over the chain, zipped across the street, and I didn't look back. At some point, the guard gave up and let me get away. I stopped and gasped for oxygen. Sweat covered my chest, and now the sweat felt south-pole cold. My spit tasted thick and acidic. I still held the crowbar. Remembering the cop shows I'd watched with Dad, I wiped the tool with my shirt and tossed it into some bushes.

After I got away from the shops and traffic signals and headed up the slope of Houston Street, I pulled out my little flashlight. I walked back in a daze, past the houses with the orange tile roofs, past the small elementary school, around the curve where the hill was covered with chaparral and white sand.

I knew two things as I made my way home: I knew I was never going to tell Dad about the windows, the mailboxes, or the gnomes, and I knew I needed to stay away from Donald. He had gone too far. At least he had gone too far for me, and I was not about to follow him to my own execution. I felt like a fool and a child.

It was about two in the morning when I got home. I beamed

the light onto the front of my house. It looked absolutely the
same—just a building where people slept and ate. The house
was noiseless inside. It stank of crusted chili cans, egg shells,
and grease. Newspapers covered the floor in front of the
television. I was glad Dad wasn't up. I didn't want to explain
where I'd been. My heart kept rocking like it was at a thrash
metal concert.

I went to my room, undressed, and crawled into bed.
I'd have the weekend until I had to face the damaged school
property. I figured Donald and I would be expelled if we were
caught. It took me a long time to fall asleep. It felt like I could
sense every small detail within the dark. The wind outside. The
spider in the corner of the window. The muscles in my throat.
Everything. Somehow I managed to drift off.

Early in the morning, when it was still black and quiet
throughout the neighborhood, the phone rang and woke me.
I heard Dad knock over a lamp in his room, and the ringing
stopped. Dad spoke in short phrases, "yes" and "uh-huh."

I found my father sitting naked on the edge of his bed. The
lamp on the floor was on, and it lit the room a strange yellow.
He held up two fingers, a way of telling me to stay quiet. I
stood and waited.

"Yeah, I understand," he said. "You better tell him."

Dad waved me over. He handed me the phone.

"Hello—"

"Cooper, this is your grandmother. I have some news."

I gripped the phone, and I felt the room, the house, the
world expand and fall away. Everything was growing; I was
shrinking. And then a dreamlike silence draped over it all. I
didn't know if I wanted to hear what my grandmother was
going to say. I held my breath. The walls contracted. Dad
picked up the lamp and set it on the nightstand. He started
putting on some clothes. I waited for my grandmother to speak.

"Your mother is here. She's sleeping in the next room."

"Is she okay?"

"She looks like she's been crying."

"Where has she been?"

"I don't know. She won't say. She was upset, and she'd been drinking. Something is wrong. You and your father need to come get her."

Grandma and I talked a little longer. I could hear her smoking, and I heard the scraping sound of her drying her lips with her shirt collar. When we finished, I told her I loved her. She told me the same, and then we hung up. I looked at Dad. He finished tucking his T-shirt into his jeans. He looked back at me as if he was waiting for me to give him an order.

"Well?" I said.

"Get dressed," he said. "Let's go."

TEN

WE HEADED EAST. DAD DROVE quickly. He was good behind the wheel, and he kept the car in control, even on the turns and in traffic. When we pulled onto the freeway, everything went quiet and smooth. The road kept coming and vanishing beneath us. Lights shimmered yellow and blue in the distance.

We were going to Camp Clark, a town in between Phoenix and Flagstaff, where my mother had grown up and my grandmother still lived. Mom never had a good word to say about the place. I had been there only a few times, when I was too young to have formed distinct memories.

I was filled with a nervous excitement, but I was exhausted, too. It felt like now—finally, after everything—we were going to get Mom back. After passing the outskirts of town, the Interstate shrunk to two lanes, flat, straight, and dark. We rode through the hills to the southern edges of the Mojave. As we approached El Centro, the air turned thick and heavy, and I smelled alfalfa, cattle, and the rich soil of nearby ranches. Dad explained that the alfalfa was sprayed with salt water because it was to be sold to the Far East, where they were accustomed to the taste of their own alfalfa having grown in seawater. Later he told me the stink of manure smelled like money to the farmers.

I tried to stay awake, but the hum of the engine and the gentle sway of the drive put me to sleep. I didn't have any dreams; there was only blackness and a soft warmth. When I awoke, it was dawn. My eyes felt crusty. My lips were a little numb. The sun bled out, and the light came rosy and sharp. Dad said we were coming to the state line. When we crossed the bridge into Arizona, I saw the Colorado River beneath us, thin and shallow, like a teal scar across a pale skin. The banks were rock and sand, and algae skimmed the surface of the water but didn't float away.

The state sign was a big copper star with alternating red and gold rays beaming from it. The state's logo reminded me of the sunrise itself, so I thought of Arizona as a place of early mornings and new days, a place people went to begin again. Dad told me he never liked the state, that it was Barry Goldwater's home; he went on to explain that he thought of the place as a safe haven for California's criminals.

We rode into Yuma and parked for breakfast at a truck stop. Cars and semis sat out front as if abandoned. The gravel lot was colorless and dusty. Cold winds blew over us as we strolled to the front door.

Dad and I took a booth. We ordered pancakes and eggs. Dad drank coffee. The sun wasn't completely up, but the place was already busy. Men in jeans and work shirts hunched over the counter, eating steaks and smoking cigarettes. In a corner, cowboys mumbled to each other across their huevos rancheros. A bell rang every time the door opened. Cooks in their undershirts stood in the kitchen flinging hash browns and sausages on the griddle. I could still hear the trucks rolling along the highway outside, carrying lumber, livestock, and feed. Everyone was going somewhere.

Our food came. I felt better after I ate. Dad and I didn't talk much, but at one point he told me he thought I was handling everything well and that he was proud of me. I said thank you, but that was all I said.

In truth, I was ignoring everything. I'd made it a point not to think. I had not told him about breaking the mailboxes or the windows. I would never mention Roxy or what she had done. To me all those things had been illusions—all make-believe, all happening to other people. Not me. Not Dad. Not Mom. It was almost as if they hadn't happened at all.

I asked Dad why he thought Mom had gone off in the first place. It seemed like an honest question, and it was one I wanted answered. Dad drank his coffee. He held on to the mug, and steam rose from it. His elbows rested on the table.

"I don't know. I'm not going to lie to you about that. There could be a bunch of explanations, some even your mother may not even realize. I don't think you'd find any of them satisfying."

Dad drank his coffee. He stared out the window. His brow scrunched up, he gnawed the inside of his cheek the way he always did, and then his jaw went tight. I wanted to ask him more questions, but I figured he was just as confused as me. I walked around while Dad paid our bill. On the other side of the café was a store and showers for truckers. The shop was filled with trinkets and candy. Dust was everywhere. I looked at knives with painted handles, scenes of deer in woods and wolves of the night. All the blades were made in China. I picked through T-shirts with cliché innuendos printed on the front. There were moccasins and dolls and belts and hats and oil and tools. I wanted to find something nice for my mother. I thought if I saw something she would like, that I'd buy it for her and then give it to her and she would keep it for always. I knew I was being silly. There wasn't anything there my mother would have wanted. I had never seen my mother really want gifts or presents. On birthdays and holidays, she never asked for anything. And when she opened presents she always gave thanks and smiled, but she never blushed or screamed in excitement.

There had been days where she'd cried in bed, her body a soft white that disappeared within the sheets, but there had been good days too. Magical afternoons and mornings. There had been the picnics, just her and me, and I'd wandered barefoot in the grass and she'd watched me on the swings. A woman's eye keen to protect her young. There were the endless days in summer, when we drove to the beach and I slept beside her on the towel, me smelling of sunscreen, lip balm, and apple juice; she being all antiperspirant, hairspray, and that woman skin smell beginning to age. I'd grown tired of the waves, my body wet and chilled, and I had collapsed next to her while she lay beneath the sun. We were creatures of the sea, born to salt water and then to the banks and the sand. All fading memories—perhaps some false or only half true—but knowing they were slowly dimming hurt the most. I prayed to hold on to them for as long as I could, like a child trying to hold sleet in his hands.

I took a deep breath and sighed. Whatever happens, happens, I told myself. It wasn't much comfort.

The rest of the drive felt unending. The desert sprawled outward, and large hills squatted in the distance. All the land stretched out beige and dry. Mirages floated against the blacktop. We searched the radio, but all we found was static.

Several hours later, we crossed through the western edge of Phoenix. We stopped for gas and headed north. Outside of town, the once white road signs were now a burnt yellow with black smears from bullet holes.

Dad cursed to himself. "Damn state is nothing but rednecks and fascists. Everybody's backward."

The desert clawed and hunched to the side of the road. The road curved and dipped into dry valleys, all dirt and creosote and prickly pear. Cliffs filled with cacti and rugged stone waited in the distance. The land looked desolate and mean.

Camp Clark was small, and you saw all of it from far back on the road as you approached. Even when you stood in the center of town, you could see past the outskirts into the wilderness. The streets were old but clean and well maintained. There was a Dairy Queen and an A&W, and there was a main street downtown where the shops still had neon signs from right after the Second World War. Pickup trucks sat in a row beside the sidewalk, and pedestrians crossed the road wherever they felt fit. It was sunny and dry, and the clouds hung large and far away.

Dad drove to Grandma's house and parked on the street. I stared at the house. My grandmother lived in a cottage behind a supermarket. A wire fence wrapped around the place. Pebbles and yucca decorated her front yard. Dad reminded me to be on my best behavior. We got out and walked to the gate, let ourselves in, and knocked on the door. The sun was bright but there was no warmth, and it was cooler in the shade of the porch. I heard a dog bark and trucks changing gears somewhere out of sight. I didn't see Mom's car anywhere.

My father and I gasped when Grandma opened the door. She looked trampled and used. Besides her wrinkled clothes and rumpled hair that jetted off in random tuffts of silver, she had the worst black eye I've ever seen on anyone. Her left eyelid sagged past her iris, and a plum half-moon ran across her cheek. Most of her face looked puffy and overly ripe. She had a few small splits in her lip, too, but these didn't seem to deter her from smoking a cigarette. My grandmother looked at us one at a time and then said bluntly, "You're too late. Arden already left."

Part of me drifted off, like being carried out with the tide. My disappointment hit hard and burned. I wasn't sure if I'd hug or hit my mother when I found her.

Grandma pushed the door open wide, and we walked in. Her house reeked of stale tobacco, like wet chalkboards and decrepit newspapers. Behind the odor of thirty years of cigarettes lay a stench of mothballs.

Dad and I sat on the couch. Grandma took the rocking chair across from us. The walls were faux wood, and all the blinds and curtains were shut. The house was dark, quiet, and clean.

"Geez, Liz, what in the name of Holyfield happened to you?"

"Where's Mom? You said she was here. You told us to come for her."

Grandma stubbed out her cigarette and then fiddled with her pack and took out a new one. She lit it, inhaled, exhaled, and picked a bit of leaf off her tongue. Dad rubbed his palms together. Grandma wiped the corner of her lips with her shirt collar.

"I had put her to bed. Figured she'd sleep until you got here. I brewed some coffee and planned on listening to the radio for the night—stay up and keep watch. I was afraid she'd do something. Wasn't sure what, but something nonetheless. Arden always liked her surprises. I was catching an old episode of *Fibber McGee and Molly* from the station on the rez when she started stirring. What she didn't know is I'd swiped her keys. I wasn't about to let her drive off. Not again. She confronted me about it. Said she had to leave, had to go. I kept telling her to go back to bed. And then she sucker-punched me. Her own mother. Can you believe it?"

"I'm sure I can try," said Dad.

"Arden and I fought, but she had youth on her side. She dug the keys out of my jeans and then . . . she was gone. I heard her peel out of here. She was long gone by the time I ran to the road. The sun was coming up. I tried calling all of you, but no one picked up. Figured you'd already left."

"I don't understand," I said. "She came here, got a few winks, and left?"

"I tried to stop her," said my grandmother. "I think that's pretty obvious. This isn't eye shadow here."

"But why?"

"Arden is going to do what she wants to do."

"Did she tell you anything?"

"She wasn't making much sense. She cried a lot. Arden isn't much of a weeper."

"What did she say?"

"Something about her life being ruined, wasted."

When Grandma said that, I paused. What had Mom meant by that? Did she mean Dad and I had wasted her life? I didn't know what I should say to Grandma or to Dad, so I didn't speak. I sat and listened.

"Did she say anything that may give us a clue as to where she went?" said Dad.

Grandma slowly rocked. She rested her left ankle over her right knee. Dad let out a short sigh. Grandma stared at us like we bored her. She was a mannish woman with sturdy shoulders, coarse hands, and short ashen hair. I'd never seen her in a dress or wearing jewelry. She wore only shapeless jeans and baggy flannels.

"What about you, Cooper?"

"What about me?" I said.

"What are you planning to do with your summer vacation, Cooper?" Grandma always called me by my full name, never Coop. She sipped her coffee and smoked.

"Hang out. Read. Go to movies."

"Doesn't sound productive."

Grandma took a drag and wiped her lips with the collar of her shirt. Smoke floated in a spiral up and away from the cherry on her Camel.

"It's called summer vacation for a reason."

"How would you feel about maybe spending the summer with me?"

"And get heatstroke?"

"That's your mother talking."

"Funny, I thought it was me talking."

"Arden had wit."

"You mean *has* wit."

"If you stayed with me, I could get you a job."

"Work?"

"That's another word for it, yes. There are some opportunities. You could also do some volunteer work."

"Doing what?"

"You could get involved with my church. They have some young-people programs. But there is always ranch work you could learn."

"I'm not sure if I'm cowboy material."

"Well, think about it. I'd love to have you, and it would be a chance to get away, maybe make some friends, perhaps even earn a dollar. And we have girls in Arizona, too."

Grandma smoked. I didn't say anything, and neither did my father. Grandma looked at Dad and then at me. She wiped the corner of her mouth with her shirt's collar. She nodded and bit her lip.

"Okay," she said. "So what do you want?"

I wondered why she asked me this, changing the subject.

"Me? I want my mom back."

This made Grandma chuckle. She stubbed her cigarette out in the ashtray on the coffee table between us. The last twirls of smoke floated away.

My grandmother was in her late sixties, but she was still strong from a life of hard work. As the years have passed, I have noticed how laborers—ranch hands, fruit pickers, construction workers—maintain a certain vigor as they age, despite decades of abuse. Some people call this "country strong," but I never called it anything other than tough. It was, and is, an aspect I think any human can attain and keep, and it is something I have always admired. There is something to be said for callused hands, muscled shoulders, and a tight, broad chest. Men and women who work office jobs, even if they exercise, never have that same build or brawn. You can spot the difference at a glance.

I had no doubt of my grandmother's power. Though her gender limited her opportunities during her era, she had worked all her life. She had given out ladles of water to migrant workers. She'd spent a great deal of time working with horses and cattle. When the war began, she entered the factories and honed her skill on assembly lines dealing with rubber and aluminum. After the war, she took a job in a cafeteria at the

VA. She'd retired the previous year, but now she did volunteer work at her church and with the 4-H. Though I never became religious, I respected churches; this was not because of their devotion to a higher power, but for the opposite reason—for their devotion to humanity, to the downtrodden and the meek. These were aspects I liked about Grandma Liz. She never complained, and she tried to help others. At the same time, she never made excuses for her or others' mistakes. Grandma believed one was responsible for one's actions, end of story. She was not about to apologize for her daughter, and I did not expect her to.

"Listen," she said as she leaned back, her hands resting on her stomach, fingers locked together. "We can ask around. Some people she might have stayed in touch with. But I doubt it. Arden was always a bit of a loner."

Dad forced a smile. All teeth with wide eyes. He nodded and sucked in his cheeks.

"Anything you can do to help," said Dad.

ELEVEN

GRANDMA SENT US TO TALK with Cady, one of my mother's old friends. We were told she worked at the rodeo grounds outside of town. There was an auction going on, and everything smelled of dirt, dung, gasoline, and the musk of horse, hog, and cow. Pickups, their wheels and sides caked with mud, parked in packs under a cold sky. Gray clouds floated in the east, but it was all blue out west. We found Cady serving soda at the refreshment stand near the bleachers. The place was loud with a man's voice, fast and clipped, rapping through the PA system. Dad asked if we could speak with her. She had a girl not much older than me take over. The girl had long hair, dark and straight.

We followed Cady outside to the back. I was careful not to slip on the mud. Cady wore jeans and a western shirt. Years of sunshine had darkened her Nordic looks, and I thought her rustic and beautiful. She had a long, deep scar across her left cheek. It didn't distract from her beauty. Still, I tried not to stare.

"You used to know my wife, Arden, back in high school?"

"She married you? So you must be her kid?"

She leaned against a fence and looked at me, but I didn't

speak. I could still hear the auctioneer: "A hundred, do I hear a hundred and twenty, do I hear a hundred and twenty?" A quick gale blew Cady's hair across her face, and she brushed the lock back behind her ear with one hand. Cady's eyes were round and blue.

"Yes. This is our son, Coop. I don't suppose Arden has contacted you, has she?"

There was a pause. I could tell Cady was thinking. She bit her lip a little and glanced to the side and down. Then she locked eyes with my father. Cady looked confident and strong.

"Arden? After graduation she was out of here so fast that she left a dust cloud in her wake. Lickety-split. Arden hated it here."

"We can't find her. Do you know where she might have gone?"

Cady shook her head. Her lips moved into something that wasn't a smile or a smirk, but a flat and straight line, as if she'd just tasted something sour. She shoved her hands into her pockets. The PA kept buzzing: "This is a prime heifer. You don't want this one to get away. Let's start the bidding." Cady looked back toward the rodeo grounds and then at us.

"Back then," she said, "Arden and me, we were pretty wild. It was the sixties. Peace, love, rock 'n' roll. She always said she wanted to do everything, go everywhere. Arden talked a lot. Stowing away on cargo ships to France. Stuff like that."

"Folks, don't let this great animal get away from you."

"You're saying we should go to France?" I said.

"No. Hell, maybe. I know she wanted to go to New York a lot. I think she thought of herself as some misplaced bohemian. We talked about getting modeling jobs in Manhattan. Big dreams. Then she ran out to California. I stayed here, had my daughter, and then my accident. I guess neither of us were destined for *Vogue* or *Cosmo*."

Cady kept talking, but I stopped listening. A flat piece of land ran behind her, all sand and stone, with large patches of sludge dashed about. Somewhere, a truck started up. The announcer declared the animal sold. Cattle mooed in the distance. They were to be sold and slaughtered or locked away and milked.

We walked with Cady back to the snack bar. She stayed a few steps ahead of us. Cady kept her arms crossed under her breasts as we moved. The girl, who I now assumed to be her daughter, was handing a snow cone to a little boy in a baseball cap. Cady went behind the counter and put a hand on the girl's back, between her shoulder blades.

"How about you come have dinner with us tonight? I might have some pictures of Arden you would want. Say seven?"

Cady wrote her address on a napkin. Dad took it and thanked her.

"Remember," said Cady. "Tonight. Seven."

"All right, folks," said the auctioneer. "We have a special coming up. Now is not the time to be cheap."

Cady's daughter had brown hair and dark features. She wore braces and had a red bandanna wrapped around her forehead. If Cady went missing, would this girl go looking for her? I wondered if Cady would ever go missing in the first place. I wanted to know what the difference was between a woman like Cady and a woman like my mother. I was not angry, just disappointed. I could imagine Cady and her daughter going home and talking and Cady offering advice or maybe just listening, and her daughter trusting her with information she'd never told anyone else. They looked satisfied, kind, and decent. I was happy for both of them.

On our way out, I glanced down a corridor that opened into the arena and briefly saw a bull. It was tan, and its horns stretched out in a dirty white. His eyes looked black, glazed over, and focused on nothing at all. I got only that quick snapshot of it as I walked by. Dad stayed in front of me. When we got in the car, he held the keys in his right hand and rubbed his lips with his left thumb. Dad didn't look at me. He gazed out his window. We sat like that for a while.

I knew what he was thinking, and I was always a little
scared when that happened. It was like he knew the answer but
wasn't going to tell me because the answer was bad news. It
made me feel stupid to be sitting beside my father, like a lapdog
who could only yip and skip away. I wanted to do more, but I
couldn't think of anything to do.

Dad started the engine. The wheels began to roll, and we
drove back to town. I know my father must have been under
a great amount of stress. He didn't deserve it. He had gone
through a lifetime of toil, and it didn't look like it was about
to become any easier. And now he was trolling around the
Southwest looking for a runaway wife. I figured he was debating
how much longer he should stay in Arizona before returning
home. Undoubtedly, he ran various scenarios in his brain while
he wondered where else to look for Mom. I also guess he tried
to think of what to tell me . . . and what not to tell me. But this
is true: I never heard my father complain. Not once.

None of this is to say my father was an uncommunicative
stoic. He liked to talk; he just knew some things were pointless to
discuss. Why bemoan work when you know you have to work?
Why debate an issue when the matter has been decided? Why
criticize someone when you know that person won't change,
only feel hurt and then spiteful? Dad chose his words carefully.
But when he spoke, you knew he believed in what he said.

Dad napped in my mother's childhood room for the better
part of the afternoon. At one point, I opened the door and
saw him lying on top of the covers with his back facing me.
He still had his shoes on. His face pressed against a pillow, and
his shoulders bulged beneath his undershirt like the desert's
hills. The walls were decorated with watercolor paintings—I
assumed done by my mother. They were all green and violet
and abstract. I closed the door without speaking, without
making a sound.

I wanted us to keep looking for Mom, but that would be
difficult with my father being asleep. I figured there were more

places in Camp Clark we could go, other people we could talk to. I wasn't sure why my mother had returned to Arizona and then left so quickly. It was almost as if she was on some type of secret mission.

My grandmother was in the kitchen. She listened to a preacher on the radio while she leaned her hips against the counter and sipped her coffee over the sink. A cigarette rested in the ashtray to her right. A wisp of smoke twirled and floated away. The air in the house felt heavy and stale. She saw me but did not say anything, at least not at first. I stood in her kitchen with my hands by my sides. She took a drag, drank some coffee, and used her collar to wipe her lips. My grandmother turned her head to look at me. Half of her face was plum-colored.

"Does it hurt?"

"Bruises don't hurt," she said. "Scars neither. They're just reminders of what not to do next time. That's all."

My grandmother stubbed out her cigarette and motioned with her head for me to follow her. She drank her coffee while she walked out of the kitchen. I trailed behind. The preacher on the radio kept talking.

"And it is clear that America is in danger," said the preacher. "In danger of sin. In danger of drifting further and further away from God. . . ."

My grandmother went to the hallway closet and opened the door. I heard my father snoring from Mom's old room. Grandma Liz kneeled and pulled out an old cardboard box from behind her coats and hangers and an ancient vacuum. The box looked as if it would rip apart in my grandmother's hands. She opened the top.

"God cannot be ignored," said the preacher. "God must be embraced. Only then will you know love and peace."

Inside the lay a pair of white gloves, a sewing kit, a small jewelry box, and some ribbons given by the 4-H. My grandmother dug through the contents and pulled out something from the bottom. At first I couldn't see what it was.

"Those lost souls who do not come to Jesus will surely find themselves deeper and deeper in the wilderness. Only Jesus can be your guide. . . ."

My grandmother had some type of book. She kicked the box back into the closet, shut the door, and guided me over to the couch. We sat together, and she showed me the cover. It was my mother's high school yearbook. Grandma Liz licked her thumb and began flipping through pages. I could see the desert outside the living room windows. Stones and cacti pocked the sand and the grit, and the land sprawled out in a dry and barren gray.

"You must turn the other cheek and offer your forgiveness. . . ."

Grandma Liz turned to a page with a photograph of women all wearing aprons. There were about thirteen of them standing around a giant cake. Beneath the photo was the caption, "Home Economics 1968." All of the women smiled, proud of their baked and frosted dessert—all of them except one.

I recognized my mother immediately. Even though she was younger, even though her hair was styled in a bouffant, and even though the photograph was in black and white, I knew it was her. She had the same eyes. Her cheeks looked a little puffier, but her eyes gave her away.

"She hated that," said my grandmother. "She got forced into that class for some reason or another, I can't remember. But she hated every second of it. It was the only class she got a C in."

"Do not listen to the false prophets. . . ."

My grandmother turned through a few more pages. Dad snored loudly. I heard him shift on the bed. Grandma Liz pointed at another photograph. This one was of prom. Boys and girls dressed up for the big formal dance of the spring. The boys wore bow ties. The girls had corsages pinned close to their hearts. There were about four or five couples in the picture. My mother's hands were clasped together in front of her navel.

"Oh, I'd forgotten about this one," said my grandmother. "Heaven is for all who believe and have faith. . . ."

"What do you mean?"

"See the boy next to your mother?"

The boy had one hand on my mother's back. His other hand stayed by his side. He had thin blond hair, and he looked skinny and chipper. He wore big Buddy Holly glasses and had a goofy grin with lots of teeth.

"He and your mother were friends. Just friends. They never dated. But he was drafted that year, and he died in Vietnam. God, what was his name?"

"Was it Alburn?"

"Yes. How did you know that?"

The door to my mother's old room opened. My father walked out and rubbed his eyes. Grandma slammed the book shut. She rose and went to the radio and turned it off. My father stood by the couch and blinked a bunch of times.

"What time is it?"

"About six thirty," said Grandma.

Dad nodded and bit his lip. He looked outside. The desert's skyline was beginning to grow dark. A strong wind blew over the house. My grandmother lit another cigarette and smoked.

"Let's get ready," said my father.

"Okay."

My father turned and went down the hall to the bathroom. When he shut the door, I asked my grandmother if Mom had said anything to her about a lady named Roxy.

Grandma shook her head.

"No," she said. "After she made it to California, your mother did not report back too much. She called when she got engaged. She called when she got pregnant. All the other phone calls and visits were simple check-ins. Arden always valued her privacy."

"The boy, the one who died in Vietnam—do you know how he died?"

"Not all the details, no. Something about jumping on a grenade. I don't even know if that's true. People like to tell stories."

I went and found the yearbook on the couch. I opened it and found the photograph of my mother and the other couples at prom. They all looked youthful and full of optimism. I heard a toilet flush, and my father came out of the bathroom. He pointed at me and told me we would leave in ten minutes.

Dad didn't tell Grandma about our plans. He just said we were going out for dinner. She smoked and read her Bible.

I tucked my shirt in and combed my hair on the ride over. I wanted to look nice, even if Dad hadn't bothered to shave. Everything felt so casual; nothing was ever formal or respectful. That wasn't how I wanted to appear or behave. I knew my mother would have worn a dress and perfume. As we drove to Cady's, I realized how stifling everything must have been for my mother—to live in Arizona with dreams of Manhattan, only to end up outside San Diego with people like me and Dad. I knew I wanted to travel and see all those faraway places. I couldn't really blame her.

Cady's street ran flat and dark. There were no streetlamps, and there wasn't any moonlight. The houses, small and simple, sat along the road as if waiting for someone who wouldn't arrive. The buildings were all from the late '40s and had small front yards of rock, stone, and sand. Paned windows stared across the sidewalks. I wondered who lived there, what they were like, and what they were doing. The world felt bigger and smaller at the same time.

We found Cady's house, and she let us in. After the desert's chill, the warmth of the living room felt like an industrial oven. My eyes baked. My mouth went dry. It took me a bit to adjust.

I could smell something cooking, and the place looked clean. The living room led into a dining area where there was a small table, already set with plates and silverware. The carpet was a creamy beige, and it still had the streaks from being recently vacuumed. The furniture looked old but nice, though not horribly expensive. I assumed most of it had been passed down through the years. Plates with painted mallards and geese adorned the far left wall, and a wooden cuckoo clock hung on the right. The kitchen was to the left of the dining area. The bathroom and bedrooms were to the right along a short hallway.

"I'm so glad you could make it," said Cady. "And you both look so handsome."

"You have a lovely home," said Dad. Cady looked different. At first I couldn't tell why, but then I realized she was wearing makeup but had applied it gently and carefully. Dad was smiling, but I didn't really want to be there. I got the feeling I should have stayed at my grandmother's.

Cady opened a bottle of Merlot and set it on the table to breathe. She asked us to sit and if we wanted anything to drink. I asked for some water. Dad requested a scotch if she had any. Cady briefly vanished and reappeared with two glasses—one for me, one for my father. Dad sipped, and the scent of the booze was strong. Cady poured herself a large glass of wine and then sat on a wooden chest in front of us, holding the glass with both hands. She wore black jeans and a green turtleneck. Her hair wasn't pulled back anymore. It curtained the sides of her face, covering the scar on her cheek. I thought it was a pity. I liked her scar.

"My daughter is hiding in her room, but she'll come out to eat. Teenagers. Dinner will be ready in a few. It's only chicken. I hope that's okay."

"Smells wonderful," said Dad.

Cady drank and smiled. She looked pretty, but she smiled the way a hostess at a restaurant smiles, as if trying not to look bored or thinking about something else.

"Tell me, Coop, what is your favorite subject in school?"

"I don't like school."

"Oh, well, that is an honest answer."

"He loves to read. The kid is a real bookworm."

"That's great. What do you like to read?"

"Books."

"I see. Let me check on that chicken."

Cady got up and left. Dad leaned in and whispered to me that I was being a jerk, that I was embarrassing him. I didn't say anything. Dad shook his head and drank his scotch. I rolled my eyes and decided to stay quiet. If they didn't like my answers, then they could stop asking me questions. I knew I was being curt, but I didn't want to toy around with small talk or formalities. I didn't have the patience for that. It felt fatty, and I wanted it stripped down, cut, lean, and tight. I was going to say only what needed to be said, ask only what needed to be asked. I would think only what needed to be thought, feel only what needed to be felt. And I'd decided that most of the time it was better not to think, better not to feel.

When Cady returned, I noticed she had refilled her glass. This time the Merlot almost reached the rim. She drank as she walked so it wouldn't splash over. She waved her free hand while she drank. A door opened and closed, and Cady's daughter drifted into the living room. She wore a gray long-sleeve shirt and overalls. It had been a long time since I'd seen anyone wear overalls, and it seemed to me an odd fashion choice for a teenage girl.

"Oh, Zoe decided to join us. Remember Percy and Burt—"

"Coop. Short for Cooper."

"Coop. Yes. I apologize. I don't know why I thought Burt. You just look like a Burt, I guess."

"Hi," said Zoe.

"Zoe, how about you show Coop your room."

"Mom."

"Daughter."

Zoe looked at me as if I was an abandoned mutt who'd planted himself on her back porch. She stared at me and then waved me over, and I got up to follow her. As we went down the hall to her room, I heard Cady whisper something and then laugh. Zoe waited for me, and when I came in she closed the door. I heard Cady laugh again, this time in a loud cackle.

"Mothership is going to get drunk. Try not to judge her."

"I won't. Dad likes his scotch. It's fine."

Zoe's room looked like all the other girls' bedrooms I'd seen, which wasn't many. The bed sat shoved against a wall, well made with a pastel comforter. Stuffed animals lay on the foot of the bed. There was a student desk by the window, but I guessed Zoe didn't use it much. The only items on it were a few school books and a snow globe. It was all too orderly, too neat. She'd used tape to hang a poster of Madonna on her door. The picture featured Madonna in all black and gold with her hands in the air. I didn't understand the craze over her; none of her songs sounded that good to me. Zoe sat on her bed with her legs crossed under her. I started to pick up the snow globe, but Zoe asked me not to touch it.

"Your room is nice."

"It's small."

"Still nice."

I pulled out the chair at her desk and sat facing her. Zoe held a stuffed bunny in her lap.

"Want some hooch?" said Zoe.

I didn't say anything. We looked at each other, waiting for one to speak. Cady laughed in the other room, and Zoe's eyes shot to her door and then back to me. Zoe leaned over and pulled a small bottle out from under her bed. She unscrewed the cap, sipped, and then smacked her lips and held the bottle out for me.

"It's okay," she said. "It isn't anything too hard. Just schnapps."

I took the bottle. The contents looked clear and smelled like mouthwash. I took a drink and let the liquor sit in my mouth for a second. It was all syrupy and tasted of peppermint. It wasn't like the stuff I'd drunk with Donald, but still my eyes, nose, and throat all burned. I'm sure I coughed and gagged a little.

"Good stuff, huh?"

"Take it."

I held out the bottle for Zoe, and she grabbed it and took another sip. The burning vanished from my face and traveled to my stomach with a cold trace. Zoe giggled at me. She covered her mouth to try to stop. I saw her braces when she smiled.

"You'll want another one in a bit. Trust me."

"I doubt that."

"Why are you and your pops here? The mothership said something about your mom."

"Your mom and my mom were old friends."

"So?"

"My mom is missing. We hoped your mom knew something."

I heard Cady laugh, and then Dad mumbled something and Cady laughed even louder. I didn't know what they were talking about, and I wasn't sure I wanted to know. I always had the sense that grown-ups were hiding information, keeping dark truths secret. I suppose they hoped if their children never knew of the painful, then they would never experience pain. But even that didn't make much sense.

"Mothership likes her wine. She caught me with a cigarette once and flipped. Such a hypocrite."

"Where's your dad?"

"Where's your mom?"

"Sorry."

"It's nothing warped."

"What?"

"Forget it. You know what I hate? I hate it when grown-ups still treat you like a kid. It's like they don't even have eyes. Like they can't see who they're talking to."

"You hate your mom?"

"No. Of course not. Well, maybe sometimes. Maybe a little. Do you hate your dad?"

"No."

"Sure?"

"Yes."

"You and him seem kinda standoffish."

"We've been driving a lot. It wears you down."

"You want that second drink yet?"

"Yes."

She passed the bottle back to me. Zoe was right. I did want another sip. That second drink felt better, tasted better. I could drink it more naturally on that try. Zoe took the bottle from me. I thought I might fall off my chair. The schnapps warmed me, and the heat blossomed throughout my core, into my stomach, lungs, and limbs. Then I was a little wobbly. I could feel the room expand, and the world outside began to enclose around us. Zoe seemed friendly and was pretty. I had a brief urge to go sit next to her, but I didn't. The heat slowly cooled, and I didn't want it to leave.

I stood and said I needed to use the restroom. I didn't, but I felt like I should splash some water on my face. Zoe tilted her head to her right and played with the stuffed rabbit on her lap. When I left Zoe's room, I peered down the hall. Cady and Dad sat on the couch talking. They faced each other. I couldn't hear what they were saying.

I went into the bathroom and gently closed and locked the door. The room was clean and white. The shower curtain and the towels were blue with gold trim. Glass and porcelain knick-knacks adorned the top of the medicine cabinet: elephants and horses and cows. A small plastic trash bin with a lid sat beside the toilet. The air smelled soapy and womanly. I leaned over the sink with my hands flat on the counter. For a brief second, I thought I might throw up. My spit felt thick, so I let it pour out of my mouth. This made me feel better. I turned on the faucet and lowered my head under the running tap. The water was cold, and it made my mind drift away.

After I'd dried my hands and face, I didn't immediately return to Zoe's room. When I left the bathroom, I saw that

Cady and my father were still on the couch. Cady seemed to be sitting closer to Dad, but I wasn't sure. I felt embarrassed and awkward around Zoe, so I decided to waste some time. I snuck down to the door at the end of the hallway, into Cady's room.

None of the lights were on, but I was fine moving around in the dark. I also feared that turning on any lights might give me away. Between the moon outside the window and the bit of light that seeped through under the door, I could see plenty. The bed lay neatly made. An old quilt, decorated with patches of corduroy, denim, and cotton, stretched over the sheets and the mattress. The pillows looked soft and lumpy. I took one quiet step after another and tried to make each breath silently fill my lungs.

I knew I had no reason to be there. It was invasive and rude. I told myself I wouldn't be there long. Dad's voice carried through the house, but his words came as unrecognizable sound. A jewelry box sat atop Cady's dresser. I pulled out the top dresser drawer. Inside were panties, lots of them, all folded and neatly piled. Some were silk, a few looked black and skinny, others just white cotton. I didn't touch any of them. I just looked. I couldn't help but look. There was something sensitive and intimate about the woman's underwear that I couldn't understand. Women were mysterious to me—their habits, their secrets. They communicated differently and they thought differently and they felt differently. I wondered if women all viewed men like that, like elements from another dimension. Some of the girls at school were already growing breasts. I'd heard about some of them starting their periods. I'd only kissed a girl once, and that had been a year ago at a picnic with a girl I never saw again. Her lips tasted like grape soda and ChapStick. I closed the drawer and decided to get out of there.

When I returned to Zoe's room she squinted at me, as if she was trying to read my thoughts. I had the feeling she knew what I'd been up to. Zoe drank some of the peppermint schnapps and watched me sit. She held out the bottle for me, and I took it, sipped, and handed it back. Now the liqueur didn't faze me. It was just good and minty.

"You were gone a while," she said.

"Sorry. I wasn't feeling very well."

"You hurl?"

"No."

"It's okay if you did. Everybody hurls if they drink too much. You're not drunk, are you?"

"I'm fine. I'm much better now. I'm fine."

"You got a girlfriend?"

"No."

"I've got a boyfriend."

"Congratulations."

"He's a senior."

Zoe lifted the bottle to drink, but she kept her eyes on me. I knew she was lying. Her boyfriend had to be make-believe. I didn't know why she was telling me stories, but I wasn't about to call her out on it.

"That must be nice," I said. I realized I hadn't heard Cady or Dad laugh in a while. The house now felt even more quiet than before. I wondered if they were still in the living room or if maybe they'd gone for a walk or if Cady was showing off the back yard. Zoe passed the bottle back to me. I took a big gulp from it and had to swallow it slowly.

"Say, does your mom have red hair?"

"Yes."

I handed Zoe the bottle. She drank. She bounced her head to the side as if listening to music. She still had the stuffed bunny in her lap, and she made the ears flop back and forth.

"I think she was here the other night."

As soon as Zoe said this it felt like the gravity in the room disappeared. My entire being became hollow and dizzy. At first I thought she was joking, trying to get a rise out of me. Maybe this was another little white lie, like the boyfriend. But then I realized Zoe was being sincere. She drank the schnapps and gave me a nod and then was about to say something else, just move the conversation along as if she hadn't said anything of importance.

"What? What do you mean?"

"Mom had somebody stop by. A lady with red hair. She didn't stay long. She was pretty upset. I heard her crying. Mom kept trying to comfort her and get her to leave at the same time. But I didn't catch her name."

"Arden?"

"I don't know. I said I didn't catch it."

"Jesus."

I stormed out of Zoe's room and into the living room. I needed to tell Dad this. I needed Cady to explain what was going on. She clearly knew something but hadn't told us. I marched with my hands in fists, ready to demand information. I was angry, confused, and confident, despite my lack of patience. This feeling did not last long at all.

When I turned the corner I stopped, frozen in place. Dad and Cady were on the couch. They were in each other's arms, kissing, and my father had his hand under Cady's shirt, running up and down her back.

"What the fuck is this?"

I don't normally swear. But I remember those words coming out instinctually, like a heartbeat. Dad and Cady stopped making out. Cady was on top of Dad. She lifted her head and brushed back her hair. By this time, Zoe had come out and stood beside me.

"Really?" she said. "Really, Mothership? You can make out with some stranger, but I can't have a boyfriend? I hate you. I really hate you. I don't want you to talk to me ever again."

Zoe ran back to her room. Cady pushed herself off Dad. She tried to smooth out her blouse, wipe the spittle off her lips. Dad looked a little flushed. His eyes were red. He didn't say anything. He just sat up and ran a hand through his hair.

"I'm sorry you had to see that," said Cady. "It wasn't what you thought."

"Save it," I said.

"Maybe we should leave," said Dad.

"No. Mom was here. She's been lying to us the whole time. What was my mom doing here?"

Cady looked back at my father and then at me. She put her fingers to her lips. The house felt hot, and now it was silent. Cady muttered a few noises, trying to think of something to say. I kept my eyes on her. I didn't want her to get away from us.

"I need to check the chicken," she said. "I don't want it to get burnt."

"You stop right there," I said.

Cady sprinted into the kitchen with her head down. Dad stood and tugged on his shirt. I thought he looked like a real bastard.

"Have you lost your mind?" I said.

"Calm down, Coop."

"No. I'm not calming down. You're married. To Mom. We're here looking for Mom. You're kissing some other woman."

"Coop, it's complicated."

"Don't give me that. You're only allowed to kiss Mom. That's it."

"You'll understand when you're older."

"Really? You're going to try to pull that on me? I'm not stupid, you know."

"Things just get messy and hard to explain."

"Try me."

"Not now. We should leave. It's time to go."

"Not yet. She needs to explain what Mom was doing here."

"Cooper."

"No, it's okay. He's right," said Cady. She stood in the archway that led to the kitchen. Cady's body pressed against the jamb. She kept her hands and arms close to her chest, and she held a wine goblet in front of her collarbone. "I suppose I haven't been entirely honest with you."

"Was my mom here?"

"Yes. But not long. And I don't know where she went."

Cady raised the glass to her lips. Dad and I watched her drink. She looked like she was trying to crawl into herself. Cady finished her wine and then sat at the table. She put her hands out in front of her as if to brace herself.

"Talk," I said.

Cady took a deep breath and slowly exhaled. Dad and I stepped forward, closer to her, waiting to hear her confession. She didn't look at us. I was angry with my father, but I tried to be stoic and focus on Cady. Her information was more important than Dad's failings.

"Arden came by the other night. At first I didn't even recognize her. She was still beautiful, just older. She explained she wanted me to go away with her. I told her no."

"Come on, Cooper," said Dad. "Let's leave. Let's go home."

"No. I want to hear this."

"Your mother and I were close. At least we used to be."

Cady kept her hands on the table, but she angled her head to look specifically at me. Her eyes were filled with a child's sadness; they were remorseful, if not guilty.

"Your mother always told me she loved me," said Cady. She moved her sight back to the table and the empty glass in front of her. "And I believed her. But I always imagined it being a sisterly love. We never did anything, I swear. Before she moved to California, she tried to persuade me to go with her. But I was too afraid. I was a child. I didn't know what I wanted, other than safety. She told me she had never stopped thinking about me. It was sweet. But between what is my nature and having Zoe, I had to say no. She was upset. I told her to go home, back to you, to both of you. She said she couldn't."

"Why couldn't she come back?"

"I guess she thought she'd already torched all of that."

"My grandma told me about some boy, a close friend."

"Yes, Alburn, the local poet. He was a year ahead of us. He read his work to us. But he and your mother were never romantic. Alburn was sensitive. He understood your mother. She wept for days when she got word that he'd been killed in Vietnam."

"Where is she? Where's my mom?"

"I told you," said Cady. "I don't know. After I got her to stop crying, she just took off and left. She wanted a new life. I guess she went out to go get it."

And then Cady gave me a look that I've felt for the rest of my life. She lifted her head slowly, not all awake, and her eyes had changed into something dull and bored—not sleepy, but almost annoyed and carved out of stone. It was an undead stare that made me feel small, ignorant, and foolish.

There wasn't anything left to discuss. Cady had revealed it all. Now it was time to head home. No reward, no greater knowledge or insight, no reversal of fortune, no purge of emotion; there was no finish line to cross, no top of the mountain to reach. We'd leave with nothing.

Dad told me we should go. He was right. It was time for us to exit. Cady started to cry. She wiped her eyes, and her back shuddered as she wept. Part of me felt bad for her . . . but only a little bit.

I told my father I wanted to say good-bye to Zoe. He gave me a nod but didn't say anything. I was still mad at him for kissing Cady, but it didn't seem to matter as much now. Dad just stood there looking at Cady. He might as well have been a statue or a calm beast of labor. I went and knocked at Zoe's door.

"Go away."

"Zoe, it's me. Coop."

"I said go away."

"I'm coming inside."

I found Zoe on her bed, faced own with her head on her

stuffed rabbit and a stuffed penguin. Tears for Fears played on a violet boom box. I went and turned off the music.

"Leave me alone."

"We will. Dad and I are leaving. I just wanted to say good-bye."

"Good-bye. Okay? Good-bye."

The stuffed animals muffled her voice. She sobbed a bit more and then raised her head. Her cheeks were red from crying.

"Do you want my phone number?"

"What? Why?"

"I don't know," I said. "In case you wanted to call me and talk."

"I don't want to talk to you, kid. I don't ever want to see you or your dad or your freaky mom again."

"Okay. Well, I enjoyed talking to you."

This was the truth. I had enjoyed talking with Zoe. She'd been nice and shared her peppermint schnapps. I found a piece of paper on her desk and wrote down my address and number anyway. Maybe we could write letters.

Right before I left—just as I put my hand on the doorknob— Zoe sat up and looked at me and told me to wait. I stopped. I'd hoped she'd tell me that she liked me and would write me.

"You know both our moms are total cunts, right?"

"What?"

"My mom—you know she did that to herself?" Zoe ran the tip of her thumb down her cheek in a line similar to her mother's scar. "She cut her face when she was young. She did it for attention."

I didn't know what to say. I didn't even know if she was telling the truth. She'd lied about having a boyfriend. And she was slightly drunk. She waited for a response. I didn't give her one. I left and closed the door.

Back in the hallway, I didn't see anyone. No Cady. No Dad. Light seeped out from under the door to Cady's room. Tears for Fears started to play in Zoe's room again. I went to the living room. Through the window, I saw Dad in the car with the engine running.

I took one last look at Cady's house. It was so normal, almost bland.

It was cold and dry outside. The desert's chill became sharp at night. It made me think of razor blades and barbed wire, a coyote's fangs snapping in the dark. When I got in the car beside my father, the only sound was the hum of the heater and the motor. Dad kept the radio off. Nobody talked.

We kept our eyes on the road that ran out into the distance, into the wilderness; a single strip of pavement that took you to places and away from places. I soon realized that Dad wasn't going back to Grandma's. I thought about asking why, about asking him where we were going. But I decided against it. Besides, it didn't really matter anymore.

TWELVE

ON MONDAY, I WENT TO school as if nothing had happened. I didn't speak with anyone on the bus. When I got to campus, I saw that the windows were being fixed. All the broken shards and remains had been cleared. Some students stood with their books to their chests and watched the men replace the plates. I went to class and sat silently.

It wasn't until third period that an announcement came over the PA system saying I was summoned to the vice principal's office. All the students made "ooh" sounds and one said "somebody is in trouble," but I didn't care. I gathered my backpack and left.

I already knew what would happen. They would ask me questions, and I would give them answers. I wouldn't be allowed to leave until I did. They might threaten me with suspension. I wondered if the school realized that wasn't much of a threat.

For the most part, that is what happened. I had to wait outside the VP's office for a while, and then his secretary told me to go in. The vice principal sat at his desk doing paperwork. He looked at me and asked me to sit down. He put the papers away in a drawer. I figured they were more props than anything, fluff to make him look busy or important to students. It didn't fool me.

"Mr. Balsam—"

"Coop, please. Call me Coop."

"Okay, Cooper—"

"No. Just Coop. Only my grandmother calls me Cooper."

"Are you aware of the vandalism that happened over the weekend?"

"No."

"You didn't see the circus out there? Nobody said anything to you?"

The vice principal held a pen in his hand and used it as a pointer while he spoke. When he listened, he held the pen in both his hands, almost as if he was rolling an extra-long cigarette.

"I like to wait until lunch for gossip," I said. The vice principal squinted slightly at me.

"I see."

I almost mouthed off and said, "No, you don't see. You don't see a goddamn thing." But I decided against it and kept my mouth closed.

The vice principal was a tall man with a thin build, save for a middle-age beer gut. His scalp was balding, and he sported a thick black moustache. He wasn't stupid, but he was institutionalized. He had been behind that desk so long he'd forgotten how all of the school's rules, all of the school district's ideas, just didn't really matter. I didn't hate him. But people like him were the reason I disliked school. Talking to teachers was like talking to telemarketers; they had their scripts they memorized, written by others for the sole purpose of making you go away. Nobody was ever interested or concerned. They got involved only to stop any future headaches. Naptime, recess, free periods—all were just ways to avoid students. This man wasn't my friend. I didn't owe him anything.

"What is this all about?" I said, trying to play coy.

"Coop, our security guard picked your picture out of the

yearbook. He says he saw you break the windows."

"Wasn't me."

"No?"

"Nope."

"Then why did he see you there?"

Fine, I thought, if he wants answers, then I can give him some. If giving up Donald was what it would take to get me out of there, then so be it.

"Donald," I said. "Donald Krisp. I watched him do it, but that's all I did."

"Krisp?"

"Yeah," I said and spelled it for him. He nodded slowly and wrote it down.

"He is a grade above you, isn't he?"

"Two grades."

"You know, a young man like yourself should be concerned of the company you keep. And destruction of school property is really destruction of your property."

He looked at me and waited for a response: a little nod, a shrug, a sorry glance at the floor. My upper lip made a quick snarl. I leaned back and crossed my arms. We were done. He knew it. I wasn't going to let him lecture me. He could talk all he wanted, but I was finished listening. School spirit, hometown pride, and goody-goody Boy Scout mottos were all empty to me. Everything was too messy and chaotic for any type of bumper-sticker philosophy. The people who subscribed to those were either idiots or so far removed that anything concrete now felt foreign.

I turned my head to the side and looked around the room. Plaques and photographs hung on the walls. He kept talking. Go on, I thought. Talk until your lips are chapped. This wasn't my problem anymore. Then he noticed I wasn't paying attention.

"Cooper," he said.

"Just Coop."

"Are you okay? You seem a bit distracted."

I looked him in the eye.

"Do I?"

"Yes."

"Don't you worry about it."

"We'll have a talk with Donald. You're not off the hook yet."

I got up and went out. I made it a point not to shut the door as I left.

After lunch, I failed a science test and decided I was done for the day. I skipped gym and drank a milk shake at the Freeze-E across the street. I read a bit more of *Hawaii*, but I couldn't concentrate, so I stopped and finished my shake while gazing at traffic.

Watching the cars rolling away made me think of my mother driving somewhere, her arm out the window or both hands on the wheel; or maybe she was parked somewhere at a rest stop and sitting on the hood and staring out at an Interstate or an open field or a dry splotch of land.

I had no place to go. I thought about heading home, but home felt like an option worse than school—dirty and haunted. I strolled the streets until I came to the bank on the corner across from my father's store. I could see him through the windows. He stood behind the counter, ringing up an item for a woman in jeans and a red blouse. The woman left, and my father stayed by the cash register, bent over and leaning on his forearms. I wanted to go in and talk with him, but I knew he'd be mad at me for ditching school. The sun was out, but there were still clouds in the west, floating in from the Pacific. A breeze rattled the leaves of the eucalyptus and palm trees that lined the sidewalk. Mexicans sat on the bench by the bus stop, and men and women in denim and sunglasses came and left the bank behind me. No one looked at me. No one noticed me. I decided to keep moving. Dad didn't seem busy, but he didn't appear like he wanted visitors either.

As I began to walk away, I almost crashed into Sebastian.

He was coming out of a taco place with a bag in his hand. At first I tried to act like I didn't know him, but it didn't work. I got only two steps ahead when he stopped me.

"Good afternoon, Captain Tsunami. What's your rush?" For a brief second I wanted to keep moving, but I turned around and gave him a small half wave. We stepped toward each other. Cars drove down the street behind me. "What type of crime-fighting are you up to?"

"I had to give it up."

"I know what time it is. No super-villains in school?"

"No one who needs me."

Sebastian nodded but didn't smile. I looked at my shoes. Clouds passed in front of the sun and away.

"I think lots of Lois Lanes and Jimmy Olsens need a person like you."

"Nah, Lex Luthor got old and retired."

"Your pops told me about Arizona."

"He did?"

"He did."

"It is what it is."

"And it's not what it's not."

"Do me a favor—don't tell Dad you saw me."

"Saw who? The invisible man? Claude Rains? Who'd believe me?"

"I'd believe you."

"You're too trusting."

"Too something."

"Don't worry. Your secret identity is safe with me, Captain Tsunami."

"Thanks."

I gripped the straps of my backpack. I couldn't look him in the eye. I was too upset with the world. Sebastian adjusted his glasses, turned his head, and looked behind him. We could both see my father inside his store.

"You know," said Sebastian, "none of this is your fault."

"Oh, cut it out. Just shut it," I said, clenching my jaw as I spoke. I hated it when people said something like that. It made me feel small and simple, like I was too stupid to understand the events around me. I expected more from Sebastian. I didn't want to hear it. I didn't want easy excuses or fuzzy cop-outs. It didn't make sense that people couldn't accept bad things as bad things. There always had to be a safety net.

"Coop—"

"No. Just forget it. Just go and smoke pot or read comic books or whatever it is you do. You're just some burned-out old hippie. What do you know about it?"

"I was just trying to help."

"Go help yourself. And then go fuck yourself. People like you and Dad make me sick. You sit around and wonder why things don't work out, and then you just shrug it off and go back to waiting to die. So get to it—go fuck yourself and die already."

"Captain Tsunami."

I walked away, his voice calling after me as I marched down the sidewalk to Houston Street, where I turned right and vanished. A part of me felt like a real jerk. But something needed to be said. I couldn't let Sebastian or anyone treat me like that, like a child in need of an emotional mattress.

I marched home with my head down. Later that day, I saw Donald and his parents pull into their driveway. Everyone got out. Jake slammed his door shut and went inside. Donald followed, his mother trailing behind him. I found out later that Donald confessed to everything, that he even broke down and cried, and that his family would have to pay for the windows. Donald would have to do eight weeks of detention or face expulsion.

THIRTEEN

DONALD AND I FOUGHT THE next day. I didn't see him at school, and no one asked me about the windows. All day I kept my eyes open; I knew if I saw him, I would need to avoid him.

When my math class ended, Ms. McMurtry requested I stay to talk. I figured she knew I'd been involved with the vandalism. I hoped she wasn't going to try to guilt-trip me, tell me she was disappointed or anything like that.

"Coop, you drew something on your quiz I think I should ask you about."

We stood in front of her desk. She showed me the last quiz. Red Xs and one green check mark went down the list of problems. I didn't need to look at the score to know I'd failed. But at the bottom of the page was a doodle. I'd forgotten I'd drawn it. I've never been a talented artist, but I recognized my crude pencil strokes. I'd drawn a woman on fire.

"Sorry," I said. She put the quiz on a pile on her desk. She crossed her arms. I looked through the open door at students walking down the hallway. It was lunch time, and I heard the students crowding outside the cafeteria, ready to gorge themselves on potato chips and small cartons of milk.

"Coop, this really isn't like you. Why did you draw this? Is this supposed to be me?"

"No, it isn't you—I swear."

I felt bad that she would even consider that. The woman in the picture wasn't anyone. I'd been thinking about the Salem witch trials we'd been learning about in history, that was all. The idea that Ms. McMurtry thought I wanted to see her be burned at the stake embarrassed me. I tried to explain it to her. I couldn't look her in the eye.

"Coop, drawings like these are troubling. I should send this to the principal."

"Please don't do that," I said, remembering my experience with the vice principal. I didn't want to have to deal with all of that again.

"Okay," said Ms. McMurtry. "I won't, but you can't draw things like this. Not in my class. You're so young. You shouldn't have such depressing things on your mind."

This angered me. Why did everyone think the world was so great? I recalled Sebastian telling me how everything would be okay, but a lot of the time, most of the time, things did not turn out okay. Most of the time things just got worse. It seemed that everyone believed if you just ignored problems, they went away.

"It was just a doodle. I was bored. That's all."

"Coop, I don't want to be nosy, but your grades and your entire attitude have taken a sharp turn. Are you sure everything is fine?"

Ms. McMurtry sat on her desk and put her hands in her lap. She wore brown slacks and an ivory-colored blouse. For a second I thought about telling her about my mother, even about Roxy. But I didn't. I just stood there.

"Coop, look at me."

I did as I was told. Her eyes were soft and curious. I didn't feel angry or upset, just tired—exhausted from dealing with Dad, waiting for Mom—and emotionally spent from putting up with the world.

"I'm fine, Ms. McMurtry."

"You don't look fine."

And then she put a hand to my cheek. Her palm and her fingers felt cool. Then, and I wasn't sure why, I went in and hugged her. I just did it like a knee-jerk reaction. I put my arms around her, and my head rested on her shoulder. My arms squeezed her. She pushed me away.

"Coop, you can't do that. It's inappropriate."

"I didn't mean to."

"Coop, maybe you should talk to—"

"I need to go," I said.

I left immediately, feeling humiliated and lame. I didn't want to see Ms. McMurtry ever again, though I knew I would. There was something so weak about hugging her. I didn't want to think about it. I headed toward the cafeteria but changed my mind, so I ditched and went home.

I spent the rest of the day up in the hills by my house, reading and watching the grass sway in the breeze. It was sunny and almost warm. I'd been lost in the book, believing I was with the characters in the islands. The wind smelled of the Pacific, which made the book feel even more true and real.

When I hiked down, I stepped on stones to avoid smears of mud. Coyote tracks dotted the trail. I held out my hand so my fingers touched the leaves, still slick with dew. The air was filled with the whooshing sound of cars and trucks rushing along the freeway on the other side.

"Hey, ass-tongue." Donald found me on the street corner. I hadn't seen him, but I turned to face him after I recognized his voice. "Come here." Donald stood on the sidewalk with his feet spread apart, his hands in fists. His nostrils flared. We stood thirty feet from each other. He knew I had told on him. And I didn't care.

Donald charged me. I had never thought of him as fast—he usually clumped along, and I don't think I had ever seen him run—but for that moment he became a mad bronco. His legs moved, and then he tackled me. I didn't have enough time to dash away. He wrestled me onto the grass and rosemary by the sidewalk. On my back, I gazed straight into the sun. Donald punched me in the shoulder, the neck, my head. The tissue around my bones turned lumpy and absorbed each hit. His body blocked the sun, and his features went dark in silhouette. I tried to cover my face. All his strikes felt distant and dull. It was as if I wasn't the person being struck, I was simply observing it.

"You know what you did?" Donald said with his jaw locked.

"Get off me."

"They say this is going on my record. What if I can't join the swim team because of you?"

He continued clubbing me. My hands flailed at branches, at soil. The brush smelled sweet and ripe. Donald smacked me across the mouth. I tasted blood.

"I'm going to kill you so bad," said Donald.

My right hand grabbed something hard and round. I knew it was a rock. Donald pulled back a fist and aimed to smash in my nose. He might not kill me, I thought, but he is going to try, and he will keep on trying because that is what he does. He can't do anything else but destroy. He was out to raze the community and laugh in his retreat. For a second, I swore he was about to smile.

I hit him in the side of his head with the rock as hard as I could.

Donald fell off me, loose and limp. I ran away in a daze, thinking I'd killed him. I knew I must have; I had bashed in his brains. Donald was dead. I had murdered him. They would send me to jail. The rest of my life would be spent behind bars for manslaughter.

Down the road, I saw my father standing by the car beneath the eucalyptus tree. He must have just gotten home. Dad stood there and waited for me. He watched me jog toward him. I started crying. I felt like everyone was out to get me, and now I had defended myself and was going to die in prison because of it. Everything needed to stop and go away and be safe or quiet or leave me alone.

I threw myself at my father like a child. My arms went around his hips.

"Donald is dead. I'm sorry, I didn't mean to. He was going to hurt me and I couldn't run and he was on top of me and I had a rock and I needed to do something and I'm sorry—"

"Coop. Look."

Dad spun me to see Donald wobble down the sidewalk, a hand to his temple. He turned a corner, and then he was gone. Dad had seen everything. I looked at him.

"You rang his bell, but he'll live. Who knows, maybe you even knocked some sense into him."

I still had my arms around his waist. I felt his body heat and his growing paunch and sides. We went inside. Dad drew a bath. Steam rose from the water. I stripped and stepped into the tub. My body ached. The muscles taut, the skin scraped and raw. The water felt good and warm. I sat there and soaked. After a few minutes, Dad knocked and asked if he could come in. I said yes. He entered and sat on the toilet and looked at me.

"You okay?"

"I'll be fine."

"You been sleeping all right?"

"Not really."

"Me neither."

I scooped two handfuls of water and splashed my face. I felt a split in my lip sting. Then my eyes began to feel watery again, so I splashed my face once more.

"Why does this type of shit always happen to us?" I said. Dad put his hands together so his fingers interlocked. I avoided eye contact.

"What? You mean Mom?"

"Yes."

Dad nodded and sucked in his cheeks. He bent over a little and rested his elbows on his knees.

"I don't know, Coop. We just need to do the best we can."

"Sometimes that isn't good enough. You ever realize that? Sometimes you have to do more."

"What else can we do?"

"You should know. You're the adult."

"Okay."

Dad stood and left. When the door shut, I threw an arm over my eyes. I stayed like that until the water cooled.

I loved my father, but right then I hated him. It pains me to say so, but I know I did. I think I aimed my rage at him because he was near, because I could. Someone had to be responsible even if no one was at fault, was my reasoning.

After I dried and dressed, I went out to find my copy of *Hawaii*. It was dusk, and everything had a tint of purple and rust. The air smelled like rain. No one was outside. I dug through the shrubs and found the paperback. It was spread open with smudged pages. The front cover was torn halfway down the spine. I dusted it off and figured it was still readable. I wanted to finish it so at least I could say I had read the whole thing. Someday, I told myself, I'll get to Hawaii and a bunch of other exotic places. I knew it wasn't true.

That night I lay in bed and read the bent and dirty pages, and I didn't think about my mother or Donald or school. Dad watched television in the living room. I heard him walk to the kitchen during the commercials when he needed more ice for his scotch.

At one point the phone rang. I heard Dad get up and answer it, but I couldn't hear what he said. After he hung up, he came and stood outside my door. I waited for him to knock, but after a while he walked away. Good, I thought. I didn't want to see him. I stayed in my room. I hadn't eaten and was hungry, but I wasn't leaving my room until I knew Dad had gone to bed. I slid Mom's journal out from under my mattress and opened it.

I wish I could say I'm happy to be a senior. But it feels more like a devil's promise. You've made the deal, but you're not happy with the results. So I'm a senior. Big whoop. Everyone is already talking about prom.

I just want to get away from the dirt and the cattle and the dung. I need to get out of Arizona and not be like all these people. I don't care about prom. I don't even care that much about getting a new dress. It's time to avoid all the pits and the hooks. Alburn tells me about a village in New York where I should live. He's afraid he'll be drafted. I think he'll be fine, with his eyesight.

Jennifer and Michael are already engaged. I bet she's pregnant. I wonder if she's happy or if she cries into her pillow, sobs in the shower. I bet she does. I bet she cries and slaps herself red. I bet she hates herself and wants to die but can't utter a word to a soul.

I shouldn't be so mean. Jennifer is nice. Dumb but nice. I still remember that skirt she wore when we were freshmen. Surely she's pregnant. Why else would she agree to marry Michael? God, I hope I never have children.

And there it was.

Mom had never wanted any of us. But I wasn't even that surprised.

At some point, I fell asleep. I simply closed my eyes one second and opened them the next, only to find that several hours had passed. I didn't feel groggy or weighed down like I usually did; I was awake and ready. It was almost three in the morning. The first thing that came to mind was that I wanted to break something. I wanted to get back at the world and leave a tiny scar. This time I wouldn't need Donald.

I snuck out of my room and moved through the darkness of the house. No moonbeams. No starlight. Just me and the furniture in a lightless building in the early-morning hours.

Dad snored from his bedroom. He would sleep until his alarm went off, and that wouldn't be for a few hours. I grabbed a jacket and went out the front door. I turned up my collar as I walked down the road.

I didn't know where I was going, but I knew what I was doing. Instead of just smashing something, I was going to break into someone's home.

I wanted to violate someone's sense of safety. I felt as if I needed to hurt some innocent bystander because my world no longer made sense. Yes, this was illogical, but that was how my mind was working. It was an immature emotional response.

All the driveways had cars parked in them. The lights inside the houses were turned off. I walked along the sidewalk and then crossed between two stucco buildings and across someone's backyard. I kept my eyes open for welcoming details. There would be something, I knew it. A stuffed mailbox. An overgrown front yard. Something.

Sure enough, a couple of streets down from where I lived, I found a house with a small pile of newspapers in the driveway. That was the one.

Nothing about the house stood out to me. Stucco walls with a wooden shingle roof and a wooden garage door. A large and crooked pine tree stood out front. The pines did not shake with the wind. The air smelled of grass, leaves, ice plant, and eucalyptus, all damp with dew. The chill stung my cheeks and the tip of my nose. I kept my hands in my pockets.

To be safe, I snuck around back. A wooden fence closed off a small patio, but there wasn't any lock. A few plastic chairs and a little table with an ashtray sat near the sliding glass door. I tried this first, but it was locked. I had better luck with a window. Once I got that open, I climbed inside. I could feel my heart beating its way around in my rib cage. I had managed to enter a stranger's house. This wasn't just some petty vandalism; this was breaking and entering. This was a felony. This made me feel better. My skin prickled with adrenaline.

The room was clearly a little girl's bedroom. Posters of unicorns decorated the walls. The comforter and pillows on the twin bed against the wall were bright pink. Stuffed animals lay about the bed and the floor. I told myself not to do anything to the kid's room. It was off-limits.

I stepped softly down the hall, even though I knew no one was home. I refused to turn on any lights. I wasn't just a burglar—I was a spy, an assassin, a ninja. I worked in the shadows. Now I just needed to decide on what to do first. Break something? Steal something? Look for secrets?

I went to the kitchen and found a few bottles of Tecate in the refrigerator. I opened one and drank. I didn't like it that much, but I continued to drink as I roamed.

I flipped on the television. Some black-and-white film played on one of the local channels. It was one of those old movies were women were called dames and all the men wore fedoras pulled down over their eyes. I watched for a second and moved on.

There was a half-empty pack of cigarettes and some matches in a nightstand drawer. I lit one up and finished the bottle of Tecate as I went back to the living room.

"Mr. Neff, why don't you drop by tomorrow evening about eight-thirty. He'll be in then," said a woman's voice on the television.

"Who?" said a man's voice.

"My husband. You were anxious to talk to him, weren't you?"

"Yeah, I was, but I'm sort of getting over the idea, if you know what I mean."

"There's a speed limit in this state, Mr. Neff. Forty-five miles an hour."

"How fast was I going, officer?"

"I'd say around ninety."

I dropped the empty bottle and ashed my cig on the floor. The movie on TV looked pretty good, but I wasn't ready to sit down and watch it. The house had a nice rug in the living room and a matching green couch and loveseat.

"Suppose you get down off your motorcycle and give me a ticket?"

"Suppose I let you off with a warning this time."

"Suppose it doesn't take."

The television sat inside a big wooden entertainment center. A stereo lay on a shelf below the set. Below that were two doors. I went and opened those and found cassette tapes, a massive collection of Great Men of Music from Time Life. Mozart's tapes came in a light brown, Strauss's tapes were the color of mustard, Beethoven came in blue, Bach was green as holly, and Tchaikovsky was a blood red.

"Suppose I have to whack you over the knuckles."

"Suppose I bust out crying and put my head on your shoulder."

I looked at all of the cassettes. I knew my mother would love to have something like that, a seemingly endless supply of the greatest music composed in the Western world.

"Suppose you try putting it on my husband's shoulder," said the woman in the movie.

"That tears it," said the man.

I didn't know who lived in that house, but I felt a hatred for them of an intensity that I have not experienced since. Right then I think I could have beaten them all with my fists, I was so angry. They were the family my mother had wanted, a family that listened to classical music, had matching furniture that wasn't just picked up along the way off of friends who'd moved away or from a Salvation Army. Even their television got better movies than ours. Fuck these people, I thought.

I went to the kitchen and found a garbage bag and then went back to the living room, the television, and the tapes. Brahms, Handel, and Liszt were coming with me. I started throwing the tapes into the bag. The bag got so heavy, I feared it would rip and there'd be symphonies and concertos everywhere.

"Know why you couldn't figure this one, Keyes?" said the man in the movie. "'Cause the guy you were looking for was too close. Right across the desk from ya."

The movie on the television came to an end, and the credits began to roll. I ran around the house and tried to wipe off everything I'd touched. Once I finished that, I swung the bag over my shoulder and headed out. I didn't bother with the television. The station gave its sign-off, a montage of bald eagles and helicopter shots of mountains, deserts, and plains.

Then the set went to static.

I went out through the sliding glass door this time and stalked the quiet streets toward home.

The bag weighed me down. I carried it like a demented Santa Claus. I'd come from the North Pole with stolen cassettes of classical music for all the boys and girls. God bless us, everyone. I found myself sucking in long breaths and exhaling with force. I had to hold the bag with two hands.

When I got back home, I dropped the bag on the driveway. It was still late and dark and quiet, and I was exhausted. My head felt empty, as if someone had drilled a hole in my skull and pulled my brains out with a coat hanger. My body trembled slightly. There was a coat of salt across my chest and down my back from where sweat had chilled and dried. I wanted a shower, a nap, and something warm to drink.

Now there was another problem: I had no idea what to do with the tapes.

I pulled open the garage door and dragged the bag inside. The garage lay in total disarray. Cardboard boxes with children's books, stuffed animals, and baby clothes from my early years sat on one side. Tools, my bike with the broken chain, and random car parts sat on the other. I hid the bag behind a tool cabinet and an old loveseat that we'd never gotten rid of. It could stay there until I decided what to do with Mr. Haydn and his friends.

After closing the garage door and turning off the light, I snuck back into my own house similarly to how I broke into my neighbor's. I didn't feel much better—at least, not as good as I had hoped I would. There had been the initial adrenaline rush when I first stepped into the little girl's room, but now all I felt was a dull sense of boredom and regret. Those people would come home, see that someone had been there, probably call the cops. They'd see some ash on the carpet, an empty beer bottle on the floor, and it would take a while for them to figure out if anything was missing. The TV would still be there. The stereo too. The secret safe (if there was one) was untouched. Then—maybe in a few days, definitely not at first—they'd see all the cassettes were gone, and they'd look at each other and say, "What?" And none of this gave me satisfaction. I hadn't really hurt anyone or taken a mindless revenge; I'd simply confused some people and forced them to buy their music all over again on compact discs. I wasn't exactly the world's greatest cat burglar. But at least I had all the adagios I could stand.

Dad shook me awake a few hours later. I hadn't been asleep long, maybe two hours. My body twisted beneath the covers. Violet light seeped through the blinds.

"What?"

I pulled the sheets up over my shoulders and rolled onto my side. Dad was already dressed and shaved. He wore jeans and a T-shirt, and his coat with the fur collar. I looked at him and then clenched my eyes shut.

"Coop," he said. "Get up. Get dressed."

"The sun isn't out yet, Dad," I said. I rubbed my eyes. My pillow felt cool and soft against my cheek. Then, like a silent stab to my sternum, I remembered breaking into the house and stealing the Time Life Great Men of Music collection. Somehow, my father knew. He'd called the cops and was turning me in. He must have found the tapes and didn't want a criminal for a son, so he was handing me over to the police.

"Coop, the bank called me. They asked if I was in Mexico."

"What?"

"My credit card has been used a few times in Mexico. Your mother is in Mexico."

"I don't understand."

"I'll explain later. Get dressed."

FOURTEEN

WE LEFT THAT MORNING. FOG covered the roads. The air tasted salty and metallic, and the world was damp and gray. I could sense the sea as we headed west. Dad drove carefully through the mist. At the border, a guard waved us through. We passed into another country.

In Mexico everything had the aroma of earth and spice. Even in the light rain, you smelled flour and peppers. Pork and poultry hung in the shop windows, and carts on the street sold carne asada, corn, and fruit. Men on the corner held parrots in cages, and the birds hid their beaks beneath their wings.

On the far southern outskirts of Tijuana, we pulled over to a cantina in a strip mall for breakfast. We ordered huevos rancheros and drank coffee with cinnamon and cream. The salsa on the eggs was hot, and my eyes watered as I ate. The cantina was cold but the food warmed me, and I didn't notice the chill by the time I finished eating.

Dad sat slightly turned to the right in his chair, one elbow resting on the table. He chewed on a tortilla. A vein pumped along his temple. I could only imagine what was free-falling through his mind. He seemed to me to be like the gambler on his last gold coin, about to break into a cold sweat but never making a noise.

"I want to warn you," he said. "We may not like what we find."

"What do you mean?"

Dad turned and faced me. He chewed his food. He wiped his mouth and then took a sip of coffee.

"What I mean is this—your mother may not want to come back with us."

Dad tossed his napkin on the table. He crossed his arms. His body looked tired, beaten, but somehow not finished.

I poked at my food with my fork and tried to act like I wasn't frustrated. Dad leaned in and rested his elbows on the table. There was no one else in the cantina, save for the employees and one old man who sat drunk in the corner, eating a bowl of menudo.

"Is Mom a good person?"

"All in all, yes. I think she is a good person."

"Why is this happening to us? This isn't normal."

"Eat your breakfast. It's getting cold."

"Fuck, Dad—"

"Don't swear."

"Mom leaves, we look for her, and now you're telling me she might not want to come back once we find her. Why are we wasting our time? Why are we doing any of this?"

"Because it is the right thing to do."

"Why is it right? Who makes these rules?"

"Do you want to quit? You want to go home? Do you?"

"No," I said. "I don't."

And then we went silent. I finished the eggs and the beans, and I used a tortilla to soak up the sauce. The drunk in the corner started having a coughing fit. A waitress ran to him and tried patting his back.

Dad examined an old map of Mexico he'd pulled out of the glove compartment. The map was ancient, and the creases in the paper were tearing apart. Blotches of coffee had stained one corner of the map a bloody brown. Dad explained that my mother had charged the card to a motel in a fishing village south of Ensenada.

The man in the corner kept coughing. Spit, thick and silvery and white, clung to his moustache and his lips. The woman who had been patting his back ran away and returned with a glass of water. Dad rubbed his chin, and I knew he was still thinking. The coughing man took a sip and threw up a little onto his table. It was just a puddle of saliva.

Dad paid, and we walked outside. We got in the car and headed south. Highway 1 was long, and it followed the curves along the coastline. There was little traffic, mostly eighteen-wheelers and the occasional rusted-out pickup truck. After a while, I saw the ocean on my right. It spread into the distance without end. You could not tell where the sea stopped and where the overcast sky began. There were no gulls near the surf, and the road was too far back to see any waves. Drops splashed on the windshield. I tried not to think.

We drove for a little over an hour. The road ran ahead in a dull gray, the same color as the clouds. Occasionally, the headlights of a large truck shined at us from miles away. I'd wait as the lights came closer and closer, and then there was finally the giant whoosh of wind as we passed each other in the fog.

All we had to go on was the name of the motel and the town. That was all Dad had gotten out of his phone call with the bank. Dad stopped and asked for directions at gas stations. Luckily, most of the people spoke English; Dad's Spanish wasn't good. My father and I didn't say anything when we came to a series of bungalows on the beach. We drove up and down the row. They were all vacation rentals for Americans. These became expensive in the summer but were cheap in the winter. Most of the cottages looked vacant. A few of the cars parked out front had California license plates. We didn't see Mom's VW Rabbit.

The cabins had all been painted purple, yellow, and green, but the main building—a lone stucco rectangle—stood separately to the south. It reminded me of the houses on the other side of the hill where we lived. I briefly wondered about the people who were staying there, why they had come and where they had come from. Everyone was going somewhere. Even if they didn't want to.

Dad pulled up to the front office, parked, and killed the engine. We sat in silence. It hadn't been that long a trip, but it felt as if we'd been driving for days. All I could hear were the sounds of Dad and me breathing and the waves breaking on the shore.

Dad got out, and I followed him. His arms swung as he walked. We went to the front door and entered. The room was dim, and it was colder inside than it was outside. A faux wooden counter half bisected the room. Nobody was there. A chair and a desk sat behind the counter. Dad rang the bell three times, but no one came. He took a deep breath and exhaled through his nose, something I'd seen him do when he was upset with me or when he argued with Mom or an irate customer. He marched behind the counter and began flipping through the ledger.

"Should you be doing that?"

"I'm improvising here. You just play lookout. Arden Balsam. Cabin número nueve. Let's go."

We got back in the car and drove down the beach to the cabin and knocked on the door. I peered in through the windows. It began to drizzle. We went around back, where Dad was able to open a window a little but not enough for him to get through.

"Come here," he said. Raindrops dotted his brow and cheeks. His pumpkin-colored hair was dark, flat, and wet.

"I don't know."

"Stop being an old maid. Come on. I'll boost you up, and you can shimmy your butt inside."

Dad stooped and cupped his hands together, and I put one foot in his palms. He lifted me, and I stuck my head, arms, and shoulders in and pulled myself through, scraping my front and back. Dad pushed at my buttocks and feet until I was all the way in. I crashed to the floor. There wasn't much furniture. A wooden chair, a white wicker love seat. A small television. A painting of white and lavender streaks hung on the southern wall near the bedroom.

I knew my mother had been there, as if there was a lingering scent, a whiff of perfume even though there wasn't any. I smelled dust and wood and cotton and the beach smells that seeped through the walls. But my mother had been there. I was sure of it. The odd quiet felt like her. I halfway expected her to walk out of the bedroom and see me and then gasp and put a hand to her chest in surprise.

Dad banged on the front door. When I opened it, I saw the colorless waves crashing in the distance. Dad came in but didn't speak. He scanned the place. He used his right hand to wipe the dew from his face. The place was silent except for the occasional lonely call of a seagull. Dad marched into the bedroom and back.

"She had to have been here," I said. Dad nodded and told me to check the other room. I went and saw that the bed wasn't made. Clothes lay on the floor. A dress and a pair of jeans. A couple of panties. Socks. An ashtray rested on the nightstand. It was filled with cigarette butts, all Virginia Slims, my mother's brand. I plopped on the bed and picked at the butts. They were all marked with a faint rose color from Mom's lipstick. I plucked one and put it to my lips, and it tasted cold and dirty with ash. But beneath that there was the faint whisper of wax and the hint of my mother. This was all that was left. There were no more memories, only sensations. Now there was only sight, sound, smell, taste, and touch. Everything else was a corrupt lie.

The sliding mirror doors of the closet stood near the foot of the bed, neither open nor closed. Bare hangers dangled inside. An olive green suitcase sat inside on the floor. I recognized it as being part of a set my mother owned. I placed it on the bed and opened it. Not much was inside: a bra, a slip, and a small rectangle purple case with a snap-lock lid. The case cover felt like velvet.

Inside the case was a golden rope bracelet with a lone ruby in the center. I ran my fingertips along the band, feeling the metal, cool and strong, yet light and delicate. There was a type of mystery and order about it that made me feel beaten and humbled. The case shut with a clapping noise. It seemed like something from a time of big-band music and tuxedoes. A time that I believed (in some misplaced nostalgia) had more tradition, ritual, and respect. I liked the softness of the case. I rubbed it against my cheek, and I could smell the fabric and the dust. I didn't know why my mother had brought it.

As I sat there, I heard a car pull up. I stuck the case in my pocket and ran to the living room, where my father stood looking out the window. A jeep, its paint job faded and blemished, rolled to the front of the cabin and stopped. The engine continued to run. I couldn't see who was inside. It was overcast even as the afternoon neared.

"Is it Mom?"

"Your mother doesn't drive a jeep. I don't know who this is."

We stood and watched. I heard the motor quit. A woman got out. She wasn't my mother. She had brown skin and hair that had once probably been jet black and silky but now looked coarse with scattered streaks and white strands like a spider's web. She wore jeans and a polo shirt and a light windbreaker. I figured her to be near fifty. She saw us and squinted and stopped, and then she made her way to the door and knocked and opened it at the same time.

"Hello?" she said. She had a slight accent. Dad and I stood there. Neither of us spoke. The woman held a set of keys in her right hand. She looked at us like we were blurry. "Who are you? What are you doing here?"

"My name is Percy Balsam. This is my son, Cooper. We are looking for Arden. She's my wife."

"Ms. Arden is gone. She left yesterday."

"What do you mean? Her stuff is here. Isn't she coming back?"

"No. She left suddenly. You can take anything she left behind."

"Was anyone else here? Was she alone?"

"She stayed alone. She was nice. She seemed sad. I'm Maria. I'm the manager."

"Did my wife say where she was going?"

"No. I come every morning to bring the paper. She was leaving. She told me good-bye. That was all."

Maria looked at me and my father. She told us we couldn't be there. I wondered why she hadn't bothered to pack her clothes. I wanted to know why she didn't take the bracelet with her. Maria asked us how we got in. Dad put his hands on his hips and paced.

"This is great," he said. "Just fucking great."

"I'm sorry, sir. You have to leave."

"No," he said and pointed at Maria. "You don't get to tell me what to do. Not here."

Dad continued pacing. The way he walked back and forth reminded me of the lion at the zoo, hungry and athletic, with eyes glazed over but still sharp and keen. I felt a little bit nervous, and I realized I was holding my breath again. I forced myself to take a breath and try to relax.

Dad stood in front of the window. He didn't make a sound. Outside the window, beyond the beach, the waves were white and the rest of the ocean was pale and lifeless. Somehow I understood that even if we found my mother, it was over. We'd lost. Everybody had lost. Nobody ever came out ahead. Dad and I had tried to play by the rules, but we'd forgotten that the rules didn't apply to anyone but suckers. We were second-place men. And losers have to make the long walk home.

Suddenly, I knew why Mom, left. You don't leave places you enjoy; you leave places you dislike. Mom took off. Mom must have disliked home. Home consisted of me and my father. Mom disliked me and my father. I guess we just weren't good enough. But that's how it is, I told myself—water is wet, the sky is blue, Mom is gone. It is okay to hate the situation, but it won't change the situation. I told myself to think of it as sport. I wasn't a good athlete with the minor exception of being a fast runner. And when I wasn't agile enough to catch a ball, I didn't break down, I didn't cry. I wasn't good enough. I missed the ball, end of story. I didn't try to understand the ball. When I played baseball, I usually struck out. I didn't enjoy it, but facts were facts. I had struck out. I had three swings, and all were misses. Game over. That was the scenario with Mom. We had messed up, and now she wasn't there. Sorry. Endgame. Go home. Move on. Nothing we could do about it. Good-bye.

"Let's go, Dad. Let's go home. Let's just leave."

"No."

Dad opened and closed the cupboards. Then he looked in the icebox and found two bottles of Tecate. He took them, opened one, and drank it all in a few gulps. After he finished, Dad held the bottle and gazed at it. He set it down and opened the second beer. This he drank slowly, smacking his lips after each sip.

"That's a good beer," he said. He smiled at Maria. She just stood there. She still had her keys in her right hand. Dad smiled at me. "Nothing quite like a good cold beer. When I first got to Nam, the boys told me that I could get a six-pack for twenty bucks, and I said there was no way I'd pay that much for a few longnecks. But sure enough, after a month and a half, I caved in and placed an order. An hour later, this skinny Vietnamese girl rides up on a moped with a cooler on the back. And that was easily the best beer I ever had. So cold. And it was just old Budweiser. Regular American lager."

Dad didn't look at either of us. He stared at the floor and bit his lip. I knew he was somewhere else, someplace lost in memory. Maria turned her eyes toward me as if asking for help. I didn't say or do anything. There wasn't anything that could be done.

"Later on that summer," said Dad, his tone now flat and lifeless, "a new guy ordered some beer. Some poor FNG. But this time, two different girls rode up. Skinny girls, their legs so thin, stretching out of their denim shorts. The new guy got his beer, and then one of the girls shot him. Nobody even saw her take out the gun. Just blamo! Everybody ran out. People were screaming. Both of the girls had guns. They started shooting. Two skinny girls. And I don't know why they did it. Hell, they could have just poisoned the beer. It would have been easier. This sniper I knew shot them both. He shot one in the head, the other in the gut. He took that one into the brush and raped her while she bled to death. God, all of that over some hops and barley. The funny thing is that it didn't last long. A short firefight, just a skirmish. I didn't even have a chance to fire my weapon. Just strange. I don't know what happened to the beer."

Dad shook his head. He looked as if he'd just heard something absurd. His eyes shot wide for a second and then went normal. Standing there—looking at my father, listening to his story—I felt both love and fear toward him. He was no longer my old man, the paternal figure; now he was Percy, a good man who had seen violence and disliked it and was now trying his best to look after the people for whom he cared. He tried so hard because he knew the world could be a terrifying and dangerous place, but cowardice was not the solution. He was as upset as I was, but he was doing the most he could to keep things running smoothly.

When I got older, I made acquaintances who looked down upon people like my father. Anyone content with a simple job and a family was a fool, they told me. I don't think any of them knew what they were talking about. They were ignorant and selfish people who had never starved or been scared.

"I guess we'll be leaving," said Dad. He set the empty Tecate bottle on the counter.

We walked past Maria. She didn't turn around or speak.

The poor woman was probably confused and startled. No one said good-bye. It was cold in the car. I had broken into a sweat, and the sweat felt freezing. I tried to be as quiet as possible as Dad started the car and headed to the main road.

Dad drove north. When we came to Ensenada, Dad said he was hungry, so we pulled over onto one of the side streets and got out. The town was a maze. The streets ran busy with cars and people. Horns and radios blared in the background. Dad and I made our way through crumbling brick alleys that felt like tunnels and passed leather and jewelry stores and small shops that sold ponchos and T-shirts to tourists, mainly college students on spring break. Tequila with the worm. Big, cheap sombreros. Dad kept walking. I tried to stay close to him.

We ate fish tacos at a stand near the beach. The fishmongers had closed for the day, and now they were cleaning up. They sprayed down the streets and washed away the blood with the grime and oil of the road. You could still smell the day's catch, iced down and fresh like cut cucumber. The ocean smell was everywhere, the saltwater and the kelp. When the wind blew off the water, I'd close my eyes and let the Pacific roll over me, taking me away and bringing me back again.

Dad ate his tacos. I ate mine. They were delicious and crisp, and the sauce was creamy and good. Dad wiped his mouth with a napkin and ordered a shot of tequila. The case with the bracelet was in my pocket, pressing against my thigh. Dad took his shot and clenched his eyes. His lips turned flat and straight. As he took a few deep breaths, I pulled out the case. Dad motioned with two fingers for a second round.

"What is this?" I said.

"Looks like a bracelet."

"No, that's not what I mean. You know that."

Dad held the glass in his left hand. He turned his head a little to look at the case. I opened it as if presenting him an award.

"Put that away," he said. He drank his second shot and set

the glass down. People walked past us, sometimes so close that their elbows and biceps brushed against our spines.

"Tell me."

"Not now. Maybe later. Another time."

"Just tell me. You've dragged me to Mexico, and now you're getting drunk. You owe me."

Dad let out a long sigh. He didn't look at me.

"I gave it to your mother. I bought it in Vietnam."

"You knew Mom back then?"

"No."

"Then explain."

Dad puckered his lips and nodded. I was starting to feel annoyed and angry. Sometimes I wanted to yell at everyone I saw; this was one of those times. But I was too tired to yell. I was too tired to even be that mad.

"I was in-country long before you were born, long before I met your mother. But I bought that bracelet over there, near Saigon. I had been walking around, and I went into this jewelry store. There were all these beautiful pieces, necklaces with gems. This old man was standing there, not saying anything. Just standing there, watching me, smoking his cigarette. I wanted to buy something, anything. I had some dough and was going to spend it. I looked down and saw that bracelet. Not like anything else in the shop. I pointed at it, and the old man pulled it out and held it in his hands like it was something holy. I told myself yes, I'm buying this. Not for me, but for her."

Dad ordered another shot but didn't drink it right away. He held the glass with both hands and stared into it.

"You mean Mom?"

"Yes. I mean no . . . well, kinda. I bought that damn thing because I knew someday I was going to get the fuck out of Vietnam, and I was going to come home, meet a beautiful woman, and make babies with her. And when I met her, when I knew it was her, I would give her that bracelet. That way whenever I saw her wear it, I'd know that no matter what was going on around me, that life was better now. It was a gift for your mother. And it was a gift for me."

Dad drank a bit more and then decided he needed to sleep the booze off, so he went and crawled into the back seat of our car. I wandered the streets of Ensenada, thinking about what all I had heard. Though I didn't want to believe it, I understood now that my father had seen a lot more in Vietnam than he let on. That was for certain. Also, it made me wonder about the conversation I'd had with Sebastian. I wanted to know where love came from. And where did it go? But it didn't come from any place. It didn't go anywhere at all.

I came to the beach and sat on the sand. I watched the sea roll toward me. Part of me wanted to cry a little, but I didn't. Looking at the sea, I felt almost enlightened, a little bit relieved, while also disappointed. A cool wind came by, and I wrapped my arms around myself to stay warm. The world would destroy you if you let it; it was just a question of time. The water looked devoid of color, but I knew that beneath the surface there were sharks, whales, and rays.

FIFTEEN

IT TOOK DAD A WHILE to sober up and drive us home. It was a long trip up the coast and into California. The sky and the sea stretched out as a long and worn patch of denim. Dad didn't talk. I stayed silent for the entire ride. The case with the bracelet bulged in my pocket, but I liked knowing it was there.

I tried not to think, even though there was a lot to think about. It was getting to be too much for me to handle, so I felt I had to ignore everything. At least for a while. I slept a little with my head against the window. The glass felt sturdy but cold.

Whenever I used to have a bad day, I would talk with my mother. She'd sit on the couch and listen to me tell her every-thing—how the boy at school beat me up, how I forgot to do my homework and the teacher scolded me, how I skinned my knee in recess or failed to catch a ball in some game. Mom would smoke and nod as I rambled on about all the things that I thought were important but would forget about within twenty-four hours.

One time I found her washing dishes, and I sat at the kitchen table and started talking. After a while, I realized she wasn't really listening. She would respond with a "Yes, dear" and an "Is that so?" but none of her comments connected back

to what I had said. I stayed in the chair and watched her put
the coffee mugs and plates on the counter. She faced away from
me. I got up and went to her and put my arms around her, and
my cheek touched the small of her back. She smelled of perspi-
ration, cotton, and soap. I wasn't mad at her. But I wanted her
to know I was there even if she was busy, distracted, or dazed.
It was okay to be all of those things. At least she pretended to
listen. She could have just cursed me and told me to go outside,
to go play, to go watch television.

Mom didn't swat me away. She didn't say anything. She
continued washing the dishes. I could smell the water, dirty with
scraps of food and leftover gunk from milk, juice, and sauce. We
stayed like that for a while, the two of us, like conjoined twins or
slabs of steel fused together by fire if not blood. Sunlight, hot and
bright with late Californian spring, drenched the kitchen and our
bodies. Her long red hair almost reached the top of my head. I
wanted her to turn and put her arms around me. Sometimes she
could be so affectionate, like when she took me to the beach or
when she took me to see the missions decorated for the Day of
the Dead. And then there were days when no one could reach
her. Or talk to her. Or see anything of her save a body and
clothes, a husk of a woman no one understood. Unpredictable,
untamed, but adored regardless.

I didn't feel confident anymore, but I knew that didn't
change anything. If I didn't have my mother to talk to, then I
could talk to my father. But Dad was shutting himself off too.
The only person I felt I could talk to was Sebastian. And I
had treated him like a stray mutt, kicked and abused. I recalled
what I'd said to him, how I'd yelled at him. I knew I'd have to
make things right with him, and soon.

Sebastian was the closest thing I had to an uncle. He was
the closest I had to a grandfather. He was the closest I had to a
brother, a godfather, and a friend. I didn't know how I would
begin to apologize. I wasn't sure if he would give me a second
chance after all I had said.

It was late afternoon by the time Dad pulled his Charger up to our house. The sun would set in a few hours, just as everyone else was driving home from work. We went inside, and my father flipped on the television. The place stank of spoiled meat and old vegetables in the garbage. Dad sat on the couch and kicked off his shoes. He didn't look at me. I knew he was going to sit there for a long time.

"Dad?"

"Yeah?"

"Nothing."

I went to my room. It was quiet there. The bed needed to be made. Books and magazines cluttered the floor. A pile of underwear and shirts lay in the center of the room. Empty and half-empty cans of soda lay about on the windowsill, my trunk, my dresser. I was boxed in, and the room was dim. I felt an ache in my throat as if I was about to start sobbing, but I balled my hands into fists and forced that feeling to go away. First, I'll pick up my room, I thought. And I did that. I took the case with the bracelet out of my pocket and placed it on top of my dresser. That way I would never lose it. Then I started picking up my laundry and trash, hoping a clean room would lead to a fresh state of mind. No more toys, comic books, and candy wrappers all over the place. No more sheets kicked to the foot of the bed or down the side against the wall.

As I put away my copy of *Jaws*, the piece of newspaper with Roxy's number and address floated out like a wounded moth. I picked it up. I couldn't tell my father about Roxy. At least I wasn't going to. But it didn't take me long to make up my mind as to what I was going to do next.

I put my mother's journal in my backpack and snuck out my window. There wasn't time to explain or lie to Dad. I had to leave and couldn't let him see me. I cut through a few yards and made my way toward Houston Street and headed down into the valley.

By the time I got to the bottom of the hill, it was dusk

and cars crowded the streets. The western horizon resembled a split apricot. The air grew cold, but I didn't mind. I stood at the corner and waited for the light to change. Cars' headlights shone out in yellows and golds like giant Christmas stars, blessed and merciful. The supermarket where my father had gotten into a fistfight lay behind me. My school was up and to my left. Dad's auto-parts store was down the way to my right on the other side of the road. The supermarket's parking lot was almost completely full. I walked past my junior high and followed the long road that led farther up alongside the hill.

I knew some kids who lived in the hills, but I had never been inside any of their homes. All the buildings on the hill north of the freeway were big and spacious with giant windows that allowed sweeping views of the valley. I'd heard that some of the mansions even had elevators. The road curved around the slope in a thin, inky streak. You couldn't really see the houses, only the driveways, which wound up and behind white brick walls, eucalyptus, and Italian cypress.

Sebastian lived in a small cabin behind a cloak of California juniper and black oak at the end of a short road. He had no driveway, just a dirt path that sloped down from the street. The cabin had only one bedroom, cut off from the main room by a heavy bead curtain. The bungalow had originally been a servant's quarters for a bigger house that had been repeatedly sold off until it was torn down. The land was then used to farm Hass avocados. At some point, whoever grew the avocados went away and left the trees to survive on their own and grow wild. Sebastian would pick the fruit in the spring and let them soften and mature off the branch before he'd bring them to my father's store for us to eat. I used to play Robin Hood in the groves as a boy when my father visited Sebastian, and I always thought his house was warm, friendly, and good.

It was dark with just a sliver of purple in the far west by the time I made it to Sebastian's. The air tasted metallic but smelled sweet like gin. Light from Sebastian's cabin shined out as a lone beacon from behind the cypress and oak. I heard music as I got close. Through a window, I saw Sebastian sitting in a chair, drinking tea, and listening to records. He wore a loose bowling shirt and boxer shorts, and he rested his feet on a purple milk crate. I recognized the music as Country Joe and the Fish, a group he liked from his "San Francisco days," as he called them. Sebastian knew a lot about music, especially the various rock 'n' roll groups of the '60s after the British invasion. He'd been to concerts all across the nation and often remarked how much he regretted not going to Woodstock.

A screen door blocked the cabin's front door, and it always slammed shut behind you. I had to knock several times for him to hear me. I could see him through the window, and I watched him get up and walk toward me. He didn't smile when he answered.

"Evening, Captain Tsunami," he said. His voice was flat. He spoke with no spark or humor; he said it just as if stating some type of fact. He stood behind the screen door and made no motion to open it or to let me in. Sebastian's face was blank and still. He stared at me.

"I need your help," I said.

"That's funny—I thought people asked *friends* for help."

I cringed when he said that. I knew I deserved it, but I didn't think I could handle any more rejection. I tried to look him in the eye but couldn't. I focused on the ground.

"Please," I said. "I'll start crying. I'll beg."

Sebastian said nothing. I took a deep breath.

"What would you do if I sang out of tune?" I tried to sing, but my voice came out weak and tinny. A frail melody in the dark as I looked at my shoes, at Sebastian's shins. "Would you stand up and walk out on me?"

"Lend me your ears and I'll sing you a song," said Sebastian. "And I'll try not to sing out of key."

Sebastian slowly pushed open the screen door. He still didn't smile. His voice, even as he sang, remained serious. I went inside and immediately felt flushed. Sebastian walked over and turned down the music and then returned to his chair. I could still smell the chicken and broccoli he had cooked for dinner.

"I owe you an apology," I said.

Sebastian sat with his hands behind his head. He kicked the milk crate toward me so I'd have something to sit on. I chose to stand.

"Isn't that an odd phrase? To 'owe' someone an apology, I mean."

"Is it?"

"Maybe you can just give me your marker. An IOU."

"I prefer to pay off my debts as soon as I can."

"You'd either make a very good or a very bad gambler."

"I'd rather be well liked at craps than hated at poker."

"What I find funny," said Sebastian as he held up both hands as if motioning for someone to stop, "is that you want to give me this marker at the same time you say you need something. Isn't that a bit, I don't know—"

"Convenient?"

"I was going to say, 'self-serving bullshit.' But hey, I'm not good at politics. You tell me. You're the one who is in school."

Sebastian put his hands on his paunch and locked his fingers. His eyes went wide and reminded me of some owl who knew all the secrets of the woods and couldn't be shocked or impressed anymore.

"I'm trying," I said. I squeezed the straps of my backpack and let go. "I'm trying to kill all the chickens with one big swing, yes."

"I thought the saying included a stone."

"Axes are sharper."

I pulled out the corner of newspaper with Roxy's handwriting and handed it to him. Sebastian adjusted his glasses as he took it. Even though the piece of paper was small, Sebastian held it with both hands.

"What's this? You got a girlfriend?"

"Not in the slightest. You know where that's at?"

"What if I do?"

"Then maybe the hot dogs are on me."

"I do like a good hot dog."

"I know you do."

"First things first. Time to cash in that marker."

"I'm sorry I snapped at you the way I did the other day."

"And?"

"And I didn't mean any of it. I was being a brat. A selfish, immature brat."

"And?"

"And I'm a no-good butthole of a kid who doesn't deserve to have a friend like you. I smell like a butthole, too."

Sebastian didn't move. He touched his moustache and moved his mouth as if to yawn.

"Sebastian?"

"Give me ten dollars for gas and we're good," he said. "But remember that you said you were buying the hot dogs."

Roxy lived a bit to the west in Lemon Grove. The town's name told you everything. The entire area used to be just citrus. Then came the suburban housing, all small two-bedroom ranch houses that sprang up in droves overnight. Years later, the streets and the buildings still resembled the '50s and the postwar boom. A giant statue of a lemon stood in the center of downtown as a reminder of the past.

Sebastian drove us there in his VW Bug right as traffic was beginning to die down for the evening. We listened to "Shotgun Tom" Kelly on the oldies station play off the hits from the days of Eisenhower and Kennedy. On the weekends, Kelly reported from a station inside the Corvette Diner downtown, a nostalgia restaurant for baby-boomers where everything looked like it was made from red-and-black patent leather. An actual Corvette sat in the restaurant. "Shotgun Tom" played some Beach Boys, Chubby Checker, and Little Eva. A Sam Cooke song ended as we rolled onto a side street where the houses were either blue, yellow, or green. Toys and bicycles cluttered the front yards. Beat-up trucks and El Caminos parked in driveways smeared and stained with oil and paint. Sebastian slowed down, and I tried to read addresses aloud.

"Eight eleven, eight thirteen . . . Not so fast. It's dark out here," I said. I was practically in Sebastian's lap as I looked out his window. Streetlamps shined on the sidewalks but not the buildings. "I don't see it. Where the heck is this place? Did she just make it up or something?"

"Here it is," said Sebastian. He pulled to the side of the road and shifted into park.

"Where?"

"There," he said and pointed to a wooden staircase that ran up the side of a house to a white door with a diamond-shaped window. "It's an upstairs apartment. Popular with college students. Coop, who are we meeting? You haven't gotten yourself into any trouble, have you?"

"Not yet. But I'm aiming to fix that."

The house was dark, but the lights were on in the apartment. I leaned back and undid my seat belt. A cold sensation shot through my veins. The last time I'd seen Roxy, she almost ripped off my genitals. Who knew what she might try this time. But I knew I had to talk to her. I just wasn't sure if she would talk to me.

"Okay," I said. "Let's go."

"You feeling all right? You look pale."

"Everything is rainbows and lollipops. Now let's go."

We went up the steps slowly. I carried my backpack on one shoulder. Sebastian stayed behind me. I heard music as we got closer. I didn't recognize the song, but it sounded like a type of rockabilly played by Dracula. I looked back at Sebastian. His face was blank. A cat screeched in an alley, ready to fight. A car burned rubber and rushed off in the distance. I came to the top of the stairs. There wasn't any spit left in my mouth, and my throat felt dry and rough. My gums tasted like copper and rubber.

I thought my legs might give out on me. And though it was a winter evening and cold enough to see my breath, I felt hot with sweat on my palms and in my pits.

"Go on," said Sebastian. "We drove all the way out here. You haven't even told me who this person is. You better knock."

"I'm still not sure how to explain," I said.

"Then don't. Just knock."

"Okay. No guts, no hot dogs."

I knocked three times on Roxy's door. I heard her yell, "Ah, fuck Nixon!" and then the music was turned off. Sebastian and I glanced at each other in brotherly confusion. The door swung open, and there stood Roxy in a black tank top and bright yellow panties. I didn't know where to look.

"Nutsack," she said. "What are you doing here?"

"I have a few questions for you." I stared at her feet. She had painted her toenails black. Her legs were pale; they looked cold and lifeless.

Roxy kept a hand on the door. She looked me up and down as she clicked her tongue. Her eyes slid sideways.

"Who's Jerry Garcia?"

"I'm the driver," said Sebastian.

"May we come in?"

"Why should I talk to you? Maybe I should be asking you the questions. Do you have any clue where Arden—I'm sorry, I mean 'Mommy'—is, Mr. Moto?"

"Maybe," I said.

"Tell me."

"Not so fast."

"I see," she said. "Looking for an exchange? A little tit for tat? Maybe I've got enough tits as it is."

"Maybe another tit is just what you need."

"Get lost, nutsack. Take wavy gravy here with you."

"No."

"No? What do you mean, 'no'? Don't you understand how this works? You're a weird little kid."

"I've been to Arizona," I said.

"Sorry to hear that."

"And I just got back from Mexico."

"Hope you didn't drink the water."

"Did my mom ever mention a Cady to you?" As soon as I said that, Roxy paused. She cut out the fast talk and went mute as a statue. Roxy leaned against the jamb. "She did, didn't she?"

"Yeah, so what? Maybe she was thinking about taking up golf."

"Let us in. Talk to us."

Roxy clicked her tongue a couple more times. A wind blew over me, and my body shuddered at the mix of the cold breeze with the warm air that floated out of Roxy's apartment. Roxy gave us a nod and stepped back to let Sebastian and me inside. After she closed and locked the door, she crossed her arms under her breasts.

"Okay," she said. "What do you want to talk about?"

"I still can't find Mom."

"Oh, well, lucky for you, Mickey Spillane, I have her here underneath my mattress."

Roxy leaned against the door. Sebastian stood to my right. I wasn't sure what he thought of all this. He probably thought I'd gotten mixed up with the wrong crowd—not that he could be one to talk.

"You cut me up, Roxy. You like being a comedian?"

"I love me some Lenny Bruce. So I'm a joker. What does that make you?"

Roxy gave a half smile. I dropped my backpack to the floor and kept my hands in my pockets. I wanted to appear as if nothing fazed me. I wasn't sure how good a job I was doing.

"I'm Arden's son. My name is Cooper Balsam. And if you have a problem with that, you should say so right now."

"What if I do?"

"How about we don't find out. Keep everything happy and nice."

"Look at you," said Roxy. She smiled and stepped toward me. She put her hands on the back of her hips, and the insides of her thighs slapped together as she walked. "You've turned into a real Mike Hammer, haven't you?"

Roxy stood close to me. She smelled of an odd mix of lotion and leather. She didn't wear any makeup this time. When she'd come to my house she had dark and fierce eyes, black with mascara. Now they were just regular blue eyes. A little bit of acne ran across her cheeks. Her hair was still dirty and greasy.

"Don't you worry about it. You boys want a beer?"

Roxy strolled past me to the icebox. Shag carpet covered the living-room floor. The kitchen, which was just a refrigerator and a stove, had fake blue-and-white tile. Her apartment was small, smaller than Sebastian's cabin. An old couch, I assumed it was a pullout, was her only piece of furniture. Books and records sat on the floor against the walls. A spider plant cowered in the corner by the window. Its leaves fell about the place like thin, exhausted green arms. Sebastian squatted and looked through her LPs. Roxy grabbed three cans of Miller Lite and handed me one as she made her way to Sebastian. I saw the top of her butt crack when she walked in front of me.

I wasn't confident I would be able to get Roxy to talk to me, but so far she hadn't assaulted me, so I felt I was doing okay. I kept an eye on Sebastian. If she tried anything like she did last time, I wanted him nearby.

"How did you meet my mom?"

Sebastian took the beer and popped it open. I did the same. Roxy sat on the armrest of the couch. She kept her knees close together.

"Still hunting down Arden? You won't find her unless she wants you to."

"You sound pretty confident about that."

"You've got good taste in music, lady," said Sebastian. He held up a Captain Beefheart record and gave a goofy smile. Roxy shot Sebastian a look and then refocused her sight on me.

She took a drink of her beer.

"Tell me," I said. "I need to know everything."

"Trust me, kid. You don't want to know everything. The details would make you squirm. Besides, how I met Arden isn't important."

"How do you know?"

"Because I was there."

Roxy ran a finger around the top of the beer can. I almost expected it to hum the way crystal would. Her mouth stayed a little open as she watched me.

I still thought I wanted to know everything too. I believed if I knew what my mother had done, when and where she'd done it, that I would be able to grasp it all. And then things would make sense again. Maybe I could even begin to make things right.

"Are you going to toy with us and waste our time, or what?"

"Just the opposite. Drink your beer. There are sober children in Africa."

Roxy took another sip of beer. I did the same but kept my eyes on her as I drank. Sebastian stood and leaned against the wall.

"I met Arden through friends, if you really want to know. But I'm guessing that just makes you more curious. Who are my friends? How do they know Arden? Where does it all really begin, ooh la la. It doesn't matter, though. And I don't really know myself. Sorry to disappoint you on this round of *Jeopardy*, but the details are of no consequence. And you'll have to trust me on that."

"Were you and my mother in love?"

Roxy grinned and looked down at the beer in her hands. I think she actually blushed, which surprised me. I didn't think Roxy could be embarrassed or shocked or titillated.

"I feel I can honestly say that both she and I were in love with her."

"Coop, let's go," said Sebastian as he stood. "This girl is crazy."

"Hey there, Merlin, I'm a woman—not a girl. Got that?" Roxy's body became stiff and at attention. Sebastian took several steps toward me. Roxy rose as Sebastian put a hand on my arm to guide me to the door.

"Stop it. Let me go," I said. "I want to hear her."

"Old man, you're in my castle now, and I say let the boy stay."

"We should really leave," said Sebastian.

"Arden didn't love me," said Roxy. She didn't look at me or Sebastian. She held her beer with both hands, almost as if in prayer. "Arden didn't even really like women that way."

"What are you saying?"

"Kid, your mom is one of those people who spends all her time looking in the mirror. Get me? I wasn't anything to her. Another amusement, a fun distraction. Just another little knick-knack, a toy, or a souvenir. Funny stuff, huh?"

"Let's go home, Cooper," said Sebastian. He started to push me toward the door, but I shoved him away.

"Get off me."

"Coop—"

"Stop it."

"I'm sorry, kid," said Roxy.

"I don't believe you."

"We should really leave," said Sebastian.

The thing that hurt, the thing that shocked me, was that I knew Roxy was telling the truth. She wasn't trying to scare me or be wild. She simply explained how it was. And deep down, as much as I hated it, I knew she was right.

"Everybody gets fooled sometime," said Roxy. "It sucks. But it happens."

"Leave him alone, lady," said Sebastian. "And put on some pants. Your cooter is about to fall out."

"You wish, you breeder."

"Shut up, both of you. Just shut up," I said. "So now what? What am I supposed to do now?"

Roxy shook her head and bit her lip. She couldn't look at me. Her eyebrows went up and down as she thought.

"You hope you don't get fooled again. And that's about it."

"No," I said. "That's not good enough."

"Then you better put on your 3-D glasses, because you're living in the movies."

Roxy drank the rest of her beer. She belched as she strolled past Sebastian and me, and she crushed the can before she tossed it in the trash.

"What did my mom tell you about Cady?"

"Cady? She mentioned the name a few times but never in a way I really understood."

Roxy turned on the kitchen sink's faucet and ducked her head down to drink from the tap. Water splashed over her lips and into the basin. She had to stand on the balls of her feet as she drank. When she finished, she wiped her lips with her forearm. She stared at me as she did so.

"She said she left Arizona because of Cady. She talked about how much she hated Arizona, but it was because of Cady that she actually left the place. I never knew what that meant."

"I do," I said, although I really didn't. But I had an idea. "Wait, what about this?"

I kneeled and pulled out my mother's journal from my backpack. Roxy watched me flip through the pages. When I found the passage I wanted, I stood and cleared my throat.

"Kid, please don't make me listen to your poetry. I'm not in the mood, and I don't dig haiku."

"Listen," I said. "My mother wrote this back in high school: 'I think individual identity is important. One should stand out. Today in gym class, I noticed we all wore white—all of us a garden of magnolias. Such a pity. Here we are in what every elder tells us is our prime, but we're reduced to monotony. I want to be special. I'd rather be special than loved. I've tried both. And the kisses and the presents and the compliments are only enjoyable if you feel you deserve them. I need to know I deserve them. This place isn't special. And the people who live here are dead inside. All except Alburn. He sees things. My Cadillac told me I was just as boring as everyone else— the only thing I can never stand to hear. Good-bye, Valentines.'"

Roxy leaned against the counter. She spun her hand in the air and shrugged.

"Does that help?"

"No," said Roxy. "Your mom was a bitch in high school. What a shock. I got news, Tiny Tim: she's a bitch now."

"I'm sorry if I wasted your time," I said and shoved the journal into my backpack. "Let's get out of here, Sebastian."

I was heading for the door when Roxy asked me to stop. I did. I expected Roxy to speak. She had a look on her face as if she was about to say something important, like a farewell speech or instructions for survival or some deep-felt apology. But Roxy didn't say any of that.

"Take care of yourself, kid," she said.

"You too, Roxy. You too."

SEBASTIAN DROVE ME TO THE beach that night, where we burned my mother's journal. We watched the pages spark, catch fire, and curl into ash. Waves crashed on the shore, only to rise and break again. Cinders floated away toward the sea. We warmed our hands over the flames and smelled the kelp and the smoke. The pages quickly smoldered and turned to embers and dust. Sebastian told me that the ocean was the great keeper of all the world's secrets. I believed him, but I didn't feel interested in secrets anymore.

We drove along the coast with the windows rolled down, and Sebastian told me to stretch out my arms. I reached through the window and let the wind rush over me. The air was cold and strong. The car sped onward, and I felt as if I was flying. Sebastian encouraged me to yell, so I yelled. He told me to scream, so I screamed. We were going so fast and everything around me was wild, free, and dark.

SIXTEEN

THE NEXT DAY, IN MATH, Ms. McMurtry took attendance. When she called my name, I raised my hand; she glanced at me with wide eyes, like a confused child. She didn't say anything to me. She continued calling students' names. Her lesson plan was simple, and we had to do a worksheet. I had no idea how to solve any of the problems, so I stopped halfway through and turned it in unfinished. I scrawled my name at the top and underlined it three times.

The bell rang, and class was dismissed. As I left, Ms. McMurtry asked me if it was true. She didn't ask me to stop. She didn't call me by name. She just asked, almost as if talking to herself, was it true. I stopped and thought about not answering her, just leaving. I didn't know why she would care. The windows were fixed. It wasn't her property; it was the school's. But I didn't walk on. I turned around and gripped the straps of my backpack.

"Ms. McMurtry, I don't know what you've heard or what people have been saying to you—"

"That you and that Donald boy broke the windows. My windows included. Did you? Did you break my windows? You must really hate me, don't you?"

"No, Ms. McMurtry."

She bit her lip and her chest heaved. She was trying not to yell or lose her temper. She kept shaking her head in disbelief.

"This isn't an easy job, you know. Coming in every day and being mocked and hated when I'm trying to help all of you. I mean, who does this? Really? And you have to go and break the windows to my classroom?"

"I didn't do it. It was all Donald."

"But you were there. You watched. You enjoyed it. And that's just as bad."

"It wasn't like that."

"You know, Coop, I used to think you were a nice and sensitive boy. But I was wrong. You're just trash."

There are moments, quick flashes and incidents, that seem so abrupt that the seconds afterward become complete silence. Ms. McMurtry's statement was such an occurrence. It may have been the cruelest thing anyone has ever said to me. It literally took my breath away. I felt like I couldn't get air into my lungs. Now, I'm not sure why I found the remark so mean, so hurtful. I think it was because she said it with such sincerity. She really thought I was scum, someone whose presence made the world a lesser place.

I didn't do anything. I didn't reply. There was no yelling or crying. All I could do was leave, her words staying with me, stinging me, like saltwater in the eyes. She didn't look at me as I left. After that, I could never look her directly in the eye.

Instead of going to lunch with the other students, I went to the far end of campus, where we ran laps. It wasn't a track—just a square dirt field fenced off with eucalyptus. A few students hid behind tree trunks, smoking cigarettes. They eyed me, ready to fight me if they thought I'd snitch. I found a rock to sit on and stared into space.

That ended up being the last time Ms. McMurtry and I spoke to each other. I still attended her class for the rest of the semester, but I wouldn't speak, wouldn't raise my hand to answer any questions. She never called on me. In fact, she stopped saying my name during roll. She'd just look to make sure I was in my seat in the back.

After my last class, I walked to my father's shop. I didn't think about Ms. McMurtry or about my mother or really about anything. I just looked at the cars on the street, the buses that stopped, and the people who got on and off.

As soon as I entered the shop, I knew my father was mad. He didn't smile at me. His eyebrows scrunched up in a scowl. I didn't know why he was upset. A woman in the store went to the counter with a bouquet of air fresheners.

"Will that be all, ma'am?"

"I think so. I hope so."

Dad rang her up. He looked at her when he spoke, but he glared at me the rest of the time. I roamed around the filters and windshield wipers as if I were browsing. I peeked out from behind a display of motor oil.

Dad smiled when he handed over the woman's change. The woman wore jeans and a green windbreaker. I hoped she would stay a bit longer so I could delay finding out why my father was pissed. I thought about leaving, running away, but figured it best to stay and take it.

The woman went out the door. Dad watched her go down the sidewalk and through the parking lot until she was out of sight. Then he turned his head toward me. He motioned with a finger for me to come to him. I took slow, small steps forward. When I got to the counter, he leaned in close to me.

"You have some explaining to do," he said quietly.

"What about? What's wrong?"

"I heard you crawl out last night, for one thing. Want to tell me where you went?"

"I didn't sneak out."

"Don't lie to me, Mr. Cooper Balsam."

"I didn't."

"Then why did Sebastian tell me you went to his cabin and made him drive you to some strange woman's apartment?"

Right as he said that, I felt the world stretch out in front of me in a vertigo type of daze. It was almost like someone punched me. My mind tried to think of a clever response, some alibi or half-truth that would get me out of the conversation.

"I'm sorry," I said. It was the only phrase I had to offer. I couldn't imagine there was anything else to say.

"You're sorry? So you did something wrong? You seem unsure about that. Do you really not know the difference between right and wrong?"

Dad's voice stayed quiet. He scratched his cheek as he looked at me. The man blinked a few times but didn't move his sight.

"I needed Sebastian's help."

"Yeah, that's what it sounded like. Why didn't you come to me?"

"I just couldn't," I said.

"Why not?"

"I don't know."

"You're full of reasonable answers today, aren't you?"

I didn't say anything. I wasn't sure how much Sebastian had told my dad, so I wasn't sure how much I really needed to tell him. I didn't know how much I wanted him to know.

"Okay, you want to plead the Fifth, you go right ahead. But you're not off the plank yet."

Dad stooped over and reached for something behind the counter. He pulled up a trash bag and set it in front of me.

"Dad, I can explain—"

"Good, I like explanations. Explain this to me, Mr. Sneak-out." Dad turned up the bag, and all the cassette tapes I'd stolen began to spill out. The Bach, the Brahms, the Chopin. Dad's head trembled as he spread the tapes around with one hand. "Let's go. Explain why I have NPR tucked away in my garage."

"I'm sorry," I said.

"Sorry? You're saying that a lot lately. You're sorry for sneaking out, sorry for lying, sorry for stealing. You did steal these, didn't you?"

"Yes."

"So you're a liar and a thief now?"

I didn't say anything. Dad shoved all the tapes back into the bag. He held out the bag for me.

"Go on," he said. "Take it." I took the bag and put it on the floor by my feet. "Well, where did you steal them from?"

"Does it matter?"

"Will you tell me why you stole them?"

"Does that matter either?"

"Coop, I just don't know anymore. I just don't know."

Sebastian poked his head out from the storeroom while wiping the grease off his fingers. A jolt of rage bolted up my sternum and into my jaw. I didn't know why Sebastian had spilled everything to my father. Sebastian shrugged but didn't speak.

"I don't know why you act like you care," I said to my father. "We all know you really don't."

"What?"

"Admit it. You don't care about Mom or me or anyone."

"Why would you say that? Why would you think that?"

"I'm the one who went looking for her. I'm the one who went out last night. What did you do? You watched *ALF*."

"Oh, so I drove us to Arizona and to Mexico for my health?"

Sebastian stepped forward. He threw the brick-colored rag onto the counter and held up both hands. Dad didn't look at him, and neither did I.

"Hey, friends, neighbors, countrymen, let's put the atomic missiles down and listen to ourselves for a second."

"Stay the fuck out of this, Sebastian," said Dad. I felt a little shocked when he spoke. Dad almost never cursed.

"I'm just trying to be the UN here, comrade."

"He's my son. Stay out of it. You've done enough for global peace today."

And then Dad walked around the counter, and I jumped back. He put a hand on my shoulder and shoved me around, picking up the sack with all the tapes as we headed toward the door.

"Cover and close up for me," he said to Sebastian. Sebastian said nothing. My father's grip was strong. I didn't even try to shrug him off. I knew it wouldn't do any good. He pushed me outside and then switched his palm from my shoulder to my wrist, and he dragged me to his Charger. It almost felt as if my arm would pop out of its socket.

He told me to get in, and I did. Dad tossed the bag with the tapes in the trunk before he got behind the wheel. The engine was loud. Dad kept his jaw clenched. He shifted gears and sped out of the parking lot. The car became a beast that snarled, roared, and lived for speed and gasoline.

We pulled into the driveway about half an hour before dusk. A cold wind shook the eucalyptus leaves. The hill was dark in silhouette, with the sun fading purple and orange in the distance. Dad got out and slammed the door shut. I listened to him pop the trunk, grab the bag, and walk around to my side of the car. He yanked open my door and told me to get out. Before I could even unbuckle my seat belt, he shoved the bag with the tapes onto me and against my chest. He stood with flared nostrils, and he watched as I stumbled out of the seat.

"Thank you, sir. May I have another?"

"Don't get smart with me."

I held the sack over my shoulder. I glanced to the side and off to the distance as I waited for my father to scold me.

"You've got choices, kid. I'm going to go inside. You can do what you want with the Tabernacle Choir. A man would return them. A punk would throw them away."

Dad pushed the passenger-side door shut behind me and walked toward our home. With the bag on my back, I marched to the house I'd broken into. I stood on the sidewalk and tried to see if anyone was around. A few children rode bicycles farther down the street.

I thought about ringing the doorbell. Confessing. Admitting my guilt. I could just leave the bag and run away. But I didn't do any of that. I doubled back and crossed Columbus, past where Donald and I had smashed the mailboxes, and went up into the hills where we had drunk and smoked. I kicked at weeds and wild grass until I found a small gulch. I dropped the bag in, and then I tossed in some stones to weigh it down. I liked the sound of the tapes crunching under the rocks. When that was done, I smacked my palms clean and walked down the slope to the pavement and the stucco buildings.

Before I went inside, I checked the mail. There were a few bills and some junk coupons. I gathered it in one hand and was heading to the house when I heard a voice shout out to me. It was Donald.

"You going to apologize?" he said.

"Apologize for what?"

"You cheated. You hit me in the head with a rock. You can't do that."

I paused. For a brief second I debated arguing with him about the errors of his logic. But Donald's logic was simple: Donald wanted what he wanted. If he didn't get that—be it a toy or vengeance—then the world was unfair, and it should change its ways for his comfort. I wasn't in the mood to deal with him. He stood in front of me, waiting for me to ask for forgiveness. The left side of his face was purple and pink. A pennant-shaped scab ran across his temple.

"Get bent," I said.

"I'll get my dad."

"Good for you."

"Where are you going?"

"I'm going home, inside. It's cold. Where do you think I'm going?"

"No."

"No?"

"No. We're going to fight."

I flipped through the mail in my hands and started to move toward the house. My eyes glanced at Donald and back at the mail.

"Good-bye, Donald," I said. I turned and began to walk away.

"Damn it, you stupid pillow-biter. Come here."

Donald grabbed my hair. He pulled hard, yanking me close to him. I dropped all the mail. The coupons fell into some mud.

Donald decided we were going to fight one way or another. The last time I'd clobbered him with a stone the size of a baseball out of a pure adrenaline rush of fear. This time I wasn't afraid. I wasn't even that angry. I was simply annoyed. Though I felt horrible the last time I'd hurt him, I now felt nothing about what I was about to do.

I snatched his hand and twisted it, cranking it off my head. Donald's wrist felt chubby and weak in my grip. The bones connecting his hand to his forearm did not want to move that way. I saw Donald wince. He clenched his jaw and broke free. I think he said something, but I wasn't listening.

Before he could do anything else, I kicked him in the groin as hard as I could. Donald cupped his crotch and bent over in pain. I grabbed his ears and sent one of my knees to his forehead. Donald tumbled to the ground. His upper half spilled into the ice plant. One hand covered his brow, and he cried a little.

I didn't think about what I was going to do; thinking wasn't a factor. There were just events that occurred—earthquakes, thunderstorms, plagues, and fires. It was like I stood outside myself, watching it happen. It wasn't me intimidating him. It was someone else.

"Beg," I said.

"What?"

"Beg for your life."

"Go lick a dog's butt."

I kicked Donald in the cheek. He turned over so his back faced me. He tried to push himself up. I kicked him again.

"I told you to beg."

Donald didn't make any noise, but he wept. I went to him and took hold of his hair, his thin, pale, corn husk-looking hair. I tugged on it, yanking his skull a bit.

"You like that?" I said. "You like it when somebody does that to you?"

"Please."

"No, we've passed that phase."

"Coop—"

"Shut up."

Then I hit him. I punched him in the face. It was a solid strike to the nose and upper lip, but it didn't draw blood.

"Listen," I said. "You come anywhere near me again, ever, and I'll fucking kill you."

I punched him again to let him know I was serious. He got up and ran away in a shuffle.

Beating up Donald had been a long time coming, but it didn't make me feel anything. Something had to be done. Now I'd done it. I scooped up the mail and shook the mud off. Dad stood in the doorway. He looked at me. He shook his head and vanished inside.

I found Dad in the kitchen, standing by the sink. The tap was running, and Dad washed his hands. He splashed his face. I tossed the soggy mail on the table. None of the lights were on, and everything looked colorless and gray.

"Went a little psycho out there, don't you think?" Dad turned off the faucet and faced me. He dried his hands with a dish towel.

"So what? Donald deserved it."

"Ah."

"That rat bastard was asking for a beating, and I gave it to him."

"You've got the skills. I'll give you that," said Dad. He tossed the towel onto the counter. He crossed his arms. "What are you going to do when he comes back with a club? Or a knife?"

"I'll beat him again."

"What if he shows up with friends?"

"Then I'd beat them up, too."

"You going to beat up everybody?"

"Why not? Fuck it all. Fuck everyone."

"Coop."

"I'll beat up anyone who looks at me wrong. You know why?"

"Coop."

"Because fuck them, that's why. That's why."

I started to cry a little. Dad stood and watched. He didn't rush to hug me. There were no consoling speeches. I wiped my eyes with my right hand's knuckles, but my face stayed wet.

"You better now?"

"No," I said.

I wiped my eyes again and went to my room where it was lightless, quiet, and cramped. The case with the bracelet lay on my dresser. I opened it, looked at it, closed it, and dropped it to the floor. I crashed on my bed, my face on my pillow. I listened to my breathing. My eyelids shut. And then I wasn't angry anymore. I wasn't crying or upset. And then I was asleep.

It wasn't Donald I wanted to hurt; I wanted to hurt Mom. But I didn't truly want to hurt her either. I wanted to hurt my mother because she had hurt me, and I wanted to hurt others because I could not hurt my mother. I couldn't go around hurting everyone. There wasn't anything I could do but take it.

My dreams came and went in a blue haze. I don't remember the details. At some point I woke up, and the house was silent, and I wasn't sure if Dad was home. Maybe he'd gone to bed. Maybe he'd stepped out. I undressed and crawled into bed, ready to sleep the rest of the night.

The next time I awoke, it was already half past two. I sat up and saw light seep underneath my door. Faint mumbles drifted in from another room. In the dark, I slipped into my jeans and an old sweatshirt. I walked barefoot into the kitchen.

Dad sat at the table. He looked haggard, his face resting in his palm. There was someone else there, facing him. Dad motioned with his chin toward me, and the other person turned around.

"Hey, sugar."

"Hi, Mom."

SEVENTEEN

MOM HAD CUT HER HAIR into a short bob. She wore black slacks and a crimson blouse. Setting her Virginia Slim in the ashtray, she exhaled a breath of gray and blue. She waited for me to run to her, to hug her. I didn't do any of that. Maybe I expected her to come to me. Maybe I didn't want to talk to her.

"Your father tells me you've been looking for me."

I nodded. Mom smiled. She picked her cigarette up and took a drag. Her eyes closed and opened as she smoked.

"Your mother is just here to get a few things," said Dad. He had been drinking, but he wasn't drunk.

"Where are you going?" I said.

"Boston."

"What's in Boston? What the fuck is so special about Boston?"

"Cooper," said Dad.

"It's all right, Percy."

"Well?"

Mom turned around in her seat. She put her hands in her lap. And then she gave a faint smile.

"Cooper," she said, "what *isn't* in Boston? I've given it a lot of thought. I need to do this while I still can. I need to be alive.

Think about it. Where would you rather be? In the ranching area near the border, or in Boston? People are alive there. I bet they're so alive they can barely stand it."

"You can't do that. People don't do that."

"You're young. You'll understand when you're older."

That was when I decided to slap her. I was going to smack her across the cheek for leaving us, for coming back for no reason other than to mock us, for driving me crazy, for making me feel angry and sad and confused, for more or less telling me I wasn't good enough for her, for being a lousy mom, a lousy wife, a lousy human being who never really cared about anyone beside herself, for going to Boston, to the stupid East Coast, for being cruel enough to let me be born and to still love her despite it all.

"You little bitch. What is wrong with you? I don't want to understand when I'm older. I want to understand now." I went to her, pulled back my hand, and smacked my palm across her face.

Mom's cigarette fell to the floor. Traces of lipstick marked the butt. Her eyes exploded big and round. Dad shot up and stood next to her.

"Cooper Balsam—"

"Tell me I don't understand."

"We do not hit women, young man."

"It's okay, Percy."

"No, it's not."

Mom looked at me. She put her hands on my shoulders. Her face was calm, and she didn't look mad.

"Coop," she said. "Look at me."

I did as I was told. Her eyes gazed at me in a wonderful bright blue. Her eyebrows scrunched together.

"Why?"

"Don't you worry about that," she said. "Things just happen. You'll get used to it. Life is simply a series of disappointments."

Then no one said anything. It was just the three of us at the kitchen table in the early morning. The light was on in the kitchen, but the rest of the house was dark.

"Percy," said Mom, "could you make a pot of coffee?"

"I can do that."

Dad went to the sink and got the Folgers from the cupboard. I watched him for a bit and then realized my mother was still looking at me. Her hands stayed on my shoulders. I wasn't sure how to act. What was the right thing to do? Do you cry? Do you scream? Do you try to make light of the situation? I reached up to touch her hands, but she stood and used her palms to smooth out any creases in her pants.

"Come help your mother pack," she said as she picked her cigarette off the floor and stubbed it out in an ashtray.

I followed her to the bedroom. She flipped on the light. A new suitcase lay open on the bed. She opened a dresser drawer and fumbled with socks and with some of my father's under-shirts. I sat on the foot of the bed and kept my hands in my lap.

"How has school been?"

"Fine."

"That's nice."

It seemed like an odd question. But I realized she didn't know what else to say. She found the moment just as awkward as I did. She was probably just as confused as I was.

"Mom? Why did you marry Dad?"

"It felt like the right thing to do at the time."

"But not anymore?"

"It's a different time now."

"I can't believe you're going to Boston. Why were you in Mexico? Why are you leaving?"

Mom twisted her head over her shoulder.

"You don't get to question me like that. That's not fair. And I'm not just a wet nurse and a maid. You have to realize that."

She turned the rest of her body to face me. Her lips went flat. She kept her hands together in front of her stomach.

"Coop," she said, "I know you want to visit the tropics. Boston, the East Coast, all of that is my version of the tropics. Does that

make sense? How would you feel if I yelled at you for wanting
to see Bermuda or wherever? That wouldn't be nice."

I didn't say anything. I looked away so I wouldn't have to
see her. Mom went back to packing.

Mom pulled out several folded pairs of pants. She put them
in the suitcase. I stared at my hands. If I ever got married, if I
ever had children, I wouldn't be like Mom—at least that was
what I told myself. Simultaneously, I understood where she
was coming from. People wanted what they wanted, even if
others got hurt.

"Have you been doing all your homework?"

"No."

"If you don't do your homework, you won't do well in
school. And I know how you want to get into a nice college.
Maybe you can go to Emerson. Then we can get coffee in
Cambridge."

"Mom. Who was Alburn?"

"A memory now," she said. "He was a sweet boy. Just a
little older than you are now. He introduced me to poetry and
art. And they killed him. They always kill the beautiful and the
special. He never got to enjoy anything. He never got to do so
many things."

"He died in Vietnam?"

Mom kept her back to me. She kept digging through the
dresser. I could see her reflection in the mirror. Mom kept her
gaze down, focusing on the underwear, separating her clothes
from my father's. I liked how the light bounced off her hair.

"Your father tells me you've been fighting."

"A little."

Mom closed the drawer and turned toward me. She leaned
against the dresser and crossed her arms. I heard my father
moving about in the kitchen. He must have been drinking
coffee and trying to stay calm. You always hear stories of
men becoming violent when discovering their wives leaving
them, but in reality most men become passive and somber.

Dad was upset, but I couldn't tell if Mom knew . . . or cared.

"You know," she said, "I bet you're going to break a million hearts when you get older." Mom took a step toward me. She threw a pair of socks into her suitcase. "Just remember that you're too good for them. My boy is too good for any of them."

Mom winked at me and went back to packing. I returned to my room and found the bracelet my father had purchased in Vietnam. I picked the case up off my floor. I didn't open it. I put it inside my pocket and then went and sat with Dad.

Dad held a coffee mug with both hands. He stared into his drink. I sat across from him, and he didn't glance at me. He scratched his cheek. I felt sorry for him. My father was a good man. He was honest and hardworking. But he was what I've come to call West-Coast-blue. Every region has its own attitude, and this is seen in the people. Men and women in the Midwest are not the same as those in the Deep South. Southerners are not New England Yankees. Most people think that no one in California is *from* California, but that is not the case. Some families go back hundreds of years. Dad's did, although he couldn't recall many names or details. My father was tough but unlucky. And this is what I think of as West-Coast-blue. The type of person who will toil day and night and go nowhere but never complain about it, apathetic toward the unfairness of the world.

I asked my father how he was doing. His eyes moved, and he looked at me. We both knew I wasn't really asking him a question. I was just trying to break the silence. Somebody needed to say something.

"Me? I'm still here. What about you, Coop?"

"I'm still here too."

"That's good. I'm glad you're here."

"Happy to be here."

"Happy to be here."

Dad smiled. I smiled too. His head tilted as if to try to look in on Mom. You couldn't see her from the table. It was just an instinct.

"Can't she hurry up?" said Dad. He drank his coffee and gave a quiet grunt. Mom called for my father, and he rose to go see her. I waited at the table. When they came out they walked side by side. Dad told me to put on my shoes. We were leaving for the bus station in five minutes.

Mom's face was expressionless. She didn't even seem tired. I wished she had at least looked a little perplexed or given just a hint of some sadness or distress.

We took the Charger. Mom didn't want to take her Volkswagen across country, and she felt she wouldn't need a car in Boston. Before we left, I touched the side of my mother's car and wondered where it had been, where it had taken her.

When we rode toward the bus station, I sat in the back. No one spoke. There was no more future. We were a car of disembodied persons traveling onward and aimless. I leaned my head against the window. The glass felt cold. Light from oncoming traffic flooded through the windshield and over us in a yellow tint. When the flash passed, we returned to the darkness of the road. At times the world looked so black, the pavement felt so smooth, there was almost the sensation that we were drifting through space.

I don't know what I was thinking as we pulled into the depot. There was no more delay. There was nowhere left to go. We had come to the end. Dad killed the engine. Nobody got out. Buses were parked at the other side of the lot, some ready to go with their motors running. Mom asked my father if she could have some money, and Dad merely nodded. I looked at my mother's reflection in the rearview mirror. Dad's hands stayed on the wheel. Mom opened her door to get out, and my father and I followed her.

A small crowd stood outside the front doors, smoking cigarettes. Everyone was waiting to go somewhere else. They all looked desperate. The men needed a shave. The women had bad teeth. They talked in calm and careful tones, and they nodded at us as we walked by. Dad put a hand at the back of my neck as we went in through the depot doors. Mom strolled in front of us. Fluorescent bulbs kept the inside bright. Rows of hard plastic chairs, colored orange and blue, waited at the far end of the building near the vending machines and storage lockers. Mom got in line. Dad and I stood and waited, and I tried not to think. I could still feel Dad's hand on my neck, occasionally squeezing and letting go.

"This isn't your fault," he said.

"I know."

"This has to do with your mom. You didn't do anything wrong."

"I said I know."

"Okay."

Dad wanted to reaffirm me, but I didn't need him to. I knew now I was not the problem. I wasn't sure what the problem was, but I knew it wasn't me. I was a good kid, a good and loving son. Or at least I thought I was. Mom's line moved, and I watched her stand at the counter. She talked with the cashier.

"You know what it's like when something historical happens?" said Dad. "Like Pearl Harbor, or when Kennedy got shot?"

"I remember last year, when the *Challenger* exploded."

"You always remember where you were, what you were doing."

Mom bought her ticket. She walked toward us, holding her ticket close to her chest like a bouquet of French tulips.

"I'm on the next one out," she said.

"Do you want us to wait with you?" said Dad.

"No. That's all right. It will be an hour or so."

"It's not a problem."

"Percy, I'm a big girl."

I believed that meant she either didn't want to be around us or she was expecting someone else. But it didn't matter. I knew she was getting on that bus and heading east whether we stayed with her or left right then. I'm sure we were all tired.

"Best of luck to you, Arden," said Dad.

Mom hugged him. I didn't understand why he was wishing her well. He probably didn't know what else he could do. A voice came over the PA system. A few people outside stubbed out their cigarettes and came in. I smelled the wet-chalk scent of tobacco as they passed by.

Mom and Dad stopped hugging. She looked at me. I wanted to break down and scream, but something inside me told me to not do that. You couldn't act that way at such a moment; it would be childish and obscene. I tried to pretend it all just wasn't real.

"Hey, Coop," said Mom.

I looked away from her. I glanced back toward the pay phones and the ugly plastic chairs. Mom sighed.

"Hey, yourself."

"Coop. Look at me."

She hunched over a little, and I looked her in the eye. Dad stood nearby in silence. Mom smelled of cigarettes, coffee, perfume, and that woman odor, all soft and powdery. She petted my cheek. I reached into my back pocket and pulled out the box with the bracelet. It had been pressing against me for the entire ride. I handed it to her, but I didn't say anything. Mom opened the case and smiled. She closed the lid and handed it back to me.

"No," she said. "You keep it. Maybe you'll meet a girl someday and you can give it to her, and she'll think the world of you for it."

My mother hugged me, but her hug was more polite than anything else. And then she kissed me on the lips, something she had never done before. Suddenly I felt like I was another person, like I was in someone else's body. I wanted to say something smart and tender and wonderful, something she would always remember, a single sentence to haunt her—but I couldn't think of anything at all. I don't even know if I said good-bye. Dad and I walked back to the car and drove home. I never saw my mother again.

EIGHTEEN

IT WAS STILL DARK WHEN we got home and cold enough to see your breath. Dad and I got out. The grass on the hill was wet and black. I knew dawn would burn away the dew. There wasn't any wind. We slammed the doors shut and started toward the house. I stopped, and then my father stopped and asked if I was okay. I told him no.

Dad's shoulders slouched. He looked tired and old. My mind sliced from fragmented thought to fragmented thought. I wondered what I could have done, what I should have done. Behind all that was a cold numbness; I didn't enjoy it, but it was better than the debris of my other thoughts and emotions. I took in two breaths, exhaled, and shook my head. I hated my father, at least I did right then. I couldn't stand to look at him. He was weak, passive, and naïve.

"This is your fault," I said.

"Coop."

"I don't know how or why, but you did this. You're to blame."

"Don't say that."

"So now what?"

"I don't know. See what happens tomorrow."

"Tomorrow? Really? Fuck you."

"Coop."

"Fuck you."

I turned and ran up the hill. My shoes slid in mud. Dad didn't chase me. I wanted to be far away from him, from the house, from everything I knew. Damp leaves brushed against my legs, leaving streaks across my jeans. I pushed myself forward and scaled the slope with my hands, knees, and feet. Clouds drifted in front of the moon and away from the moon. I didn't know where I was going. All I could hear was my breathing, the long drags of oxygen bellowing through my body. I gnashed my teeth. I wanted to beat, claw, and bite everyone's face, anyone who smiled or laughed. My insides shrank and went tight.

The top of the hill spread flat, all gravel and stone. Rain puddles, brown and serene, scattered across the ground. I caught my breath. The anger began to drip away. From the peak, you could see the freeway. Lamps lit the pavement, and few cars drove by. Oncoming headlights came white and gold. The taillights beamed red and disappeared. I squatted and rested my knees on the ground. I washed my hands in placid water. A breeze blew over me and then vanished. Everything stayed still.

I watched the Interstate and the traffic. People sped east and west. Metal and glass shimmered under the lamps. I imagined myself crossing the lanes, sedans and coupes rushing past me. An eighteen-wheeler blowing its horn as it barreled toward me. And then I imagined being struck by some vehicle, breaking my shins, my ribs, knocking me back, my body skidding across the cement, the wheels running over my mangled self. Blood everywhere in smears and flecks.

I started to laugh. The crazy violence of my imagination came so unexpectedly, I didn't know what else to do. Suicide by truck had a ridiculous air to it. People would hear about it on the news and shake their heads, wondering what the world was coming to. I don't know why my brain went there.

Of course I didn't want to die; I just wanted everything

to stop and to make sense. There needed to be some type of peace out there. Maybe not in abundance, but somewhere in gems and pockets and under smooth stones in a field. I remembered the bracelet in my pocket. I took the case out and opened it. I thought about throwing it away, burying it on the hill. The ruby looked like a large drop of blood. I shut the case. I muttered my mother's name.

After I caught my breath, I splashed some water on my face and dried my chin and cheeks with the front of my shirt. I stood and wiped my palms on the side of my pants. The traffic on the freeway below me sounded like a gentle storm.

I pulled out my flashlight and pressed the button, but it didn't turn on. I tried a few more times and then tried shaking it. The painted-on green snake had almost all been chipped off. Now it was just a regular little machine. The batteries had died, so I removed them and tossed them into the bushes. I put the flashlight back in my pocket and started walking down the hill in the dark. I was tired, but I didn't want to go home. I didn't want to be inside that house. Dad might be up waiting for me, and that idea was enough to keep me away. I felt bad for yelling at him. He had not deserved that. I tried not to think about it.

Almost all the shops were closed. Only the convenience stores and gas stations had their lights on. I wandered the sidewalks. All the rage I'd felt was still there, but now it was smothered with a sense of desolation. The roads were deserted. Traffic signals still shined red, yellow, and green. The blacktop reeked of gasoline and sewer fumes.

A 7-Eleven stood at the corner. The lights behind the windows beamed white like fresh linen. The glow made me think of heaven. A purple streak grazed the hilltops in the east. My limbs ached. My throat felt brittle and dry. I went inside to buy a drink.

Rows of chips and candy stretched across the store. The back wall consisted of refrigerated soda and beer. A young woman waited behind the counter. A pink smear ran through her blond hair. She looked pale and bored and cynical. She read a magazine she had spread out on the counter between her elbows. Her cheek rested on a fist. She glanced at me as I entered and went down an aisle. The building was empty, save for us.

I grabbed a bottle of milk. When I went to pay, the girl put away the magazine and looked at me but didn't smile. I set the bottle down. I dug in my pockets and pulled out a crumpled dollar bill. She rang me up.

"You okay, kid?" she said.

She was thin but not pretty. She wore a white hoodie, and she kept her hair pulled back in a crooked ponytail. I must have been a mess. Mud stained my front. My face was dirty. The sun was about to come out, and I was walking around alone. Who knows what she thought. Her light-brown eyes stared at me with what I thought was concern. Maybe it was. Maybe it was just confusion, or perhaps annoyance. I can't ever say for sure. But it was enough of an affectionate gaze that it made me melt. I didn't care about my mother right then. All of the tightness within me went away.

I walked around and behind the counter.

"Kid, you can't be back here."

I didn't listen to her. I went to her and wrapped my arms around her waist, and I put my head to her sternum just below her small breasts. I breathed in the cotton and polyester of her clothes, and I could feel her ribs, her spine, and the warmth of her blood within her. She was alive and real, and part of me didn't want to let her go. At first she threw up her hands, startled by my hug. But then she touched my head. And then she touched my shoulders.

"Kid, it's going to be okay. What's wrong? Do I need to call somebody for you? Where are your parents? Kid?"

I stepped back. Her hands stayed on my shoulders. Now her eyes looked kind and deep. Up close I could see she had acne and had tried to cover it with too much makeup, layers

of sheer finish pressed powder and concealer. A name tag
clung beneath her left collarbone, but it twisted to the side so I
couldn't read it. I wish I had tried harder to.

"Here," I said. "I want you to have this. You deserve it."

I took the bracelet from my back pocket. It felt heavy. I
handed it to her. She looked at the box, and then she looked
at me.

"Go on. I want you to have this."

"What is it?"

"Whatever you want it to be. It has come over a decade and
a half, all the way from Vietnam, and now it belongs to you."

The girl gently took the case from me. She used both hands,
and she stared at me all the while. As soon as the bracelet was
with her, in her possession, I ran off. I grabbed my milk and
rushed out the door. I glanced over my shoulder. I saw her
open it, look inside, and then look at me through the window,
her face in shock and wonder.

NINETEEN

THE SUNRISE CAME SLOWLY AND without warmth. I marched the sidewalks as the streets swelled with morning traffic. My teeth chattered. I rubbed my arms to stay warm. I tried drinking some of the milk, but I didn't like it; I poured it out and threw it away. The air turned crisp and dry, and now icy winds blew in from the west off the Pacific. I saw birds struggle to fly in the breeze, their feathers thick and ruffled like fur.

I took a shortcut by crossing through an empty lot overgrown with grass and weeds, all dead and yellow. I kicked at a rusted can. Shards of broken glass gleamed in the dawn. It was all trash beneath the break of day.

When I got to the main avenue, I stuck out my thumb. I had never hitched before, but I was tired of walking and figured I would try it. Eventually a pickup pulled over. I got in. The driver was an old Hispanic gentleman with a moustache the color of ash. He wore jeans, a denim shirt, and a hefty cargo jacket. He had a beaten straw cowboy hat, which he constantly adjusted. A large brown paper bag sat between us on the middle of the bench.

"Where you going?" he said. He kept his eyes on the road. He steered with both hands.

"Home, I guess."

"Good place to go. Where's home?"

"I don't know."

"You don't know?"

"Off Columbus."

The old man nodded. His right hand stuck out toward me, and we shook.

"Coop," I said.

"Santos. You're a little young to be out here."

"Maybe. Maybe not."

"You been in trouble?"

I didn't know how to respond to this. The sun had finally cleared the eastern edges, and it thawed the frost and mist from the night. The corners of the windshield were still glazed. We came to a stop sign, and the engine snarled when we moved again. I felt safe in the truck.

"No," I said. "I'm not in trouble. No trouble at all. Just confused. That's all."

This made the old man laugh.

"Get used to that," he said.

Santos laughed again. His eyes twitched and steadied. He patted the sack between us, and he told me to help myself. He said he could tell I was hungry, which I was. I was starved. Gently, I opened the bag and peeked inside and saw burritos, big ones, wrapped in tinfoil. I pulled one out and peeled it free.

"My wife makes them," said Santos. "They're good."

I took a bite. It was all eggs and cheese and chorizo and onion and potatoes and spice—some of which I recognized and some I did not. A curl of steam floated from the center. My body warmed with the hot breakfast. I savored every bit.

Santos drove on. He came to the corner of Columbus, and I told him to turn right. I finished the burrito. I almost asked if I could have another one, but I thought that would be rude. I crumpled the tinfoil and shoved it in my pocket because I didn't want to leave trash in the man's truck. My stomach felt full, which made me sleepy. All I wanted to do now was take a hot shower and climb into bed. I didn't want to think about Dad or Mom or anything.

Santos drove up Columbus. Eucalyptus lined the road. The bark of the trees broke away in large, brown scabs. We were getting close. I told Santos he could pull over and let me out. When he put the truck in park, I held out my hand and we shook one last time.

"Thank you," I said. "You have been more than kind."

"No problem."

"Why did you stop and help me?"

"I don't know. Why does anybody do anything?"

The old man smiled, and I got out and shut the door. I waved as he drove on. The road looked frozen and gray.

I climbed a patch of ice plant and passed through someone's yard. It was quiet, and no one was outside. I could smell the earth and the dust, and I could taste the humidity. Snails clung to the sidewalk, and I put them back in the grass and rosemary that grew along the way. I knew someone like Donald would have just stomped on them.

I turned onto my cul-de-sac. Dad's car sat under the eucalyptus tree. I walked in the middle of the road. Birds chirped, but I couldn't see them. The sky spread out in a pale blue. My house didn't appear to be any different. Everything was still as it always had been.

Dad stepped outside. He saw me but didn't wave. He strolled across the front lawn to get the paper. He wore jeans and an undershirt. I wondered how angry he was with me.

I was thinking about this—about the conversation I would have to have, the apology I had to make—when a huge paw grabbed my shoulder and spun me around. Suddenly, I stood in a large shadow. It belonged to Donald's father, Jake. Donald stood to his left and a few steps back.

"My boy tells me you've been picking fights with him."

"What?"

"He hit me with a rock," said Donald. "And he did it for no good reason. Let him know he can't do that."

Jake gripped the collar of my shirt. I thought he would pick me up, but he just held on to my shirt. The muscles in his forearm flexed. His breath reeked of something dark and sour. Veins pumped in his neck and along his temple. Donald crossed his arms and smirked.

"If you like to fight, then I'm going to teach you who not to fight."

And then he slapped me. The side of my face went red, and my cheek burned. I could feel my eyes begin to water, so I looked at the ground. I was afraid, and I was ashamed for being afraid. My lips curled and trembled. Jake didn't let me go. Donald laughed, and I thought that was cruel. Jake slapped me two more times. I cried, but I didn't make any noise. It wasn't even really crying, just water dripping from my eyes. And then Jake said something, but I couldn't really hear him. All I could do was stare at the road, black and rugged with gravel beneath layers of tar. Donald laughed again. Jake leaned in and hissed something close to my ear. I sensed him making a fist and pulling back his arm. He was going to break my face, and all I could do was take it.

"You shouldn't cheat," said Donald. "You shouldn't hit people with rocks."

I closed my eyes and waited. Jake's shadow moved, and then I felt the sun shine on me. A cool wind drifted by and stirred my hair.

When I opened my eyes, Jake stood to my left. My father held Jake's wrist in one hand. I had not heard him walk up. He was just there. He squeezed Jake's wrist and pulled it to the side. Dad and Jake stared at each other, jaws clenched.

I know they stayed like that only a few seconds, but it seemed as if they froze in that stance for minutes.

Someone started a lawn mower. An ambulance rushed away, and its siren roared and faded. The lawn mower's motor gagged and sputtered and then began to hum. What happened next has never left my memory.

Dad head-butted Jake. Then he head-butted him again. The bridge of Jake's nose began to bleed. Jake pulled away, breaking free of Dad's grip, and swung a punch at my father. But Dad dodged it and stepped to the side. Dad hit Jake in the kidneys. This made Jake grit his teeth and let out a short, graveled howl.

I didn't see anyone else outside. I didn't hear the men grunt or curse. Only Donald and I saw what was happening. He and I didn't acknowledge each other. The lawn mower was still going too, and I knew it was nearby because I could smell the exhaust fumes.

Jake tried to rush my father, tried to barrel him over, but they clashed into each other and stood there locked and grappling. Jake's muscles bulged beneath his clothes. Dad's arms looked thin, his gut lumpy. The lawn mower stopped, and then whoever was pushing it pulled its chain to start it again; it took several times.

Dad rammed a knee into Jake's groin. Jake shrieked, but his voice quickly cut out. Dad put one hand on Jake's shoulder, and he used his other hand to punch Jake in the stomach. He hit him four times, each strike scooting the bigger man back a step.

I honestly don't know what Donald was doing. He stood several feet away from me, but all my attention was on my father and the fight. I know Donald screamed when Jake collapsed, but I don't know what he screamed or if it was just anger and noise.

Jake coughed and gagged and tried to get up. Blood trickled from his nose down his cheeks and into his beard. The red streak looked like a lightning bolt. Jake couldn't seem to breathe. He wheezed and gasped. I heard a sharp *chink* as a sling blade chipped at a rock.

Dad stood before Jake. Dad was breathing heavy, too. He looked like he was about to throw up. Dad reached out and grabbed Jake's hair. He pulled the man's head back and punched him across the jaw.

"Stay the fuck away from my son," Dad yelled and punched Jake again. He put his whole body into the swing, and after the strike he lost his footing and almost fell down. Jake spat blood onto the road. Both men panted. They stared at the ground.

Donald ran to his father. Jake gently pushed the boy away. I didn't know what had just happened. It was brutal but brief. I was glad it was over. Dad stumbled to the grass and vomited.

"You're a real jerk," said Donald.

Dad wiped his mouth with the back of his hand. He looked at Donald, and Donald said nothing. The lawn mower kept buzzing in the distance.

Jake and Donald retreated in a slow stagger, like two prize-fighters from skid row. They each had an arm over the other's shoulders. I wondered what they were thinking, and then I wondered if they would ever come back. Donald turned his head to look at me, and I could see in his eyes that they wouldn't.

For a second I wanted to yell some mean curse at them, but there wasn't any real reason for that. I didn't want to deal with them, and now I didn't need to. I went to my father. His eyes squinted in pain. He kept a hand to his paunch as if to make sure it was still there.

Donald's mother stood by her front door. She wore her blue bathrobe. Donald and Jake slowly went to her. Their Westie stayed by her ankles and barked.

"Asshole, you freak!" she yelled at my father. She picked up the dog, but it kept yapping.

"I'm sorry," said Dad. He held up one arm. His other hand stayed on his gut. "I didn't mean to."

"You psycho! You asshole psycho."

"Karen, I'm sorry. Son of a bitch. Christ."

Jake and Donald and Karen disappeared inside. Donald never bothered me again. His parents never spoke to me either. That was okay. They would hate me and my father, but it didn't matter. I'd see Donald now and again at school, but he'd keep his head down and avoid me. I don't know if he ever made the swim team. I sometimes thought about trying to talk to him, but I knew that was pointless.

Dad walked to the house. I followed him. We went through the front door, and it was dark and quiet. Dad rinsed his face and hands at the kitchen sink. He pulled off his shirt and dropped it on the floor. Water dripped off his lips and chin. He grabbed a beer from the fridge, opened it, and took a sip. He held the bottle to his cheek, and his eyes closed and opened. We went to the living room, and he sat on the couch while I perched on the chair across from him.

"That's the last time I do that," he said, but he said it in a way like he was speaking to no one, not even himself.

"You okay, Dad?"

"Yeah. Going to be sore tomorrow. But yes."

Dad took a long drink of his beer. He held up his free hand so it hovered palm down in front of him. His hand trembled.

"Haven't seen that in a while," he said. He put his hand down.

Dad drank his beer. And then he didn't say anything. He titled his head back, and he smacked his lips and shut his eyes.

I couldn't tell if he was sleeping or just resting. His chest rose and fell as he breathed. I tried to stay quiet. If he was sleeping, then I didn't want to wake him.

END

ACKNOWLEDGMENTS

IF I HAD TO THANK everyone who has helped me in some way while I wrote this novel, this section would be longer than the book itself. So you'll have to consider this the condensed version.

Many thanks to my parents who always believed in me and my writing—even when I didn't. Thanks to everyone in my family.

A big thanks to Mark Gottlieb at Trident Media Group for being a super agent. Huge hugs to Stephanie Beard, Jon O'Neal, Jolene Barto, and Kathy Haake at Turner Publishing for making this book so much better than I thought it could be. Thank you to Kevin Tong for the amazing artwork. Cheers to Scott Blackwood, John Benditt, and Jeff Johnson—I owe all you guys a tall glass of scotch.

I also owe a giant debt to Rob Antus, Chis Boyd, Carl Christensen, Jason Coates, Doug Dorst, everyone in FLD Productions, Tom Grimes, Caroline Herd, Emily Howorth, Daniel Keltner, David Latham, Debra Monroe, David Norman, Tim O'Brien, Gloria and Jerry Record, Mark Sibley-Jones, Penny Smith, Octavio Quintanilla and Marc Watkins.

ABOUT THE AUTHOR

WILLIAM JENSEN GREW UP IN California and Arizona.
His short fiction has appeared in *The Texas Review*, *North Dakota
Quarterly*, *Stoneboat*, and other various journals and anthol-
ogies. This is his first novel. He now lives in Texas. Learn
more about him at www.williamjensenwrites.com

CPSIA information can be obtained
at www.ICGtesting.com
Printed in the USA
LVOW11s1457090517

533873LV00003B/645/P